DEATH ON LINDISFARNE

Also by Fay Sampson

For adults:

> The Land of Angels
> The Flight of the Sparrow
> A Casket of Earth
> The Island Pilgrimage
> The Silent Fort
> Star Dancer

The Aidan Mysteries:

> The Hunted Hare

The Suzie Fewings series:

> In the Blood
> A Malignant House
> Those in Peril
> Father Unknown
> The Overlooker

The Morgan le Fay series:

> Wise Woman's Telling
> Nun's Telling
> Blacksmith's Telling
> Taliesin's Telling
> Herself
> Daughter of Tintagel (Omnibus edition)

For children:

> The Sorcerer's Trap
> The Sorcerer's Daughter
> Them
> Hard Rock

The Pangur Ban series:

> Pangur Ban
> Finnglas of the Horses
> Finnglas and the Stones of Choosing
> Shape Shifter
> The Serpent of Senargad
> The White Horse is Running

Non-fiction:

> Visions and Voyages: The Story of Celtic Spirituality
> Runes on the Cross: The Story of our Anglo-Saxon Heritage

Death on Lindisfarne

Fay Sampson

The second volume in The Aidan Mysteries

LION FICTION

Published by Lion Fiction
an imprint of
Lion Hudson plc
Wilkinson House, Jordan Hill Road,
Oxford OX2 8DR, England
www.lionhudson.com/fiction

ISBN 978 1 78264 025 7
e-ISBN 978 1 78264 053 0

First edition 2013

Cover design: Lion Hudson; waves © GeraKTV/depositphotos

Agent: Joanna Devereux at Pollinger Ltd: www.pollingerltd.com

A catalogue record for this book is available from the British Library

Printed and bound in the UK, March 2013, LH26

Author's Note

This story is set on Holy Island, off the coast of Northumbria. It is also known by its Anglo-Saxon name of Lindisfarne.

Although the setting is real, the living characters are fictitious. There are several retreat houses on the island. I have warm memories of the hospitality of the Open Gate, run by the Community of St Aidan and St Hilda, and of the helpfulness of the warden of Marygate. But the guesthouse of St Colman's and the Fellowship of St Ebba and St Oswald are my own inventions for the purpose of this novel. James's True Gospel Church is not based on any real church, in Huddersfield or elsewhere.

I am very grateful to Joe Baynham for information about the Holy Island Coastguard and Rescue Service and about local tides and currents. Needless to say, any mistakes in interpreting this advice are my responsibility alone. No real-life members of the team, or of the Northumbrian police, are portrayed in this book.

The poem in Chapter 6 is from "The Death of Urien" in the *Red Book of Hergest, XII*. My warm thanks are due to the Northumbria Community for permission to quote in Chapter 8 from their liturgy for Compline, published in *Celtic Daily Prayer* (HarperCollins, 2005). It can also be found at www.northumbriacommunity.org. The prayer in Chapter 16 is from *Carmina Gaedelica,* that rich source of Gaelic spirituality collected and translated by Alexander Carmichael in the nineteenth century. He was told it by the Argyll crofter Ann Livingstone.

Further Reading

Bede's *Ecclesiastical History of the English People*, or *A History of the English Church and People*. Various editions.

John Marsden, *Northanhymbre Saga* (Kyle Cathie, 1992).

Janet Backhouse, *The Lindisfarne Gospels* (Phaidon, 1981).

Fay Sampson, *Visions and Voyages* (Lion, 2007).

Fay Sampson, *Runes on the Cross* (Triangle, 2000).

Historical Characters

Aethelfrith "the Ferocious". Sixth- to seventh-century king of northern Northumbria. He gained control of southern Northumbria by killing the males of the ruling family.

Agilbert. Seventh-century French bishop of Wessex. Led the Roman party at the Synod of Whitby.

Aidan. Seventh-century Irish monk who became the first abbot of Lindisfarne.

Alchfrith. Seventh-century son of King Oswy and sub-king of southern Northumbria.

Bebba. Sixth- to seventh-century British princess. Married Aethelfrith, king of northern Northumbria. Gave her name to Bamburgh.

Bede. Seventh- to eighth-century monk of Jarrow and historian.

Benedict Biscop. Seventh-century warrior and monk. Accompanied Wilfrid to Rome. Founded the abbeys of Wearmouth and Jarrow.

Caedmon. Seventh-century worker at the abbey of Whitby. Composed poems in the English language.

Chad. Seventh-century pupil at Lindisfarne. Became bishop of York and Lichfield.

Colman. Seventh-century abbot of Lindisfarne. Led the Celtic party at the Synod of Whitby. Moved to Ireland after the Celtic Church was defeated.

Columba. Sixth-century abbot of Derry and founder of the abbey of Iona. Greatly revered by the Celtic Church.

Corman. Seventh-century monk sent by Iona as chaplain to King Oswald when he conquered Northumbria.

Cuthbert. Seventh-century prior and bishop of Lindisfarne.

Eadfrith. Seventh- to eighth-century bishop of Lindisfarne. Scribe of the Lindisfarne Gospels.

Eanfled. Seventh-century daughter of King Edwin of Northumbria. Brought up in Kent after Edwin's death. Married King Oswy of Northumbria.

Ebba. Seventh-century daughter of King Aethelfrith of Northumbria. Fled to Scotland when her father died. Became abbess of Coldingham.

Edwin. Seventh-century prince of southern Northumbria. Fled to Wales when Aethelfrith killed his father. Became king of all Northumbria.

Fiachna. Seventh-century king of Dalriada in Scotland and Ulster. Joined Urien's campaign to drive the Angles out of Northumbria.

Hilda/Hild. Seventh-century great-niece of Edwin. Abbess of Whitby.

James. Sixth- to seventh-century Roman missionary to the English and choirmaster.

Kevin. Sixth- to seventh-century abbot of Glendalough.

Melangell. Sixth-century Irish princess who became abbess at Pennant Melangell in Wales.

Morcant. Sixth-century king of the northern Britons. Joined Urien's campaign against the Angles but believed to be responsible for his assassination.

Oswald. Seventh-century son of Aethelfrith. Converted to Christianity on Iona. Returned to Northumbria to seize the kingdom from the Mercians.

Oswin. Seventh-century cousin of Oswald and king of southern Northumbria.

Oswy. Seventh-century brother of Oswald. Granted northern Northumbria by the Mercians and seized southern Northumbria by killing Oswin. Victorious over Mercians. Presided over Synod of Whitby.

Paulinus. Seventh-century Roman missionary. Accompanied Eanfled to Northumbria as bishop. Fled to Kent when Edwin was killed.

Penda. Seventh-century king of Mercia. Conquered Northumbria. Killed in battle with Oswy.

Rhydderch. Sixth- to seventh-century king of Strathclyde. Joined Urien's campaign against the Angles.

Taliesin. Sixth-century British poet, associated with the court of Urien.

Urien. Sixth-century British king of Rheged in northern Britain. Led an unsuccessful campaign to drive out the Anglian invaders.

Wilfrid. Seventh- to eighth-century. Went to Lindisfarne in Aidan's time, then travelled to Rome. Successful spokesman for the Roman party against the Celtic Church at the Synod of Whitby. Abbot of Ripon and bishop of York.

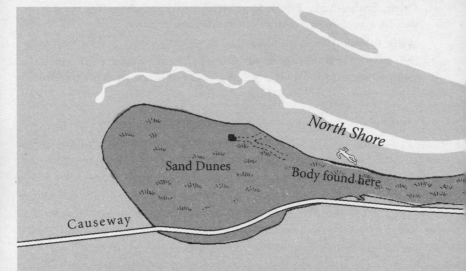

North Shore

Sand Dunes

Body found here

Causeway

Pilgrims Way

HOLY LAND SANDS
(*covered at high tide*)

Tide Times

These are the times when the causeway is open during the course of the story.

Saturday	11:05–19:10	23:40–07:30 (Sun)
Sunday	11:55–20:20	
Monday	00:30–08:40	12:50–21:35
Tuesday	01:30–09:45	13:55–22:35
Wednesday	02:40–10:45	15:00–23:25
Thursday	03:45–11:40	16:05–00:05 (Fri)
Friday	04:45–12:20	17:00–00:40 (Sat)
Saturday	05:35–12:55	17:50–01:15 (Sun)

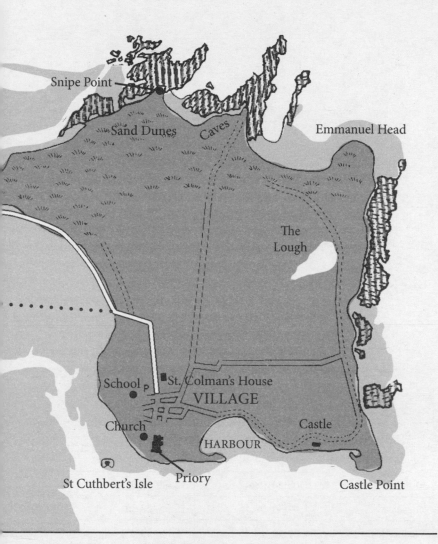

Holy Island or Lindisfarne

Chapter One

"DADDY, ARE YOU *SURE* this is a good idea?" Melangell tilted her pointed face towards her father. Her eight-year-old voice had the patient reproach of one used to dealing with a wayward parent.

Aidan looked ahead at the line of slender poles which led the way across the glistening sands towards the eastern end of Lindisfarne. Blue sky was reflected in the pools left by the receding water. He glanced to his left. Now the tide was falling there was a steady traffic of cars crossing the modern causeway to the island. But even that would be submerged at high water. Lindisfarne – Holy Island – was only intermittently linked to the mainland.

"Of course I am. Walking across the sands is the only proper way to come to Lindisfarne. That's how the pilgrims always came in the past. And the monks who lived here back in the time of St Aidan and Cuthbert. You wouldn't rather drive here in a *car*, would you?"

He was pleased to hear the cheerful confidence in his own voice. He had got his calculations right, hadn't he? He had parked the car for a week on the Northumbrian coast. He had helped Melangell pack a small rucksack with spare clothes. He had shouldered a larger one himself and his all-important camera bag. And he had consulted the tide tables with considerable care.

The sea channel that separated the island from the coast had been falling for a while, uncovering pink-tinged sand. It was jewelled with shells and pebbles. He must try to resist the temptation to take dozens of photographs of the miraculous and unique patterns the shells and quartz revealed at every step. He needed to time this journey right, so that the water had retreated from the Pilgrims' Way, but not leave it so late that the tide turned and swept back in over the sands before they could complete their crossing.

He gave a grin of delight and drew a deep breath of anticipation. "Come on, then. To Holy Island."

The wet sand oozed slightly round his boots and Melangell's trainers but held firm. Aidan had abandoned his modern walking pole for a wooden staff. It seemed more appropriate.

"Mummy said the king used to come and talk to St Aidan on Lindisfarne. But he only brought a few men and he never stayed to dinner, because he knew the monks were poor and didn't have much to eat. It's in her book."

Aidan stopped short. He couldn't help himself. The loss was still too new, too raw. He glanced down at his daughter with her mop of light-brown curls and her freckled elfin face. He had feared for Melangell. Seven had been terribly young to lose her mother last year. But she had seemed to accept the bereavement better than he had. She could talk of Jenny easily and fondly, as if her mother were still a real presence, someone she could turn to whenever she wanted.

Perhaps she is, Aidan thought. *I ought to believe that, oughtn't I? That Jenny is here, now, watching over us.* But the pain was real. They had come to Lindisfarne together, researching the first of Jenny's books about Celtic saints and kings. There was a row of these small books in Melangell's bedroom, her constant companions. All of them were illustrated with Aidan's photographs. The Lindisfarne book had been a special joy for Jenny and Aidan, because the saint who founded the monastery here had shared his own name.

The camera case hung heavy on Aidan's shoulder. He still carried it dutifully with him wherever he went. He still took photographs. If he was lucky, he sold some of them. But the chief purpose of his photography had been taken away from him. Without Jenny's enthusiasm, her pursuit of Celtic history and visions, he no longer knew with any certainty what he was taking photographs for.

Just now, his attention should be concentrated on following the line of poles to mid-channel.

Melangell stopped doubtfully at the edge of a deeper pool.

"You told me we could walk across."

The Easter sunlight had drifted behind a bank of high cloud. The sand looked more brown than pink, the rippling water in front of them grey and cold.

"You can. As long as you don't mind getting your feet wet. If we want to get to the other side before the tide catches us, it might be better to get our boots off."

He unlaced his own and slung them round his neck. Melangell picked up her trainers and held them in her hand. He took her other hand and they stepped into the shock of the shallow current.

"Ow, it's *cold*!"

"It's the authentic experience, though, isn't it? You have to imagine all the other visitors who came this way. Northumbrians, Scots, Irish, missionaries from Rome. All paddling across this little bit of the North Sea. Like us."

"Did they have nuns on Holy Island?"

"Sadly, no. St Aidan was a great friend of Hilda. But she had to go and set up her own monastery at Whitby. Only hers had men as well as women."

The water swirled around his ankles. With the coming of spring he had seized the opportunity to put on shorts for walking. Melangell was having to roll her jeans higher.

"OK? Do you want a lift?"

"I can *manage*," she retorted.

A few steps later they gained the wet sand on the far side. Halfway ahead stood a refuge box on stilts. They pressed on towards it.

As they stood in its shadow, the low spit of Lindisfarne looked suddenly much closer. All the same, Aidan turned his eyes seaward. The North Sea was a grey line along the horizon. It was hard to judge distances with no vertical features to mark perspective. How long before the tide turned? Had it done so already? How fast would that line of sea come sweeping in across the sands where they stood?

They would be leaving behind the only place of safety on this route.

The wood of the pole beside him was still dark and dank from the previous tide. There were only a few hours a day when it was possible to cross on foot safely.

Yet now they had passed the mid-point, he felt sufficiently confident to unfasten his camera bag and take out his Nikon. His hand hesitated over which lens to use, rejected a wide-angle and settled on an f2.8 telephoto one.

The first glimpse of the village on the tip of Lindisfarne sprang into instant life. No longer just a water tower and a smudge of roofs against the grey background. He could see now how the line of poles would lead them safely up the shore.

He moved the camera, trying to find how best to frame the shot that would capture that sense of arrival. The end of pilgrimage. As yet, the ruined abbey and the statue of St Aidan were still out of sight. But this view was not unlike the one that would have greeted King Oswald, or St Cuthbert, or all the other famous names of the past whose histories had led them to this island.

He steadied the lens, then gave a sudden start. He had not intended to photograph people. This was all about the sense of sacred place. Yet there were two people framed in his shot. A man and a woman, perhaps? Or a girl. The smaller figure looked quite slight. Even with the lens's magnification, it was not possible to be sure of their faces or ages, or even their gender. The one he thought was a girl wore a red sweater or jacket, the larger figure something brown.

They seemed to be holding each other. A couple of lovers? Or was the man holding on to the girl? As he watched through his viewfinder she broke away from him. Instinctively Aidan snapped the shutter.

She was not exactly running away from him now. More floundering, as if through softer sand than the damp pebble-strewn bed he and Melangell stood on.

He lowered the camera, and suddenly the pair were distant specks. The island shore was further away than the zoom lens of his camera had made it seem for those few moments.

He took a few more shots, focusing this time on the composition of poles and shoreline. Then he slung the camera back on his shoulder.

"Come on," he said. "This is not the place to stand about wasting time."

"You're a fine one to talk." It sounded an adult phrase. Had she picked it up from Jenny?

That pain again.

Melangell started forward. Then she paused. "Are those people over there? If they want to walk across to the mainland, they'll have to hurry, won't they?"

He looked round at her in surprise. "You've got sharper eyes than I have. I didn't notice them until I used the zoom lens."

"I can see a little red dot and a darker one."

"I don't expect they're coming across. They've just come down to the beach for a walk. Perhaps they're waiting to see if *we* make it across before the sea gets us."

"It won't, will it?" The upturned pointed face was momentarily anxious.

"No." He put a reassuring hand on her shoulder. "Not if we don't hang about."

They toiled on across the barely shelving sands. He took Melangell's hand. When at last they passed the line of sea wrack that marked the high tide point he lifted her up and swung her round in celebration.

"Told you! We did it. Now wasn't that much more fun than driving across the causeway?"

She tumbled down into softer sand and let handfuls of it fall through her fingers. She sat up to see what she had found. A blue-black mussel shell, the white-ridged fan of a cockle, a scrap of amber seaweed. Suddenly she dived to capture something that had fallen into the sand by her leg. She lifted it up triumphantly.

"She must have dropped it. One of those people we saw when we were halfway across."

She held out her hand, palm upward. Nestled in it was a single earring. A little golden beast with a scarlet tongue. Its tail twisted into Celtic knotwork that twined around to form a ring.

"Interesting," said Aidan. "It looks like something from the pages of the Lindisfarne Gospels."

He looked around. He hadn't been watching the shoreline since he took that photograph. The couple he had seen briefly grappling on the beach were nowhere to be seen.

"Hang on to that," he said. "Maybe we should put a card in the village shop to say we've found it. Now, let's see if we can find St Colman's House. I don't know about you, but I've worked up an appetite for tea."

He kept to himself the pain he feared might be lying in wait for him.

Chapter Two

THEY WALKED UP THE ROAD towards the village. Memories came rushing back to overwhelm Aidan. Here was the large sand-blown car park, where visitors driving across the causeway left their cars.

That was what Aidan and Jenny had done, until Jenny was seized with the idea that she wanted to walk across the sands to the island, as all those Anglo-Saxon and Irish pilgrims had done. She had cajoled Aidan into driving back across the causeway, against the flow of incoming traffic, and they had started again on foot. The same traverse along the line of poles that Aidan and Melangell had just completed. It had been rash, and they were breathless, hoping they hadn't left it too late, praying the tide would not come sweeping back before they arrived for the second time. They had collapsed laughing in the soft dry sand.

Where Melangell had tumbled onto the bank and found that earring.

He was not going to be able to push these raw memories away. Perhaps he should not have come back.

Almost immediately Lindisfarne Castle reared over the skyline on its thumb of rock.

"It's a real castle, isn't it?" Melangell exclaimed. "Even if it is a tiny one."

The first houses were beginning to line the road. Daffodils shouted the triumph of Easter in their gardens. Near the top of the road, Aidan stopped in front of one.

"St Colman's House. This is it."

Two palm trees rattled their leaves in the North Sea wind. Behind them rose a double-fronted house. It was painted pink, with the woodwork picked out in white. Pointed eaves jutted above the upper windows and there were skylights in the roof.

"I thought it would be... older," Melangell said.

"In the monks' time, you could have stayed in the guesthouse at the abbey, or later at the castle, if you were posh enough. Don't worry. There'll be plenty of history to see."

He turned to smile encouragement at her. After the anxiety-tinged laughter of crossing the sands, her pointed freckled face looked wistful, tired. This was the end of a long journey. He hoped he had been right to bring her; that the Reverend Lucy Pargeter's talks about the saints of this historic island would not be over her head.

A little voice chided him. Melangell might still be only eight years old, but she could probably give a pretty good talk herself about St Aidan. He was a particular favourite, because he shared her father's name. And she had read all about him many times in the book Jenny had written about the saint.

That shock again. The knowledge that everywhere he went here, every story from Lindisfarne's history, would carry with it the memory of Jenny bringing him here to research her book.

Even the Nikon round his neck weighed heavier. Aidan's contribution had been to take the photographs for Jenny's books. A perfect partnership. Uncharacteristically, he slipped the strap over his head and stowed the camera away in the bag that hung from his shoulder.

"Shall we?"

He held the front gate open for her and they walked up to the door.

The expression on Mrs Batley's face held more challenge than welcome as she opened the door.

"Yes?" She was a middle-aged woman, with carefully waved hair and a discreetly made-up face.

A fraction too late, her landlady's professional instinct caught up with her. A smile flowered across her features.

"You'll have come for the course?"

"Aidan Davison, and Melangell."

Mrs Batley threw a curious look at the child beside him, but made no comment.

"Two singles, wasn't it? I've got some lovely chalets in the garden, but they're family rooms or doubles. I've put you on the top floor."

Up in the eaves. Servants' quarters, Aidan thought to himself. He would have to get used to this new reality of single life.

"That'll be fine, I'm sure."

The hall was more welcoming. A bronze plaque opposite the door bore the figure of Christ, not bowed in suffering but robed in glory. Aidan recognized it. He had seen the original on an ancient book cover in a museum in Dublin. A bowl of hyacinths and primroses stood beneath it.

Mrs Batley went to the small room behind the reception desk and reached down the keys.

"Eleven and twelve. I'll show you the way, shall I? I'm afraid we don't have a lift."

"We're fit, aren't we, kid?"

Melangell was very still, thoughtful. He wondered if it was just because she was tired. She lifted her small rucksack, which she had slipped to the floor.

The front door behind them burst open. Two women swept across the hall towards them. Or rather the foremost forged ahead like a ship under full sail, while her companion glided obediently in her wake.

"Haccombe and Grayson." The large woman in the brown tweed suit, with the brutally severe haircut, had a surprisingly musical voice. Grayson, behind her, favoured softer colours and fabrics. A violet jumper and heather-coloured skirt, and a sky-blue coat.

"I'll just check you in. Then I was going to show…"

"We've booked a double room." The tweed-suited Haccombe seemed to fill the space before the reception desk. She cast a brief look at Aidan and Melangell, then turned back to Mrs Batley, as if they were of no importance.

"Is that Mrs or Miss Haccombe?" The landlady's pen was poised over her register.

"Doctor."

"Oh, and your friend?"

"Miss Valerie Grayson, if you must know." Dr Haccombe answered for both of them.

"I've actually given you a family room in the garden. That's a double and single bed, instead of a twin. En-suite, of course. If you'd like to wait here while I show Mr Davison and his daughter upstairs…"

Dr Haccombe's large hand descended over the key in Mrs Batley's grasp. "If we can navigate from Oxford to Lindisfarne, I'm sure we can find your garden chalet on our own. Which way?"

"Round to the left, past the dining room. There's a glass door."

'Valerie. Get the luggage. No, belay that. I'd better help you."

"Thank you, Elspeth."

It was the first time Valerie Grayson had spoken. She spoke firmly, with a smile. Her eyes flicked across to Aidan's, almost with apology. Just for moment, she winked at a startled Melangell.

Then they were gone, out to the small car park, like an eddying gust of wind. It left the entrance hall suddenly still.

Aidan was just picking up his rucksack to follow Mrs Batley upstairs when someone came almost running from the glass door the landlady had indicated, which led to the garden. A voice called with an edge of anxiety.

"Rachel?"

A woman of about thirty came bounding into the hall and pulled up short. She wore navy-blue lycra jogging pants and a grey sweatshirt. A crop of corn-gold curls topped a healthily tanned face. She poised, balanced on the balls of her feet, in trainers. Her eyes went swiftly over the three of them, then to the open front door. She was clearly searching for someone else. There was no mistaking the concern in her expression.

"Have you seen Rachel?" she asked Mrs Batley.

"That'll be that young one that looks as if she could do with a good tonic? No, I haven't."

Blue eyes swung back to steady on Aidan. He watched the effort it took her to switch her mind from the missing girl. But the smile she gave them was genuine.

"Hey, I'm sorry! I should have said hello."

"These'll be another two of yours, Reverend," Mrs Batley said. "Mr Davison and… Mel… Melly…"

"Melangell," Melangell said. "You don't *look* like a Reverend."

Chapter Three

LUCY PARGETER FOUND HERSELF staring down into the grey-blue eyes of a freckled face, surmounted by a mop of light-brown curls more unruly than her own. The child looked tall but thin, as though a gust of wind might blow her away.

Lucy cast startled eyes at the girl's father. When Aidan Davison had signed up for himself and his daughter, it had not occurred to Lucy that Melangell would be so young.

"How old...?"

Her first thought was that Aidan Davison looked like a red-haired gnome. He was barely as tall as she was, with hair that tended to stand up as though he had just run his hand through it, and a pointed beard. He wore khaki shorts and his legs were smeared with mud.

Grey-blue eyes, like his daughter's, were looking back at her challengingly.

"Why don't you ask her?"

Lucy felt herself blushing. Of course. It was the "Does he take sugar?" syndrome: assuming that only able-bodied adults could speak for themselves. She should have known better.

She pushed aside her alarm for the vanished Rachel and made her eyes warm for the child.

"Hello, Melangell. I'm sorry. When your father booked for you to come on my Mission to Northumbria holiday, he didn't tell me how old you were."

"Eight."

Her eyes had a very direct stare. Despite the childishness of her other features, those eyes looked... old.

"I hope you enjoy it, and that it won't be too difficult for you."

"Melangell probably knows more about Northumbrian saints than half the people here." In spite of his earlier reproof, Melangell's father was speaking for his daughter now.

"I know about St Aidan," Melangell said. "That's Daddy's name. That's partly why we've come."

Lucy looked across at Aidan, considering. Separated from his wife, probably. Access rights. Bringing the child here for a holiday. It happened all the time nowadays. Fractured families.

Next moment, the hall was suddenly full of people as the front door swung violently open. Belatedly, Lucy realized there were only two of them. A large, brown-suited woman towing an oversize case on wheels, and a thinner one with soft grey hair almost blocked from view behind her.

For the second time, Lucy geared herself up to play the part of the welcoming host. She had never run a course like this before. She knew how much its success depended on the quality of her leadership.

"Welcome! You must be…"

"Haccombe and Grayson. Never mind about that." The larger woman forged past her, brushing her welcome aside. "Let's get these things stowed in our cabin. We can do the formalities later."

As they swept in the direction of the garden door, Valerie Grayson threw Lucy a secret smile of resignation.

Mrs Batley was making for the staircase with Aidan Davison and Melangell. Lucy was left standing in the hall. Four more additions to her party, and already she was feeling her quiet assumption of authority as leader slipping away from her.

And Rachel was missing.

She stepped out into the refreshing breeze of the front garden. At the gate, between the palm trees, she looked up and down the road. No sign of Rachel.

It was early to be worried. She had known she was taking a risk bringing the troubled teenager with her. But this had seemed a healing place to bring her. Away from the pull of drugs and drink. Rachel had been clean for several months. Yet she would always live on a knife-edge. There were pushers only too keen to get her back. Or the pressures of her difficult life could tip her over the edge.

Lindisfarne. Holy Island. It had offered the promise of sanctuary. How many pilgrims had come this way across the sands to find the meeting place with God St Aidan had created here? She had fled here herself, at the lowest point of her life. Would it work for Rachel? She must pray that it would.

But where was she? She ran her fingers through her tangled hair.

Lucy told herself it was not unusual for the girl to take off on her own.

Maybe it hadn't been such a good idea to combine taking Rachel away for a holiday with running a course for a group of strangers. Could she really do her best for both?

Should she call Peter to look for Rachel?

Peter might be only twenty, but he was a tower of strength.

Lucy's feet shifted restlessly. She longed to be active, to launch into a loping run, covering the ground effortlessly to search around St Colman's House. But she had other duties. Mrs Batley would soon be serving tea to the new arrivals. She ought to be there.

The procession of visitors making their way from the main car park up to the village had thinned. But the flow of people leaving was growing. Her mind ran down the list of names. Just the Cavendishes to come.

She looked once more for any sign of Rachel. With a sigh of frustration she turned back to the house.

The hall was empty now. She made for the garden door and the chalet she was sharing with Rachel. Would it have been better to book two singles upstairs, like Aidan Davison and Melangell? A haven of quiet for herself. Privacy for Rachel.

She pulled a face. It had been enough expense to pay for Rachel to share a double with her. The church had helped. The rest had come out of her modest salary as a probationary Methodist minister. The numbers who had signed up for her course were not going to bring her a great deal more than her expenses.

But still. A week on Lindisfarne. It had to be worth it.

She hurried on. The glass door opened on to the back garden of the house. Mrs Batley had made it a welcoming area. Flowering bushes surrounded the lawn. Tables and seats were set out invitingly. Tulips and forget-me-nots made colourful borders. Along one side a row of chalet bedrooms gave on to a covered passageway to the house.

Someone sprang up from one of the garden seats.

"Lucy! Have you been outside? You haven't seen James, have you?"

Sue English: a rather pallid and plump young woman with worried brown eyes behind her glasses. Lucy had met her only briefly this afternoon, and then she had hardly spoken. Not that she had had a chance. Sue had simply watched with a mixture of awe and admiration as her companion – partner? Lucy struggled to define their relationship – had strode into the guesthouse as though he owned it. There was something unbalanced here. James was occupying a chalet room that would probably sleep three. Sue was in the singles under the eaves.

He had accosted Lucy as if he were the course leader rather than she.

Now, without James, Lucy felt as though she was seeing Sue for the first time.

"Has he gone out?"

"I don't know. He didn't tell me. But he's not in his room. I last saw him from my window upstairs. He was down here talking to that girl with the spotty face."

"Rachel?" Lucy asked sharply. She was suddenly defensive. Yes, Rachel was a teenager with unhealthy skin. Drugs had taken their toll. But that shouldn't be the first thing anyone noticed about her. Her defining feature.

"Yes. But she's not here either."

Lucy stared at her with dawning understanding. Sue had come all this way with James Denholme from – where was it? – Huddersfield.

She must have been looking forward to a week with the man she so obviously adored. And now, they had hardly got through the door before James had taken an interest in a younger girl.

Rachel. Was that where she was? The unease that had gripped Lucy when she found the teenager was missing so soon after their arrival took on a more solid edge. What sort of man was James Denholme?

She remembered an enthusiastic handclasp. A man about her own age, well built and good looking, with the self-confidence of one who knew it; his cry of, "We've come for mutual inspiration, haven't we? 'Mission to Northumbria.' That's what this country needs."

Yet behind his wide smile and hearty words she had felt his blue eyes assessing her shrewdly. His bearing exuded authority. She had an uncomfortable feeling that he was sizing her up and finding her inadequate.

If Rachel *was* with him, was she in a fit state to stand up against that male authority? And what might James want from a vulnerable eighteen-year-old girl?

New anxieties came crowding in.

Behind her, Mrs Batley called from the door, "Tea's ready in the lounge, Reverend."

She threw what she hoped was an encouraging smile at Sue. "I'm sure they'll be back soon."

Chapter Four

AIDAN WAS RIGHT ABOUT the small rooms under the eaves. His had a bed which might just have served as a double. Melangell's, next door, was narrower. Both rooms had washbasins. The deep-set windows had curtains patterned with cornflowers.

"There's a bathroom and a toilet at the end of the corridor," Mrs Batley told them. "There'll be tea downstairs in five minutes."

Aidan thanked her.

The skylights they had seen from the road lit the corridor. The bedrooms themselves had dormer windows looking out over the garden. He could see the row of newer bedrooms that opened on to it. Miss Grayson, who had briefly winked at Melangell, was standing outside one on the edge of the verandah, looking at the flower beds.

He wondered whether he should have booked one of those larger en-suite family rooms for himself and Melangell. Would anyone have raised eyebrows at his sharing with his eight-year-old daughter? The question had never arisen when Jenny was alive.

"Look! You can see the castle!"

Melangell was bouncing on his bed on her knees. She leaned across to the windowsill.

He raised his eyes to the longer view. She was right. Beyond the garden, colourful with the same spring flowers he had seen in the hall, stretched sheep-scattered fields and then that sentinel turret on its narrow rock. In the harbour before it, boats were beginning to rock on the incoming tide.

"The water's coming up over the causeway, isn't it? If we hadn't hurried, we'd have been swept out to sea or drowned." She sounded excited rather than fearful. "It's a good job you didn't hang around taking photographs, like you usually do."

Photographs? Like the television adverts that tempt an addict to reach for a drink, Aidan's hand strayed towards his camera bag. This was a high angle he hadn't taken before, looking out over the grey slate rooftops of the village. It wasn't usually possible on this low-lying island, except from the castle.

He leaned further out and turned north to catch the tumble of sand dunes that skirted the coastal road, back towards the mainland they had left behind.

For a while, he was busy with lenses and angles. He tried to close his mind to the voice that told him there would be no book of Jenny's to illustrate this time.

Yet, as he focused on the advancing line of grey water, he felt a surge of joy returning. There was always something special about being on an island towards the end of the day, when the tourists have gone, and only the residents and the longer-term visitors remain. It was all the more marked on Lindisfarne when the tide rose to cut off access.

"It's just us now, isn't it?" Melangell said, catching his thought. "Once the tide comes in, no one else can come."

"I expect they have boats for emergencies."

She made a face. "Spoilsport."

Aidan was just turning away from the window when a movement below caught his eye. A man came striding into the garden, not from the house, but angling across the lawn. From above, Aidan couldn't see his face to judge his age, just his thick crop of golden-waved hair and his brown bomber jacket.

A woman sprang up from one of the garden seats. Aidan hadn't noticed her before. In all the time he and Melangell had been looking out of the window, she must not have moved. She almost ran to meet the newcomer. A plump young woman, with long straight hair. She seized his arm.

Even from here, without hearing what he said, it was plain to see the impatience with which the man shook her off. She stepped back, repulsed, but she was still talking to him. The man made as if to stride past her to his chalet. But then he checked. He turned back and put his arm around her shoulders. Aidan's eye showed him, in imagination, the impatience in the man's face turn to a cajoling smile. For a moment, he saw again that couple clasped together on the beach.

The woman's shoulders relaxed. She sidled against him as they went across the grass to one of the doors. Then, to Aidan's surprise, he shut the door firmly on her. She was left standing on the verandah. She seemed to watch the closed door for a while, then turned for the main house.

Aidan's eyebrows rose. So, not a couple, then. Or not officially. But the golden-haired man in the brown jacket was not slumming in the servants' bedrooms under the eaves. Did he have another partner, a friend? Or had he booked this spacious family room for himself?

He sat down on the bed and began to review the photos he had taken. He came to that distant couple on the beach. The red top and the brown. The image was too small to see more. His thumb lingered over the delete button, but curiosity stayed his hand.

A gong rang faintly downstairs.

"Tea," Aidan announced, turning from the window and stowing his camera away.

"Yay!" Melangell leaped from his bed. "I'm starving."

They were starting down the stairs when a young woman shot past them, running up towards the top floor they had just left. She was dressed entirely in black. A fall of dark hair, none too clean, swung aside as she turned her head to them. Aidan saw a flash of interest in her brown eyes. Her lips curved in a cheeky smile.

Then the spark faded. The lank hair fell back, hiding her face. She turned at the top of the stairs and headed for one of the bedroom doors.

Aidan grinned wryly. For a moment, there had been something provocative in those curving lips. But he was forty, ginger-haired. Nothing there to excite a sexually active teenager.

The grin stiffened. Jenny hadn't lived to see forty.

There were voices coming from the sitting room. As they crossed the hall, Aidan's eye was caught by a red jacket flung across a chair. It had swept a hyacinth from the bowl of flowers. Something about the cut of it told him it was a woman's. It might have been dropped by someone coming through the front door, or the door from the garden, or even from upstairs.

Peony red. The colour that had appeared briefly in that shot he had taken of the couple on the beach.

The lounge, with its floral-upholstered sofas, seemed crowded. There was the curly haired minister Lucy, who had greeted them. She still looked athletic in sweatshirt and jogging pants. The oddly matched pair of older women who had stormed through reception were there. The golden-haired man Aidan had been watching from above had shed his jacket and now appeared in a high-necked Aran jersey. Close up, he was younger than Aidan and undeniably handsome and well built. As so often, Aidan wished that he himself was taller and did not have such flamboyantly ginger hair. He shot a glance of sympathy at the long-haired, overweight young woman standing just a little behind as this Adonis threw his dazzling smile around the other women.

In a corner of the room he noticed, belatedly, an older couple he hadn't seen before. Either they had been in their room when the Davisons had come, or they were late arrivals. The man was balding, in a crumpled brown linen suit. His grey-haired wife wore a baggy green cardigan over a ruffled white blouse. They stood retired from the rest, teacups in hand, making no attempt to engage strangers in conversation.

Melangell wriggled deftly through the adult bodies to the table against the wall. It was set with teacups and plates of what looked like homemade cakes. She poured herself a cup of milk and piled her plate with a slice of carrot cake, an iced cupcake and a triangle of shortbread.

She raised her eyebrows at Aidan, and took his grin as permission to add a piece of fruit cake to her hoard.

"If you'd like to take a seat," Lucy Pargeter was saying, "we'll introduce ourselves, and I'll tell you what I plan to do this week."

Melangell perched on the arm of Aidan's sofa. The woman in the green cardigan smiled at him apologetically.

"Is it all right if we come and join you?"

Her bald-headed husband leaned across and beamed at Melangell. "Hello, young lady. I wasn't expecting to find any children here. I hope you won't be bored."

Aidan gritted his teeth. He was growing tired of the need to defend Melangell's presence. It would sound too much like a doting parent to say that Melangell was not like other children, but it was true. It had been a bittersweet joy to think of bringing her here, the first real holiday they had had since Jenny died. She would be walking in her mother's footsteps, reliving the stories of Northumbria's past, which Jenny had revelled in. Many of them Melangell knew already. He had not the slightest doubt about her capacity to keep up with the other participants.

He was rescued from the need to reply. Lucy Pargeter was beginning the introductions.

"It's only fair to start with myself. I'm a Methodist minister from a small town in the middle of Devon, but I've got Northumbrian blood in me. Since I was a teenager I've been fascinated by the stories of Northumbrian kings and saints in what we used to call the Dark Ages, before we found out all the brilliant things that were going on then. A particular favourite of mine is Hilda of Whitby. Now there was a strong woman." She shot a look across at Elspeth Haccombe, as though expecting the Oxford don to agree with her. But Dr Haccombe's face was set in a sceptical frown, though her friend Valerie smiled.

Lucy continued with undaunted enthusiasm. "Mother of one of the most famous abbeys of its time, with both men and women under her authority. I did think of holding this course at Whitby, but then it seemed better to come here, to Lindisfarne, where it all began. Anyone else ready to tell us who they are and why they've come? ... Sue?"

Her eyes found not the handsome male figure in the armchair opposite her, but the plainer, more self-effacing woman on a less comfortable chair beside him. Sue's plump face, behind the glasses, looked startled.

"Me?… I'm Sue English, from Huddersfield True Gospel Church. But I'm only James's assistant. I help with the admin and stuff. He's the one you should be asking." She shot him a sidelong smile of encouragement.

Her companion was already leaning forward on the edge of his seat, only too eager to take centre stage. But Lucy held up an authoritative hand. "All in good time, Sue. I want to know what brought *you* here."

Sue looked flustered by the question. Aidan suspected that what she wanted did not figure largely in the relationship.

"I… that is… Well, it was the title, 'Mission to Northumbria'. I mean, that's what we're here for, isn't it? To spread the Lord's word? I didn't… I mean…" She looked nervously at James. "I didn't think it was all going to be historical."

James rounded on her. "You mean you've dragged me all the way up here for a bunch of thousand-year-old superstitions! A workshop on mission, you told me. New fields of evangelism in the north."

It looked as though he was going to strike her. Aidan was halfway out of the sofa. Lucy gave a sharp cry and moved forward.

Elspeth Haccombe harrumphed loudly from the far side of the room. "Speak for yourself! If I'd thought this was going to be some sort of charismatic crusade, I'd have taken myself somewhere else. Valerie assured me nobody would try to convert me."

"It's OK," Lucy tried to reassure her. Her cheeks looked pale and she was breathing fast. "We've all come with our own agenda. That's the richness of this place. There's something here for everyone. We don't need to take away the same things from it."

She turned back to James, who settled back into his seat defiantly. She lifted her eyebrows enquiringly. James seized his opportunity, a little too forcefully for Aidan's liking.

"James Denholme. It sounds as though I've been brought here on false pretences. I'm not living in the past. Like Sue says, if you want to know about Huddersfield True Gospel Church, I'm the one you ought to be asking. I'm not just the pastor there. I set it up. And the Lord is doing wonderful work through me. People are streaming through the doors. I can assure our sister over there…"

"That's great, James." Aidan's estimation of Lucy grew as she cut in deftly to stem the flow. That moment of fear he had sensed in her had passed. "But all the details of this week were on the website and in the brochure. How did you think this course could meet your needs?"

"I took Sue's word for it." He glared at her. "I don't believe in all this stuff about Catholic saints and miracles."

"Celtic saints," growled the formidable Elspeth. "Not Roman. At least, to begin with."

"Whatever. And Lucy, I have to tell you you're wrong that women like your Hilda should have authority over men. All the twelve apostles were male. And didn't St Paul say women should keep silent in church? No, I'm here because there's a tide of paganism sweeping over England these days. It breaks my heart to look at the sinful world around us. Fool that I was, I thought you would have some ideas for doing something about that."

His blue eyes went challengingly round the room, as though the respectable array of people there were the epitome of drink, drugs and violence.

"It's true that I take my inspiration from the saints of the past," Lucy countered. "But the last session will bring us up to date on what that means today."

The door behind her opened suddenly. A teenage girl with long, lank hair stood there. Acne marred her sallow face. Her brown eyes looked frightened.

It was the same girl who had passed Aidan and Melangell on the stairs. And yet she was not the same.

The provocative smile had gone. As she looked around the room full of people from under hooded lids, she flinched like a startled animal. She turned for the door as if about to bolt.

Lucy was swiftly on her feet. Her hand went out to stay the girl.

"This is Rachel," she said to the others. "Rachel Ince. She's a friend of mine. We came up together in my car from Devon. Rachel's here because… well, mainly because she needs a holiday."

She spoke in a lower voice to the girl. "Are you all right? I missed you."

The girl nodded silently and tugged the sleeves of her sweater down over her hands. She let Lucy lead her to a chair beside her own and sat down. Aidan was close enough to see that she was trembling.

"Welcome back, Rachel!" James Denholme was looking across the room at her intently.

She hung her head and did not meet his eyes.

Chapter Five

"**E**LSPETH HACCOMBE. DOCTOR. Senior lecturer in history, Lady Margaret Hall, Oxford." She bent a condescending smile on the rest of the group.

Then her keen eyes went back to Lucy. "Don't look so alarmed, padre. I'm a medievalist: thirteenth and fourteenth centuries. I shan't be trampling on your toes. I'm not a specialist in Anglo-Saxon Northumbria. And in case you're wondering what I'm doing on a church-based holiday, Valerie likes this kind of thing. She's got a soft spot for your Celtic saints. Sentimentalism, if you ask me."

Lucy forced a smile, trying to keep the sharpness out of her voice. "You're right there, Elspeth. There *is* a lot of sentimentality about the Celtic Church. That's just what I'm hoping to lift the lid on this week. It wasn't all attuning to nature and talking to the birds. There were bitter disputes that tore the community apart. We'll be looking at those too. And by the way, I'm Lucy. There's no need to stand on ceremony."

She could feel the disturbing undercurrents in the room. For a moment, James had frightened her, when he raised his fist to Sue. It had brought back terrifying memories. He obviously thought that Lucy had no right to wear a dog collar. He certainly thought he could run this course better than she would.

And Dr Haccombe regarded her with barely disguised contempt. *She may be right,* Lucy thought ruefully. *I'm no scholar. I just want to share my enthusiasm for this special place.*

She had missed Valerie Grayson's soft-spoken introduction: "… assistant bookshop manager. And yes, Elspeth's right. I've always loved the stories of the Northumbrian saints. The Venerable Bede's history. I'm looking forward to you telling us more."

She has a lovely smile, Lucy reflected. *I can see why even someone as prickly as Elspeth Haccombe loves her – if that's the right word. She makes me feel she knows I'm feeling a bit bruised, that she's on my side.*

She gave Valerie an answering smile of gratitude.

"Aidan?"

She saw the red-headed man start. He had been sitting on a sofa in the corner, his foxy face watching everyone else. Suddenly he found the spotlight of her attention turned on him. She watched him struggle to come back from wherever his thoughts had taken him.

"Aidan Davison." He answered more curtly than she had expected. "Photographer."

He stopped, as though unwilling to go on.

"And you've come here because… ?"

His eyes levelled on hers, almost with dislike. He swallowed. "I had… happy memories of this place. I wanted to show Melangell."

The gruffness of his voice discouraged further questions. There was something more here. Would a week be long enough for him to trust her, to tell her more?

"Right. That leaves you." She turned her smile on the couple sharing the sofa with Aidan.

Melangell's hand shot up. "Please, Miss Pargeter… Sorry! Lucy. You forgot about me."

I've done it again! Lucy cursed herself. *Acted as though an eight-year-old child couldn't speak for herself.*

"Oh, Melangell! I'm so sorry. What did you want to tell us?"

"I'm Melangell Davison. Melangell after a Welsh saint. I'm eight years old and I go to St Nicholas Primary School. And I really, really wanted to come on your holiday, because I've got *loads* of books about St Aidan and St Cuthbert and St Chad, and all the rest of them. My mother wrote them."

The girl was sitting so close to her father on the arm of the sofa that Lucy could not help seeing the shock that stiffened him.

He really hadn't wanted Melangell to say that. I guess it must have been a painful marriage break-up. Yet why come back here to awaken those memories?

"Thank you, Melangell. If you've got any of those books with you, I'd love to see them."

Now there really was only the elderly couple on the sofa.

The bald-headed man beamed round at all of them. "David Cavendish. Retired. A gentleman of leisure now. To tell you the truth, we didn't set out looking for this sort of holiday. But we've always loved the north-east: Robin Hood's Bay, Scarborough, Alnwick Castle. And when we looked up on the internet to see where we could stay, this came up. And we thought, well, that sounds a bit different. Let's give it a go." He turned to his wife. "Isn't that right, Fran?"

"Yes, dear. I'm Frances, by the way. Call me Fran. And like Dave says, we're retired. Used to run a children's home. We love kiddies." She turned a warm smile on Melangell.

Lucy's heart sank at the same time as she heard the stifled gasp from Rachel beside her. This was all she needed. Rachel had spent much of her troubled childhood in a residential home. It was something she found difficult to talk about. Lucy had no idea what had happened there, but it had clearly not been a happy experience.

She glanced at the teenager with concern. Rachel was curled up in her chair, like a frightened animal that expects to be hit. Her face was covered by her hanging hair.

Lucy sighed. The Cavendishes were clearly an innocent, well-meaning couple who loved children. But their very presence and the associations they brought might be enough to undo the healing Lucy was trying to bring to Rachel.

It was only the first day, and she was already beginning to question the wisdom of bringing this disparate group of people together, with their human problems. But she was committed now.

She put a hand reassuringly on Rachel's knee. The girl was shivering.

Chapter Six

AIDAN SAW THE DOOR BEHIND LUCY burst open. She turned sharply.

A large untidy young man in horn-rimmed glasses rushed into the room. He stopped abruptly. Dark hair flopped over his broad face. He was panting.

"I haven't found her," he said to Lucy. "I've looked everywhere. I…" His dark eyes went past her. "Rachel! You're back!" A grin flowered over his perspiring features.

He looked around at the crowded room, as though he had only just noticed the others. "Sorry, everyone. I'm Peter. I guess I've missed the intro. Typical."

Lucy smiled at him warmly. "Peter's another friend of mine," she told the group. "An archaeology student." She looked at her watch and seemed to make a decision. "Right, people. I think we've got time before supper to make a start. If you'd like to get your jackets and meet me by the front door in ten minutes, I'll show you where, for me, the story begins. And I can assure Elspeth it's not sentimental."

Melangell jumped down from the sofa arm.

Frances Cavendish struggled to hoist herself off the cushions. She grumbled, "No one told me this was going to be a walking holiday."

Lucy caught the protest on her way out of the room. She turned in apology.

"I'm sorry! I should have asked. Does anyone here have mobility problems? It's not far – honestly. I'm not taking you on a route march before supper."

David Cavendish helped his wife up. "Don't listen to her, love," he said cheerfully to Lucy. "She'll be fine. We may not be as young as we were, but there's life in the old bird yet."

"Here! You mind who you're calling old!" his wife retorted.

As they made their way upstairs to fetch their coats, Melangell turned to Aidan on the landing with a bright light in her eyes. "Did you see? That girl? She had a tear in her ear. There was blood on it. As if someone had pulled her earring off. Bet you it was the one I found."

Aidan gave a start. His normally sharply focused eyes had not noticed this.

"You'll have to ask her about it."

Aidan had half-expected the shrinking Rachel to be missing from the party that gathered outside the front door of St Colman's House. But she was there, a huddled figure beyond the edge of the group. Instead of the red jacket, she wore a shapeless black coat that reached nearly to her knees.

Lucy looked flushed. He wondered if there had been an argument. The large ungainly student Peter was standing behind the girl, like a protective sheepdog.

As he stepped out into the keen breeze of late afternoon, Aidan's eyes sought Rachel's face. Had Melangell been right about the blood on her ear, the torn lobe? Could anyone here have used force on the girl, so soon after their arrival? Who? Why?

Her limp curtain of hair made it impossible to see.

It occurred to Aidan to wonder whether it had been wise of the young minister to bring such a problem with her when she already had the responsibility of leading this group.

And where did Peter fit into their story?

Lucy led them down the now quiet road. The strait ahead was filling. Soon there would be no more traffic across the causeway.

Past the car park, she turned off onto the sands. Melangell tugged Aidan's sleeve.

"It was here, wasn't it? Where we came across the Pilgrims' Way? Where I found the earring."

Aidan looked out along the line of poles that marked the route they had taken from the mainland. The water now lapped around all but the nearest ones. Out in the middle, the current would run deep and strong. There was that little refuge on stilts. It hadn't been foolish of him to take Melangell across that way, had it?

Lucy walked down on to the beach and seated herself on a grass-tussocked bank of sand.

"It's best if you face the water."

Elspeth Haccombe made more of a fuss of arranging her tweed skirt than was necessary, wanting to assert her presence rather than let Lucy take centre stage.

Then there was silence. An absence of voices that gradually filled with the whisper of the waves and the sigh of the wind in the grass.

Out of that stillness, Lucy's voice came with more authority than Aidan had expected.

"I want to take you back to the year 590. The future of Northumbria hangs in the balance. Celtic Britain has been Christian for centuries. Don't believe those who tell you Augustine brought Christianity to us in 597. They're only talking about the heathen Anglo-Saxons in the south-east corner of England. Here in the north, the Anglian invaders are only just getting a foothold. Do you see there, down the coast, those ramparts on the cliff?"

The square silhouette was just visible in the early evening light.

"Bamburgh. It was a stronghold long before the Normans built that castle. By 590 the Angles had seized it. But all across the north there were the old Christian kingdoms of Britain. And the greatest of their kings was Urien of Rheged. From his capital in Carlisle he ruled from Galloway to Shropshire. He summoned the other Celtic kings to his banner to drive the invaders out: Rhydderch of the Clyde, Fiachna of Ulster, Morcant, whose land here the Angles had taken, and many more.

"The Irish king Fiachna captured Bamburgh from the usurpers. They harried the heathen and drove them back to this last redoubt, here on the island of Lindisfarne, which the Celtic Britons called Metcaud. They were on the brink of beating the invaders completely and driving them from our shores. Urien and his host were massed on those sands opposite us. They blockaded the Angles on this island for three days and three nights.

"They almost did it. They were in sight of total victory. But something terrible stopped them. Over there, just across the water, someone assassinated their leader, King Urien of Rheged.

"Rumour has it that it was Morcant, who had been king here before the Angles took his land. He was bitter that Urien had given Bamburgh to Fiachna of Ulster, and not back to him.

"However it was, the blood of the greatest British king of the sixth century was spilled in the sand. And with it went the hope of a Christian victory. The lesser kings quarrelled and broke up. The heathen Angles took back their conquests. Lindisfarne was never called by its Celtic name of Metcaud again.

"The bard Taliesin sang the praises of Urien in the oldest surviving poem in Europe:

"A head I bear by my side,
The head of Urien, the mild leader of his army,
And on his white bosom the sable raven is perched."

Her voice died into the weeping of the waves.

In spite of himself, Aidan shivered. He had not known this story.

After a while, Frances Cavendish stirred. "Very nice, I'm sure." Her tone meant something else.

"And what exactly was the point of that?" Elspeth said more loudly. "Though I grant you it certainly wasn't sentimental. Unless you mean to show us the capacity of the Celts to snatch defeat out of the jaws of victory."

Lucy laughed. "Something like that. I rather hoped you might contribute your own thoughts about what it might mean. And yes, that's a start."

There was belligerence in James's voice. "You sound anti-English. Aren't you English yourself?"

"A mixture, like all of us, I suppose. I have ancestors on Tyneside. I like to think that some of my genes go back before the Anglo-Saxons to the Celtic Britons of the north, the people who fought the Northumbrian Angles."

"Well, I'm proud to be English. I don't like the way you rubbished Augustine of Canterbury. Because of him, the English spread the word of God across the world."

"Don't worry, James. All in good time. I can assure you there are plenty of Anglo-Saxon saints to come."

The discussion became more general.

Aidan looked across at Rachel. She was sitting a little apart from the rest, with her knees hunched before her. Her head was lifted now to stare across the strait at the once bloodstained beach opposite. The wind lifted her hair. Just for a moment, Aidan saw what Melangell had: the slit in her earlobe, as though someone or something had torn the ring through her flesh.

Was it the earring Melangell had found? Who, then, had been that larger figure in his photograph?

He looked around him, at the brown leather bomber jacket James was wearing; Elspeth Haccombe's brown tweed coat. Even Peter, who had been searching for her, wore a shapeless khaki anorak.

"Well," said Lucy, getting to her feet. "I guess Mrs Batley's supper must be on its way."

As they trooped back to the road, Melangell stayed looking out over the grey water.

"Is it really true? Where we walked down to the crossing this afternoon – that's where he was murdered?"

Aidan laughed to reassure her. "That was a bit more bloodthirsty than I expected for a start. But you don't have to worry. That was more than a thousand years ago. I'm not expecting a murder on the sands while we're here."

Chapter Seven

"I DON'T LIKE LEAVING YOU ALONE." Lucy stood at the door of the garden bedroom, tense with indecision. "At least come and get something to eat."

"I'm not hungry." Rachel's voice was muffled.

"I'll get Mrs Batley to keep something for you and I'll bring it back with me."

"You've got things to do. Never mind about me."

"I *do* mind about you. I mind a great deal." Lucy longed to go back and put her arms round the girl again. None of the comfort, the coaxing, the prayers she had offered seemed to be doing any good. Rachel still sat curled in a tight ball on her bed, hugging her unhappiness to her.

Holy Island, which Lucy had hoped would cast its healing spell over her, seemed to have had the opposite effect. Rachel had been quite animated in the car, joking with Peter and singing songs as Lucy drove them north. But now it seemed as though a door to her soul had slammed shut. Nothing Lucy did or said could get past it.

Had something happened to upset her? James? Had the golden-haired pastor taken Rachel off this afternoon? Lucy's nails dug into her palms as she clenched her fists. It was one thing for James to openly challenge her leadership of this course. But if he had done anything to undermine Rachel's fragile rehabilitation...

She took a deep breath, trying to still her anger. She looked back into the twilit room. As so often, Rachel's long brown hair hung forward, obscuring her sallow face. Lucy's heart ached with pity for her.

She shaped a silent prayer.

She stood for several moments, letting this picture of the girl imprint itself on her mind. Then she straightened her shoulders and headed for the dining room.

Back in the house, Aidan and Melangell were getting ready for their first supper with the group. Dusk was thickening. Aidan went to close the curtains of his bedroom.

There was a movement in the garden below. He saw Lucy come out of one of the chalet bedrooms. She turned her head to speak to someone inside. Was it Rachel?

Yet hadn't he met Rachel earlier, bounding up the stairs to these single bedrooms? Who else was on the top floor?

He watched Lucy make her way into the house. Then a larger figure came out of another door into the shadows of the verandah. Aidan flipped through his memories of the afternoon. Wasn't that the room Valerie Grayson had stood outside? It could only be Elspeth Haccombe. She disappeared into the room Lucy had just left.

Aidan felt his eyebrows rise. It had not occurred to him to think of Elspeth as a motherly person who would go out of her way to comfort a troubled teenager. It was definitely not her style. Perhaps there was a softer side to her she kept well hidden. Maybe that was what attracted the gentler Valerie to her. He might be too ready to spring to conclusions about people.

"Daddy!" said Melangell's reproving voice from the door. "Aren't you ever coming? I'm starving."

He turned, rearranging his face into a smile. "I don't believe it. After all that cake?"

The meal was finishing. Lucy found herself growing uncomfortably nervous. She had imagined herself sharing her enthusiasm for the stories of the Northumbrian saints with a circle of eager listeners. The reality was proving more difficult. Elspeth was clearly sceptical. James didn't want to be here. He showed every sign of trying to wrest the leadership out of her hands. If he had his way, he would take the course down a more evangelistic road than she had planned. She doubted that the Cavendishes were really interested in seventh-century history.

Had she made a mistake in beginning with that bloodthirsty story of Urien's murder on the sands? She could have started with something more attractive, like St Cuthbert's playing with otters on the beach.

But she did not want a Christianity wrapped in cotton wool. It was the messy reality of life as it had been lived that attracted her. Conflicts within the Christian community and without. There had been plenty of those in Northumbria.

She stood, with what she hoped was an encouraging smile.

"Coffee in the lounge. Then you have a free evening. I've put out a collection of reading material about the Celtic and Anglo-Saxon Church in the north and Lindisfarne in particular. Feel free to borrow stuff, as long as I get it back before we go. Tomorrow morning, I've got permission for us to hold our own service in the ruins of the abbey when it opens at nine-thirty. The causeway's closed until noon, so there shouldn't be too many visitors about. I'd be happy to see any of you who would like to join me for that. We'll start our next session for everyone there at ten, to go on with the story I started this evening."

"You haven't said anything about prayers tonight," James's voice challenged her. "If that's too much for you, I'll lead them."

Lucy felt the blood mounting in her cheeks. She tried to keep her voice level and friendly.

"Thank you, James. That's a kind offer. As it happens, I have an order of evening prayer from the Northumbrian Community I was going to use. Mrs Batley's given us the room across the hall for a chapel. Perhaps you'd like to read the lesson?"

She felt his pale blue eyes on her, cold, assessing. Was this going to be the pattern for the week? This struggle for control of the group?

As the others slipped away for a comfort break, all Lucy really wanted to do was to step outside into the cool of the night and spend a few minutes in prayer. Another pull of conscience told her she ought to look in on Rachel, to take her the supper Mrs Batley had promised to put aside.

She walked into the kitchen. There were two covered plates on a tray.

"Is this for Rachel?"

"A piece of pie and some apples and custard. I hope she's all right."

"Thanks. Yes. She's had a bad time recently. She needs time to herself."

Lucy hoped that was all it was.

She carried the tray along the verandah and tapped at the door. No answer from inside. Manoeuvring her burden precariously, she tried the handle. The door was unlocked. It was only then it struck her that there was no light on inside. She felt for her own bed and set the tray down there, then turned for the light switch. There was a tension in her throat. She could not have said what she feared to see.

The spacious bedroom was empty. The covers on Rachel's bed were rumpled, where she had been curled up when Lucy left her. Fighting down her growing alarm, she moved to the bathroom. The door was closed. She knocked gently.

"Rachel? Are you in there? It's me. Lucy."

It took a moment to summon the willpower to open the door. She was praying she would not find Rachel in the bath, with blood from her wrists turning from shocking red to pink as it emptied away into the water.

Her first reaction was enormous relief that there was no one there. Then renewed alarm. It was dark outside now. She had no idea where Rachel might be.

For a moment, she leaned against the doorpost, feeling dizzy. Then the practical training for the life she had led before she became a minister asserted itself. Rachel had gone missing this afternoon. She had come back on her own. At the first meeting she had looked more upset than when she had arrived, certainly. But her emotions had been in a fragile state ever since Lucy had known her. It was part of the reason for bringing her to Holy Island. It was too soon yet to panic, wasn't it?

She stepped outside into the cool of the garden.

"Rachel?"

The girl might be sitting on one of the seats on the lawn, unseen. But there were lights along the covered verandah that led to the house. There was no sign of a hunched figure on any of the benches. No one replied.

Again, Lucy wrestled with her duties. Inside the house, nine other people would be gathering in the lounge. They would be expecting her to join them. She could slip away again for a while before evening prayers. Rachel would be back in their bedroom by then, wouldn't she?

She turned reluctantly for the house.

Chapter Eight

THE LOUNGE WAS ALREADY HALF-FULL of people when Aidan and Melangell entered. Aidan crossed the carpet to the coffee table with a sense of trepidation. He had been hoping that he could tuck himself away in a corner sofa again and listen to another of Lucy's stories about Northumbria's past. There would have been no compulsion on him to say anything. He would not have to join in the discussion, or reveal anything more about himself.

Now he felt exposed. He faced a wall of almost-strangers, any one of whom might turn an interested face to him and engage him in conversation. Aidan was not by nature unsociable, but he knew from recent experience that even the most innocent of conversations could soon turn to the question of why he and Melangell were here without Jenny.

Without Jenny.

That one irreversible reality that was a wound too dreadful to touch.

He poured himself a cup of coffee and took it quickly to a chair beside the window where no one was sitting yet.

Melangell helped herself to a chocolate biscuit and came to curl up on the carpet at his feet. A tug of conscience told him he ought to find something to amuse her. There was a cabinet in the corner with books on shelves and a cupboard below which might contain games.

Peter, the archaeology student, was bending to open it. His floppy dark hair fell forward as he searched inside. After a moment, he straightened up. He came towards the Davisons, waving a chessboard and a box of chessmen. His grin was directed at Melangell, not Aidan.

"Do you play chess?"

"Of *course* I do." Melangell scrambled to her feet.

"I thought you looked as though you might."

He laid the board on the floor and settled his ungainly bulk beside it. Melangell took up her favourite position, flat on her stomach, with her elfin face propped up on her hands. Aidan felt a rush of gratitude towards Peter.

His relief was cut short when the Cavendishes settled themselves into the sofa next to his chair. Frances took out some white knitting. A baby jacket, by the look of it. She turned to him with what he was sure was meant to be a friendly smile.

"It's lovely to see the kiddies playing, isn't it?" She nodded to Melangell. "She's a bright one, your Mel..."

"Melangell."

"We said to ourselves, Dave and me, it's a pity her mum couldn't be here as well." Her pale eyes turned to him enquiringly.

There it was. Hardly three sentences into the conversation and the wound was gaping wide.

"Yes." He took a gulp of his coffee. He had a sudden wish that he smoked, so that he could make an excuse to escape into the garden.

The best defence was to turn the questioning back on her.

"Where was the children's home you ran?"

"On the Kent coast, near Broadstairs. We always liked to be beside the sea, Dave and me."

"Can't keep away, can we? Seaside holidays," her husband joined in.

Aidan sat back and let the reminiscences of the pair wash over him.

A detached part of his mind roamed over the rest of the room. He sensed an absence. Lucy still hadn't returned. He had seen her coming out of the kitchen with a tray of food, presumably for the missing Rachel.

His photographer's gaze framed James and Sue sitting on a sofa across the room. They were physically together, but with a tension in their body language that made the gap between them seem wider than it was.

Valerie Grayson sat alone in another corner. Belatedly, Aidan wished he had gravitated towards her, rather than being cornered by the garrulous Cavendishes. He sensed a delicate reserve about Valerie. She would not have pressed him for information he did not want to give. She had one of Lucy's books on her knee, but she was not reading it. She looked slightly worried.

There was no Elspeth Haccombe. The room seemed emptier without her large presence.

The moment Lucy entered the room, Aidan could see that something was wrong. She threw a distracted look around the group, as though she had forgotten they would be here. Then he saw her make the physical effort to gather herself together. Her rounded chin went up. She shook her head so that her fair curls danced for a moment. She squared her shoulders. Then, with a smile she succeeded in making look more genuine than professional, she headed for the only person sitting alone: the grey-haired Valerie.

"If you ever want us to do some baby-sitting, don't be afraid to ask," Frances was saying at his elbow.

"What? Oh, that's very kind of you. But really, Melangell's no trouble."

"Still, we'd be glad to take her off your hands. Play some games with her," David Cavendish put in.

"We miss the children," Frances agreed. "And they do need someone to mother them, don't they?"

He could stand it no longer. "Excuse me." He got up. "I think I could do with a breath of fresh air."

Melangell's clear voice cut across the room. She had lifted her tousled head from the chessboard and was looking up at Valerie.

"My mother wrote that book you've got. It's the one about St Cuthbert, isn't it?"

Aidan flinched.

Both Valerie's and Lucy's heads shot up.

The image of the small, glossy-covered book on Valerie's knee burned on his brain.

Lucy exclaimed, "Jenny Davison? I never realized." She looked more closely at the cover. "Of course! Photographs by Aidan Davison. Aidan, I'm so sorry! I never made the connection."

Aidan felt as though a storm was churning in his head. He couldn't handle this.

Valerie smiled. Her quiet voice spoke the words he dreaded: "What a pity Jenny couldn't be here as well."

Lucy laughed. "She could have led this course better than I can."

He could stand it no longer. The words were torn from him, in a voice so harsh he hardly recognized it as his own: "I didn't come here to discuss my wife!"

He found himself standing outside the house, hardly knowing how he had got there. He was shaking.

The road was quiet now. A string of lights beaded its way towards the village, still hardly visible beyond the trees that lined this street. The sky was not completely dark. Stars shone hazily through the slight mist. The air was welcomingly cool and damp on his cheek, as though someone were pressing a satin cloth against his skin.

"Are you all right?" He jumped as a voice spoke beside him. He had not heard Lucy's light step in those trainers.

He felt his hairs prickle. She was the last person he wanted to talk to. He knew what she must be thinking – what everyone in that room would assume – a broken marriage. It happened all the time. It would be her job to show a pastoral concern for him.

He could not bring himself to tell her the truth.

"Yes," he said curtly.

He ought to apologize for his outburst, but he wasn't going to. The words stuck like a hard knot in his throat.

It felt threatening to have her stand beside him in the half-light. He tensed, waiting for the next question that would probe beneath the armour of his reticence. *Please don't ask about Jenny,* he prayed.

"Sorry! I guess I put my foot in it back there," she said quietly.

He didn't answer.

"You probably don't want me crowding you." She moved away towards the road and drew a deep breath of night air. "I feel the same.

I'm fairly new to being a minister. Sometimes I think I can't hack it. Then I come to somewhere like Holy Island and the spirits of all these marvellous people who worked and prayed here come out of the mist to hold me up and give me peace. I think of all that they had to suffer: invasion, betrayal, violent death, the loss of everything they held dear. And somehow my own problems don't seem quite so insurmountable."

He clung grimly to his silence. Whatever problems she had, they could be nothing like his own pain.

Lucy sighed. "I ought to be getting back to see to the rest of my flock. I'll leave you to the night and the peace."

"Yes." He turned an ungracious shoulder.

He heard the whisper of her rubber soles fading towards the door. A solitary seagull ghosted between the street lights.

It was only the thought of Melangell in the room behind him that made him turn.

He thought he was far enough behind her, but Lucy was waiting in the hall. He stopped abruptly at the front door. He tried to avoid the probing blue eyes. All he wanted was to be left alone.

"I'd better see if Melangell's beaten Peter yet," he said gruffly.

"She's special, isn't she?" Lucy paused by the lounge door.

"Yes," he said, again abruptly. He couldn't bring himself to tell her that Melangell was all he had.

"And I need to see if Rachel's back. She wasn't in our room. It's probably nothing. She goes off sometimes when things get too much. She's had a lot to put up with. The sort of damage no one can ever quite heal."

He saw her square her shoulders and lift her head as she pushed the lounge door open, like a soldier preparing for combat.

"I hope she comes back soon," he said with a stiff attempt at politeness.

She threw him a brief smile over her shoulder. "There's a voice in my head telling me the things I used to say in my previous existence, when other people reported a teenager missing. She's eighteen, an adult. Lots of teenagers walk out when things get too much. They usually turn up pretty soon. It's too early to send out a search party yet."

As she took a step into the crowded room Aidan's mind caught up with what she was saying.

"Your previous existence?"

"A policewoman. In this area, actually. I haven't been a Methodist minister very long. It probably shows."

Aidan halted in the doorway. He did not think he could face the rest of the group tonight after that dreadful cry of pain. All those curious eyes.

Melangell's head shot round. She scrambled up from the chessboard. Her smile was bright with excitement.

"Did you say you were in the police?"

Faces turned, all around the room. The murmur of voices stilled.

Lucy laughed uneasily. "That's a conversation-stopper, isn't it? My sister's a maths teacher and she gets the same response. But it was a few years ago now. My guilty past. I'm not going to be checking up on you all. My work now is less about crime, more about forgiveness."

"We'd better watch ourselves, though," David Cavendish laughed. "Once a copper, always a copper, I'd say. Better mind our Ps and Qs."

"Oh, please!" Lucy had coloured. "Being an ordained minister can be barrier enough. Don't hold that against me as well."

There was a disturbance behind Aidan. He saw all the eyes in the room swing past Lucy to the newcomer.

Elspeth Haccombe strode into the room. She clapped a hand on Lucy's shoulder. "You can stop worrying. There's a light on in your room. She's back."

Lucy felt a flash of joy. In spite of her confident words to Aidan, she felt that Rachel was on a knife-edge.

Then, as the pressure of Elspeth's hand on her shoulder lifted, a thought struck her. How had the Oxford don known that Rachel was missing? Lucy had told no one except Aidan. Others might have read anxiety in her body language, but Elspeth hadn't been in the lounge after supper to see it. Hers and Valerie's room was next to Lucy and

Rachel's. Had she simply seen the darkened windows and made her own assumption?

She was aware that Peter had hoisted his bulk from the chess game on the floor and was looking at her with consternation and reproach. Should she have told him? Peter was always so sweetly protective of Rachel. But Lucy had not wanted to spell out her greatest fears before the whole group. She had just prayed that Rachel would come back soon. Apparently she had.

With a quick word of apology, she made for the door before she could meet Peter's accusation.

Melangell had run to throw her thin arms around Aidan. Lucy brushed past them both. Aidan Davison was a prickly customer. The way he had shouted at her made her wonder if he might even be violent. Was that why his wife had left him? A memory of her own past made her shiver.

The garden was quiet, softly lit by the lamps along the verandah outside the chalet bedrooms. It was a joy to see that Elspeth was right. There was a glow behind the curtains of her own room.

She tapped briefly and stepped inside.

Rachel was back where Lucy had left her, sitting on her bed, with her feet tucked under her.

But there was something different. This was not the huddled and fearful figure, shrinking from the world, that she had been this afternoon. Rachel's long hair was tossed back from her face. Her eyes were bright. The food on the tray had gone.

"There you are!" Lucy said, trying to keep her voice light. "You gave me a fright when I found you'd gone."

"Why?" Rachel's voice sounded stronger. "I can go where I like, can't I? It's not a bleeding prison."

"Of course not! I only meant… Well, it's after dark, and you didn't tell me you were going out. I just like to know where you're heading, and when you'll be back. So I'll know when to start worrying."

"I don't have to tell you anything. You're not my mother."

No, Lucy thought with a flash of anger. *I'm not the woman who was so under the power of drink and drugs that they had to take you away from her, for your own safety. I actually care what happens to you.*

She swallowed back the retort before it sprang to her lips. She strove for the professional tone of calm and cheerfulness that years of training for life on the beat had instilled in her.

"You're right. I'm not your mother. But I was hoping we were friends. Friends trust each other. They tell each other stuff."

"Yeah. Like that Jamie creature kept saying. Like Jesus was my best friend and so was he. And he was going to save me, if I'd just confess my sins to him. Creep."

Lucy sat down on her own bed and gave a sigh. "I'm sorry about that. I truly am. I didn't think there'd be anyone like that on this course – the sort that tries to ram Jesus down your throat. It doesn't work like that. It really doesn't. That's what I want to tell people this week: saints like Aidan and Cuthbert, they weren't that sort of tub-thumper. They *lived* the gospel. And that was enormously attractive."

A thought flashed across her mind. James, the self-opinionated evangelist. Was that whom Rachel had been with this evening?

No. Common sense caught up with her. James and Sue had been at supper with everyone else. Lucy had left them in the lounge.

Uneasiness was returning. There was an unnatural brightness in Rachel's eyes. Her policewoman's instincts alerted her. Drugs? But Rachel was in rehab. She'd been clean for months. This was just one of her bipolar highs.

A scowl darkened Rachel's face. She tossed her head angrily and gave a bitter laugh.

"You could tell he took one look at me, out of everyone else here, and thought, 'Right, we've got a proper sinner here. Let's clock her up as my next convert.' He's right, isn't he? I'm rubbish."

"Rachel! That's not true. You've been more sinned against than sinning. You're doing marvellously. You've been clean of drugs for ages."

"Huh!" Rachel flounced off the bed and slammed the bathroom door behind her.

A selfish part of Lucy wished she had booked a single room upstairs for herself. She had enough to worry about as it was. And now she would have to spend the night with a volatile teenager who could swing from deep affection to open hostility. It was a big responsibility.

She looked at her watch. She had wrested authority back from James by saying she would lead evening prayers herself. She picked up the liturgy of the Northumbrian Community and thumbed through the pages.

She found the service of Compline for Saturday evening:

In the name of the King of life;
in the name of the Christ of love;
in the name of the Holy Spirit:
the Triune of my strength.

It would be among the service sheets she had duplicated for use this week.

I am placing my soul and my body
under Thy guarding this night, O Christ.
May Thy cross this night be shielding me.

Where *had* Rachel been in the dark?

Chapter Nine

"*T*HAT'S MORE LIKE IT."

They turned a corner between the houses and Melangell gave a little skip as the ruins of Lindisfarne Priory came into view. Aidan couldn't help it. His hand closed round his camera. He already had shots in plenty. Shots he had used to illustrate Jenny's book. But the broken pillars, the single perfect arch soaring above the short green turf stood out against the blue sky in a way that called to him irresistibly to capture them through his lens.

They reached the statue of St Aidan: tall, lean, calm-faced. You could tell the encircling sea was in his uplifted eyes. Golden lichen peppered his shoulders and tonsured head.

Melangell stroked the reddish concrete folds of his robes, almost possessively. "Hello. I've wanted to meet you for such a long time."

St Aidan's namesake could see the knot of people gathering on the turf that had once been the nave of the Norman priory's church. It was too soon yet to be certain of faces.

The woman in the entrance booth waved them through. The solid figure of the student Peter, his shaggy hair flopping over his dark-rimmed glasses, was waiting inside. He handed them their tickets.

"Hi. You found it."

"It's hard to miss."

"We're special, aren't we?" Melangell turned up a happy face to Aidan. "We can come in as soon as we like. Everybody on the mainland will have to wait until the tide goes down."

It was early enough on an April morning for there to be an edge on the breeze. But the clear sunshine was warming the sandstone to a rosier red. Melangell ran across to one of the pillars. She let her hand caress the chevron pattern incised in the stone. Then she turned, and Aidan was rewarded by her gasp as she saw the high rock of Lindisfarne Castle perfectly framed by the slender arch that had once spanned the chancel. Between the priory and the castle, boats were drawn up on a curve of pale sand.

It was as perfect as he remembered it. As perfect as it had been when it had captured Jenny and Aidan's hearts.

His finger stilled on the shutter.

He was near enough now to see the group of people around Lucy in her blue trousers and anorak. To his surprise, Rachel was there. Yet even now, she seemed poised to flee, like a bird that might take flight at the slightest alarm. Aidan was less happy to see the pastor James and his companion Sue. Last evening, James had made disparaging remarks about Lucy's use of the Northumbrian Community's liturgy. But the cadences of the threefold Celtic prayers had fitted perfectly with their setting.

Valerie was there, slim and elegant in heathery tweeds and a violet anorak. Not surprisingly, the non-believing Elspeth was absent from this morning service. Or was she? Just for a moment, Aidan caught a movement in the open space beyond the ruined church. No doubt the history don was seizing this opportunity to explore the site before the place was overrun with visitors.

Aidan and Melangell joined the group. He felt it difficult to meet the others' eyes after his display of temper last night. He was conscious that they were looking at him warily. Lucy caught his shifting gaze and gave him a brief smile of encouragement. A slight frown creased her forehead. He thought she looked nervous.

His eyes went back to Rachel. The teenager's hands were thrust into the pockets of her black jacket. She seemed unable to look at anyone directly. She shifted uneasily, still not seeming certain to stay.

"Hello," he said. "How's things?"

"'Lo," she returned curtly. She did not answer his question.

Aidan looked around again. There were still people missing, weren't there? It took a moment to place the absentees. David and Fran

Cavendish. Even as he remembered their undistinguished presence yesterday, he saw them coming through the gate. Peter followed behind like a shepherding collie.

David was looking ahead with a smile on his face. He increased his pace as he realized they were the last. But Frances had her head turned to him as she picked her way in heeled shoes across the still wet grass. Her voice came clearly on the breeze.

"I hope she doesn't expect me to sit down on this. And I'm not standing all the way through a church service. Beats me why we can't go to a proper church with chairs."

Lucy must have heard this, but she greeted the pair with a bright smile.

"Hello. You made it. Good. We're just about ready to start. No chairs, I'm afraid. But you're welcome to sit on the remains of the walls. I promise not to keep you too long. I thought we might manage a hymn to begin with."

Peter came forward and passed around sheets of paper. The little congregation broke valiantly into "Guide me, O thou great Jehovah".

As the words died away, Aidan heard a stifled cry. He turned in time to see Peter put a protective arm around a trembling Rachel. He looked round quickly to see what might have caused it. But the rest of the group were looking expectantly at Lucy. Only Elspeth strode between two far-off pillars and disappeared.

Lucy kept her service short. The rhythms of Celtic liturgy lapped around them like waves on the shore. But she brought things sharply into the present day when she reminded them of Urien's murder on the sands by someone on his own side.

"And all the time we fight each other, Jesus is calling us to go out into the world, as he did. Not to give people a theological examination, but to live the gospel where they are: male or female, black or white, churchgoers or secularists, Protestant or Catholic, straight or gay."

Aidan glanced around. The faces of the Cavendishes were impassive.

He would not have been surprised if Lucy had touched on at least one of their prejudices.

James's indignation was more evident. Aidan saw Sue gripping his wrist, restraining him from jumping to his feet to protest. Just what in that list had upset him? Several things, probably.

He suspected that Lucy might know this. She stood firmly erect, like the pillar of red sandstone behind her. The dog collar showed as a flash of white at the neck of her sapphire-blue fleece. The breeze teased her short hair.

"Lindisfarne's story is sown with dissension. We like to think of it as Holy Island, a place of peace. And so it can be. But it has known a violent history, and the discord hasn't always come from enemies outside."

Her blue eyes challenged them.

James stayed where he was, perched on the ruined wall of the church. A lingering fury scored lines in his face.

When the brief service was over, Lucy led them through the cloisters, past the statue of St Cuthbert with his knees calloused by prayer, to the outer court. Lindisfarne Castle loomed nearer on its pinnacle of rock. Across the water, the larger fortress of Bamburgh reared mistily on the far clifftop. Clouds were beginning to form. The sunshine was more fitful now.

This time, Elspeth joined them as Lucy settled her group around her again. She loomed bulkier than before in tweed trousers. She thrust a shooting-stick into the turf and settled her voluminous hips on the folding seat.

"They might have told us to bring a cushion," Fran Cavendish protested. "My bottom's getting sore, sitting on all these old stones."

Further behind, Aidan heard James's voice approaching. He looked round. He already suspected what he would see. James was walking close beside Rachel, talking to her with a savage intensity. "It means the difference between life and death. *Your* death."

She tried to break away, but he caught her arm.

The Celtic earring flashed into Aidan's mind. The blood on Rachel's ear where it had been torn away. A shudder of distrust ran through him.

He jumped down from his perch on the wall.

"Hi, Rachel. I meant to say earlier. I think Melangell may have something of yours. Is it back at the house, Mel?"

His daughter gave a grin and fished in the pocket of her yellow and pink anorak.

"No. It's right here."

The little mythical beast from the Lindisfarne Gospels lay in the palm of her hand. Sunlight winked on the red and gold enamel.

Rachel reached out her hand with more animation than Aidan had seen her show before.

"I thought I'd lost it!" Her fist closed round it, possessively.

"It was in the sand." Melangell's eyes turned up to the older girl's face. "But you won't be able to wear it, will you? Your ear's hurt."

The shutters came down over the teenager's face. Her head drooped, and the curtain of hair fell over her eyes.

Aidan looked past her and met the fury in James's face. Beyond him, plump, plain Sue looked bewildered.

He felt the undercurrent of dissension that ran through even this small group.

As he settled himself on the wall again, he feared for Rachel. Peter was watching her with concern.

James had talked about a struggle between life and death.

A metaphor, of course, but the words rang chill on the strengthening breeze in the scream of the gulls.

Lucy lifted her fair head. Aidan thought she looked more confident, now that she was back to storytelling.

"Yesterday, we left the heathen Angles triumphant on Lindisfarne. After Urien's murder, the Christian army fell apart. Northumbria was in the hands of the invaders.

"But they had blood feuds of their own. The young Anglo-Saxon Prince Edwin was the last of his family left alive. He fled before his uncle Aethelfrith the Ferocious. Astonishingly, he found sanctuary in the Christian west, with a Welsh king on Anglesey. And there he was baptized into the Christian faith. But Aethelfrith came striding west and slaughtered the British army at Chester. Edwin was on the run for his life again."

Aidan let the familiar story wash over him. Edwin's wandering through the heathen Anglo-Saxon courts, abandoning his new faith for the old gods Woden and Thunor. The mysterious stranger who promised the return of his kingdom. Storming back to Northumbria to slay his murdering uncle and reclaim the crown.

Then his marriage to a Christian princess of Kent, who brought her bishop, Paulinus. How they tried for months to convert Edwin. Then that fatal night. The attempted assassination of Edwin in which the king was wounded. The queen going into labour and the birth of a baby daughter. With all three saved from death, Edwin gave in, and was baptized for the second time. Thousands followed him into baptism in the rivers of Northumbria.

"But easy come, easy go. When Penda, the heathen king of neighbouring Mercia, swept into Northumbria and killed Edwin, his Christian queen fled back to Kent with her children. Bishop Paulinus fled too. The light of the Christian faith went out in all but a few places.

"But light was shining somewhere else. When Edwin killed Aethelfrith the Ferocious, the old king's children had fled. As Edwin had done, the heathen princes found sanctuary among Christians. For them, it was the holy island of Iona, off the west of Scotland. There Prince Oswald fell in love with Christ."

"We're getting to you, Daddy!" Melangell whispered to Aidan.

"He recruited an army of Scots and Irish. They marched into his homeland, and the Northumbrians flocked to his standard, determined to throw the invading Mercians out. With his own hands, Oswald raised a cross on Hadrian's Wall. Then he went into battle. Penda of Mercia and his allies were routed. For a second time that century, Northumbria had a Christian king.

"And one of the first things Oswald did was to ask the chaplain he had brought from Iona to preach the gospel to his Northumbrian army.

"But he picked the wrong man for the job. Corman was a bitter preacher. Instead of telling them about the love of God, he ranted at them for being wicked sinners." Lucy's eyes settled on James. "They wouldn't listen to him. In disgust, he packed his bags and stormed back to Iona.

"He told his story to the brothers in the abbey. 'You'll never convert those English heathens. They've hearts of stone. I was wasting my breath on them.'

"A quiet voice came from the back of the room. 'Maybe you were going about it the wrong way, brother. They're like babies. And you were giving them tough meat. It would be better to feed them the bread and milk of the gospel, the love of God. When they've digested that, and grown a bit stronger, they'll be ready for the harder stuff.'

"All eyes swung round to the speaker. It was Aidan, a scholar from Ireland…"

Melangell tugged her father's arm in delight.

"Well, you know what it's like if you come up with a good suggestion in a meeting. Everybody jumped to the same conclusion. 'That's right, Aidan! And you'd be the best man for the job.'

"So Aidan packed his satchel and came here to Northumbria. He was an Irishman who couldn't speak the Anglo-Saxon language at first. The king himself stood beside him and translated his words to the troops. And this time, the Northumbrian soldiers saw that here was a man who loved them, just as they were."

In the few moments' silence, Lucy's eyes ranged round her troop.

James stirred restively. "What about sin?" he said, aggressively enough for Lucy to hear.

Elspeth snorted loudly. "I thought I'd skipped the sermon."

A smile teased Lucy's lips. "I'm sorry. It's difficult to talk about Celtic saints without bringing in Christianity. Anyway, the Roman bishop Paulinus fled before the Mercians. Corman went back to Iona in a huff. But Aidan stayed. He worked here until he died.

"King Oswald had fallen in love with Iona, the island that had given him shelter and taught him the faith. He wanted to give Aidan the nearest thing in Northumbria to Iona. And this was Lindisfarne. Almost an island." She let her eyes roam round this little sea-girt world. "Imagine it without the sand dunes. They came later.

"And of course, Aidan's abbey wasn't the Norman priory you see today. Think wood and thatch. Paulinus had lived at court. Aidan kept a sacred distance. Look, you can see the fortress of Bamburgh from here. Aidan could visit the king, but he never stayed the night. And the king would come to this island, bringing only a small retinue, when he needed to get away from the cares of his kingdom and seek Aidan's wisdom.

"Aidan and his monks travelled far and wide, along the coast and into the hills, taking the gospel. They didn't baptize people in thousands, but as month followed month the heathen Northumbrians came to love and trust him. They saw the monks rolling up their sleeves and helping with the harvest. They saw them giving away the treasure and money people gave them to feed the poor. They watched them *living* the gospel. And when times turned bitter again for Northumbria, they had a faith this time that lasted."

Now her eyes challenged James directly.

He was on his feet. "Is that all you think the gospel is? Doing good and telling people that God loves them? What about the wrath of God? What about sin? You rubbished Paulinus because he baptized thousands. At my church, yes, we have people streaming through the doors. Because I tell them the truth about sin and hellfire."

Lucy's eyebrows rose. "I didn't rubbish Paulinus's preaching. I just pointed out that when things went pear-shaped for Northumbria, and the Mercians invaded, Paulinus did a runner and his conversions melted away. Aidan's was a gospel that put down roots. Like him, it stayed."

"And that's what you're telling Rachel here, is it? That it doesn't matter what she's done in the past? She's not a sinner?"

"*James!*" There was real outrage in Lucy's protest. But her expression turned to dismay.

Aidan, like everyone else, was turning round to look for the unfortunate girl who had become a battleground between these two.

Rachel was not there. Nowhere on the wide expanse of green that was the priory's outer court. No dark shadow flitting between the sandstone walls and pillars. No solitary figure on the slope down to the beach. Other visitors were beginning to arrive, spreading out among the ruins. Nowhere was there anyone who looked like Rachel.

Chapter Ten

L UCY LOOKED AROUND IN CONSTERNATION. How could she have been so wrapped up in her storytelling that she had not noticed Rachel's absence for so long?

She felt a rush of unchristian fury against James. Why was he always putting her on the defensive, challenging her? What had he said to Rachel? How much harm had he already done? Rachel was too often overwhelmed by the sense of her own worthlessness. Wasn't that what had driven her into the arms of the drug dealers? Lucy had struggled so hard to convince the unhappy teenager that, underneath, she was better than that. That God loved her just as she was, whatever she had done, whatever had been done to her. Nothing could ever make her so soiled, so untouchable, that Christ would turn his back on her. Hope, like a tiny seed, was what Lucy had tried to sow.

What could happen to Rachel if James smashed down that fragile growth?

She was aware that Valerie was intervening, trying with her gentle voice to steer the session into calmer waters.

"I expect that Rachel's gone away to find some peace on her own. Didn't I read somewhere that that's what Aidan used to do? Even on Lindisfarne?"

Lucy took her eyes away from the contempt on James's face. She tried to bring her shaken thoughts under control.

She threw Valerie a grateful smile. "Yes, you're right. It's something you read a lot about Celtic abbots. Columba on Iona, Kevin on Glendalough in Ireland, Aidan here. They needed a place where they could be alone

with God and lay the cares of the monastery at his feet. To become a
spiritual child again, seeking help from their Father.

"For Aidan, in the great fast of Lent, it was one of the Farne
Islands. Out there. You can hardly see them, they lie so flat against
the sea. But you can make out the lighthouse, where Grace Darling
and her father later rescued shipwrecked sailors in a rowing boat
in a storm. We'll talk more about Inner Farne when we get to
St Cuthbert.

"But Aidan had a little sanctuary closer than Farne. Hobthrush
Island, or St Cuthbert's. Just a pile of rocks, and a bit of grass, cut off
from Lindisfarne at high tide, just as Lindisfarne itself is cut off from
the mainland. I can show you, if you like. It's not far."

She felt an urgent need to be moving. To do something. She sensed
that many of the group, too, were glad to lift themselves from wherever
they had found dry stones to sit on. But it made everything so much
more real to tell these stories where they actually happened. To fill your
eyes with the same meadows and waves and beaches they had seen. To
feel the same wind sharp against your skin and the spatter of rain that
had been part of their daily life.

But she knew that Fran Cavendish, at least, would have preferred
the comfort of an armchair in the lounge. And David was probably
looking forward to Mrs Batley's Sunday roast.

Elspeth must have had something of the same feeling. She hoisted
her bulk off the shooting stick. "Lead on, then. Might as well work up
an appetite for lunch."

As they walked down over the grass to the narrow beach, Lucy's
eyes were flitting from side to side, longing for a sighting of the elusive
Rachel. The tide was falling. Could anything have made her so desperate
that she would try to leave the island when the causeway opened?

Peter shambled alongside her. "Do you want me to go and look for
her?"

Lucy badly wanted to say yes. But she shook her head and smiled
bravely. "Let's not start panicking yet. If I'm right, and James has been
getting at her, she may need some time on her own. I try to help, but
she doesn't always want to talk to me."

"Let's face it, Rachel doesn't often want to talk to anyone." His hands were in his pockets, head thrust against the breeze.

"Cheer up." Lucy smiled. "You've been wonderful with her. Yesterday you had her singing in the car half the way up the motorway. I've rarely seen her look so happy. I thought we were getting somewhere. Then, once we got here, everything changed."

She remembered uneasily that there had been a different brightness about Rachel last night. Lucy had come back from the lounge to find her brilliant-eyed and defiant, refusing to say where she had been.

"There!" she called to the others. "That's Hobthrush Island. The building you can see is Saxon, but it's later than Aidan and Cuthbert."

A simple wooden cross marked the low spit of rock. Stone walls stood not far from it. The tide still ran between the litter of stones and seaweed that separated the islet from the beach where they were standing. A much wider strait cut it off from the mainland beyond.

"I bet I could get over there. If I jumped across the stones." Melangell was looking speculatively at the receding shallows and the emerging mud.

"You'll do better waiting till this afternoon. Keep your feet dry," Aidan said.

Lucy watched him warily. She had felt shaken by his anger last night. But she saw how his eyes strayed past his daughter, as though he was searching along the shore for another girl. Could she count him as an ally, after all?

She caught up with her thoughts so sharply it was as if she had slapped herself. This wasn't about her. This wasn't about who was or was not on her side. All that mattered at that moment was Rachel. Could something, someone, have pushed her over the edge of what she would find bearable?

There was an empty chair at the dining table between Aidan and Lucy.

Mrs Batley swept in, bearing steaming plates of roast beef and Yorkshire pudding.

"Will she be coming?" she said sharply to Lucy. "I hate to see good food going to waste."

"I'm sorry, Mrs Batley. I know it's difficult for you, but I really don't know where she is."

A spatter of rain threw itself against the windows.

Lucy's knife rang against her glass. The conversation stilled.

"Today, you've got a free afternoon to explore the island. Some of you may want to go across to Hobthrush while the tide's out. You should be safe for the afternoon. The forecast is for scattered showers, so go prepared. Or you could spend time in the Priory Museum. Or you might just want to sleep off Mrs Batley's excellent lunch."

The kitchen door was partly open. Their hostess must have heard.

"It's a good job I brought plenty of knitting, if we're going to get rained on," Frances said.

"We'll meet again this evening at eight o'clock in the lounge. I want to tell you more about the kind of man St Aidan was, and how he died."

When conversation resumed, the living Aidan leaned across the gap and spoke in a low voice. "I know you and Peter are worried about Rachel. I would be. If it's any help, Melangell and I will keep an eye out for her. Is there any part of the island you'd particularly like us to check?"

He could see the relief in the minister's eyes.

"She could be anywhere. As I said yesterday, she's officially a grown woman. She came back last night before too long. She's only been gone a couple of hours. A bit early to call out the Coastguard and Rescue Service." She gave him a wry smile.

He could imagine the arguments going on within her. The worried pastor against the practical policewoman she had once been. She could only have been in the force a few years. What had compelled her to make the life-changing decision to leave that and train for the ministry? It was not the sort of question he could ask her at the lunch table.

Did he have the right to ask her at all? He had fiercely resented any attempt from her to question his own private life.

"Well, partner." Aidan turned to Melangell with a brighter smile. "What do you fancy? Going across to Hobthrush Island?"

"The castle." The reply was eager and determined.

"It's only a small castle. And not all that old. Just a few hundred years."

"This is a small island. So its castle ought to be small, oughtn't it?"

"Whatever you say."

He looked up and caught Valerie's amused smile.

"Don't forget your waterproofs," she said.

He raised his eyes to Lucy again. "We'll keep our eyes open for Rachel."

Aidan was surprised to see the number of people setting out. In view of the weather, he had thought the Cavendishes at least might have settled for the comfort of the armchairs in the lounge. But Fran was there with David. She had changed her heels for more sensible shoes, with a green raincoat and a headscarf. He watched them heading for the car park in front of the guesthouse. To his surprise, they climbed into a red Honda CR-V. It had not occurred to him that such a suburban-seeming couple would drive a 4x4.

Nearly everyone seemed to be setting out for the village or the shore. Only Peter and Lucy were missing. Aidan guessed they might already be out looking for Rachel.

As he and Melangell turned their faces towards the castle there was rain on the wind. But the sky showed bright blue in the gaps between the clouds. Light danced across puddles. The walk to the castle took them out of the village. The path past the curve of the harbour was less than a mile. They could have covered the ground quickly if Aidan had not kept lifting his camera to catch the bright reflections in standing water. Along the sandy ridge beside them, upturned boats, converted to sheds, were irresistibly photogenic. Their keels made sharp-edged roof ridges against the sky. They passed the blue-painted doors of the Coastguard Service hut.

The Castle Rock reared ahead of them. Turrets rose above the curtain wall, which ran diagonally down its ridge like a dragon's back.

The house within was almost hidden.

A storm of rain caught them when they were out in the open, on the grassy flat between the village and the rock. They pulled up their hoods and ran to shelter in the lee of the boatsheds. As they stood panting, with their backs against the planks, Aidan wondered where Rachel was now. Lindisfarne was almost treeless, except for the avenue planted along the road from the car park to the village. Buildings elsewhere were few. Most of the island was either fields or the long spit of sand dunes to the east that stretched towards the causeway and beyond. There was little shelter.

The shower swept over and the sun broke through again.

"We're in luck," Aidan said. "They're flying the National Trust flag from the castle. That means it's open for visitors."

"Isn't it always?"

"Depends on the tide. Everything does on Holy Island. They open when visitors can get across the causeway."

"Or the sands. Like us."

"Of course."

They climbed the ramp to the gate and bought their tickets. From the lower battery they stepped down into the massively pillared entrance hall. Aidan knew that, to Melangell, Lutyens' Edwardian renovation must look satisfyingly medieval.

He followed her eager steps through successive rooms, letting her choose which displays to linger over. But he couldn't let her miss the little scullery, which still had the pulleys and weights to raise the portcullis.

"So it *is* a real castle, isn't it?"

She ran down the long shallow steps to the Ship Room, where a model of a three-masted merchantman hung from the ceiling. They climbed the stairs to the Long Gallery and found the bedroom whose painted door revealed that it had once been used as a gunpowder store.

At last they came out onto the roof and the upper battery. High up, the wind caught them and blew Melangell several steps backwards. Light hit them. Brilliant sun illuminated the North Sea. It made the approaching bank of cloud even blacker. Once more, Aidan had his camera out, trying to capture that dramatic contrast.

At last he put it away reluctantly. "I don't know about you, but I think it's time we were heading back, or we'll get a soaking."

"It's a good job Lucy's doing her next story indoors, isn't it?"

Aidan paused to look over the parapet. Not far away, he could see the walled garden Gertrude Jekyll had designed. It seemed to be deserted.

They had turned to begin their descent when a voice Aidan recognized rose from the steep grassy slopes immediately below them.

"I was not *pursuing* her. For heaven's sake, Sue! She's a child of God who needs rescuing. And I can't imagine that a woolly liberal like Lucy Pargeter is going to do it. What that girl needs is a real fear of hellfire."

"So why is it always teenage girls?" Sue's voice protested. "Elspeth's been far more outspoken about atheism. But I don't notice you turning on the charm to try and save *her* from hell. You didn't drag her off for a walk on the sands on your own the moment you arrived."

"Be reasonable, Sue. Elspeth Haccombe is a hardened sinner. She's thrown up a wall like granite around her. Rachel's young. She's not set in her ways yet. I can get through to her, I know I can."

"Like you get through to all those girls at True Gospel? You have your fan club drooling over you, all hoping for a special smile from those big blue eyes. Don't think I haven't seen you taking them off to the vestry. For personal shepherding, was it?"

"Sue! That's an outrageous suggestion. I'm doing the Lord's work."

Aidan came to suddenly. He shouldn't be here with Melangell, listening to this. He started to hurry her down the steps.

A last shout floated back to him.

"Sue! Come back here!"

They set off down the cobbled ramp, heading back towards the village. The plump figure of Sue was already hurrying away from the castle. But not along the road that would lead her back past the harbour to St Colman's House. In spite of the approaching storm, she was taking the footpath that headed north between the fields and the rocky eastern shore.

Chapter Eleven

"Y ou're back, then."

Mrs Batley was setting out teacups in the lounge. There was no one else about at St Colman's House.

"Perhaps the others are taking shelter in the Priory Museum or a teashop," Aidan suggested.

"Or they've gone to their rooms to get dry." Melangell squeezed the rain from her fringe expressively.

"Point taken. We'll be down in a minute, Mrs Batley. That chocolate cake looks good."

Up in his room, he changed into dry trousers. He'd have done better to stick to the shorts he had worn in yesterday's sunshine.

When he and Melangell came downstairs again, there were two people in the hall, shaking rain from their waterproofs: Lucy and Peter. One look at their faces told Aidan all he needed to know.

"You haven't found her?"

Lucy shook her head. He was alarmed to see how exhausted she looked. He was already regretting his behaviour towards her last night.

Peter was trying to sound cheerful, though the naturally lugubrious downturn of his face made it hard to be convincing. "Holy Island's bigger than you think. We checked the village and the shoreline out to Castle Point. It's rocks and stones all the way north to the light at Emmanuel Head. Then you're into a wilderness of sand dunes and more rocks. There's any number of gulleys, caves and things. We couldn't do it all."

Lucy sighed. "She might have gone the other way – east along the coast road and the dunes out on the Snook."

"We were up on the castle roof," Aidan offered. "We didn't see a sign of her. Or on the way back."

"Sue and James were there," Melangell said. "They were quarrelling."

Lucy was hesitating. "I know what I said, about it being too early to report her missing. But I'm getting a bad feeling about this. There aren't any police on the island, are there, Mrs Batley?"

"No, it's the Coastguard and Rescue people get called out if someone's missing. I didn't like the look of that girl when she first arrived. That peaky face, and she'd never look at you straight, behind all that hair. That girl's trouble, I said to myself."

"I'm worried about what might have happened to her. Not what she might have done," Lucy snapped. "She's not a criminal. At least…"

She'll have a police record, Aidan thought. *Even if it's only for shoplifting. Possession of drugs? What else?*

He had little idea of the murky lives teenagers like Rachel lived. Lucy had said she'd been in care. But how caring was that? Would she have had anyone she could turn to, once she had passed sixteen?

Lucy was in a corner of the lounge, talking quietly into her mobile. Aidan helped himself to tea and cake, watching her, but trying not to make it obvious.

She snapped her mobile shut with a sigh. "Predictable. I'd have said the same myself. 'She's eighteen? How long has she been gone, madam? Since mid-morning? Has she done this before? And she's always come back? Then I don't think that warrants sending out a search party just yet. Don't worry. She'll probably come back when it gets dark.' He said I could call him again if she doesn't. Thanks! I should have asked for the coastguards straight away."

She pulled off her raincoat and poured herself a cup of tea. Rain had made her fair hair darker. Beads of moisture dripped from the tips of it.

Aidan felt helpless. "Do you want more of us to go out looking? I'm sure James and Sue would, if they're back. And probably Valerie and Elspeth." He was less sure that he could imagine Frances Cavendish combing the sand dunes in the rain.

Lucy sank into a sofa. Mrs Batley had gone.

"I really hope she's back for supper. I know it sounds petty, but I can't face the thought of apologizing to Mrs Batley for her missing three meals in a row."

"She was here for breakfast," said Melangell.

"But she hardly touched a thing," Peter countered.

"Did something happen to upset her?" Aidan was aware that he was treading on delicate ground.

"I don't know." Lucy frowned. "She seemed really cheerful in the car coming up here. She was looking forward to it. She's never had much in the way of holidays. I know Lindisfarne may not be the most exciting place for a teenager, but at least it was somewhere different. And then… we'd hardly got here before her mood changed."

"Could she have met someone? Somebody in the group who said the wrong thing? … James?"

"I could screw his neck if it was him. Oh, gosh! I shouldn't be talking like this, should I? I'm getting into police mode, and forgetting I'm a Methodist minister now. And even as a policewoman, I ought to be more detached than I am. I feel responsible."

Aidan looked past her at the window. "Look, there's an edge of brighter sky out to the west. Let's wait for this storm to blow over, then we'll split up the island between us and go over the rest."

"Perhaps she's gone away." Melangell's high voice broke in. "Across the causeway. Or the sands."

Silence fell over the room.

"It's possible," Lucy said reluctantly. "Anything is."

Lucy nerved herself to take command of the situation. She sent Aidan and Peter to do a round of the rooms, recruiting everyone they could find to look for Rachel. Some of the group had shown up for Mrs Batley's afternoon tea. Some had not. The square hall at the foot of the stairs was filling. Elspeth, in a voluminous waterproof cape over her tweeds, seemed to take up an inordinate amount of the space. Valerie, slender beside her, looked grave and businesslike.

David Cavendish was flushed. Lucy had half heard an argument between him and Frances. But he was buttoning up his beige raincoat, determined to come.

Peter came in from the chalets. "I can't find James."

At the same time, Aidan was coming downstairs, followed by an uncharacteristically sulky-looking Melangell. She was trailing her yellow and pink waterproof jacket.

"I *can* come. I'm not a bit tired," she said to Aidan's back.

"I know. But it's hard work, walking over sand. And there are a good few miles to cover, if we do it thoroughly."

Frances put a possessive hand on Melangell's shoulder. "You can leave her with me. I'll look after her. We'll have a nice time together, won't we, sweetheart?"

Melangell wriggled away. "I want to go."

"No, love," Aidan sighed. "That's an order. Thanks, Fran."

He turned his harassed face to Lucy. "Everyone accounted for upstairs except Sue. She's not in her room. We saw her when we were at the castle earlier. But she was heading away from the village then. Out towards Emmanuel Head."

"James is with her, I suppose."

"Not when we saw them. I think there was a row… Over Rachel," he added awkwardly.

Lucy digested the news in silence. Then she straightened up. "So, that leaves – what? – six of us. I was hoping for eight. I'm going to need to call in some help. Still, let's see how to divide the island up between us."

She led the way into the lounge and spread the map out on the table, where Mrs Batley had cleared the teacups and cake plates. "Elspeth and Valerie, perhaps you could take the village. I know several of us have been around that area this afternoon, and haven't seen her, but you could ask around. Gift shops and cafés. And try the harbour again. If one of the sheds is unlocked, she might have gone in out of the rain."

"Will do," Elspeth responded firmly.

"I need to go out to Snipe Point, and check the caves there."

"I'll come!" Peter put in eagerly.

"No. I have a couple of friends in the village I'm going to call on. I want you and Aidan to take the North Shore and as much of the dunes to the east as you can. If anything happened to her on the south coast, I'm hoping someone would see her from the road. The tide's down, so you can take Aidan's car for a mile or so."

"Sorry!" She saw him start. "I'm fine to search that area, but I don't have the car with me. We walked across the sands."

Lucy digested the information. She looked more doubtfully at David. "Could you do that? It'll be a hard slog over the dunes."

David looked pointedly down at his polished brown shoes. Then he shrugged his shoulders. "Whatever you say, ma'am."

To her relief, the antipathy Aidan had shown the day before had been swept aside for the moment by concern for Rachel.

"Let's get going," he said. He chucked Melangell under the chin. "Sorry, partner. I'd love to take you. But Peter and David and I need to cover the ground as fast as we can. We've some serious walking to do."

Lucy watched Melangell's lips press together in a mutinous line. She turned her eyes to Fran's. "Thanks for staying with her." Lucy managed a smile. "I hope you get along OK. I really need Aidan."

"Don't worry about us. We'll be fine, won't we, love?"

There was no answering smile from Melangell.

Lucy folded up the map and slipped it into her pocket. She held out leaflets of Holy Island with smaller maps to the others. "There. I've marked off roughly how we're doing it."

The front door opened on a rush of cold damp air. Aidan had been right about the storm passing over, but the yellow sunlight that replaced it had a cold, watery gleam. It glistened off wet roofs and leaves.

Lucy tried to sound more confident than she felt. "Right, folks, we'll give it two hours. Back here for supper at seven o'clock. We mustn't let Mrs Batley down. Between us, we've a good chance of finding Rachel."

"If she's on the island." Melangell's voice came from behind them.

Lucy was leading the way down the steps towards the road when she halted suddenly.

A figure came staggering through the gate. He seemed to be having difficulty walking in a straight line. He was holding his hand to the side of his head, but through his fingers Lucy could see the bright blood trickling down the side of his face.

"James!" she cried.

She ran forward to catch him.

Peter was on the other side of James, helping to take his weight. Together they steered him up the step into the house.

Mrs Batley rose to the occasion. Lucy was afraid she would complain about this rain-soaked figure dripping blood and trailing wet and mud across her floors. But she gave one look, turned away and then came bustling downstairs with a pile of old towels.

They sat James down on a chair in the hall. He seemed to be semi-conscious, looking around him vaguely.

Lucy turned back the hood of his anorak. "Get me some water, please."

She wiped the mud away gently and patted the head wound dry. There was a sizeable area of broken skin and bruising. Blood still seeped from it. Without the rainwater, the flow was slowing. It looked darker, more vividly red.

She was assessing swiftly whether this could be the result of a fall, or whether something had hit him.

"What happened?"

James frowned. His blue eyes tried to focus. "I don't remember."

His voice was shaky, unlike the confident assertion with which he had challenged her this morning.

"Did you hit it, or did it hit you?" Elspeth's decisive mind had gone straight to the vital question.

James tried to shake his damaged head and winced.

"Shouldn't somebody tell Sue?" Valerie's voice came from the edge of the group. Everyone looked round, but there was no sign of the pastor's faithful assistant.

"As far as I know, she hasn't been back since lunch," Lucy said. "Aidan saw her going away from the castle."

"And *I* did." Melangell had appeared from the lounge with Frances.

Lucy turned her face up to Mrs Batley. "Is there a doctor on the island?"

She guessed the answer before it came.

"No. You need to get to the surgery on the mainland. But they won't be open on Sunday."

Lucy felt her security receding. She had always thought of Lindisfarne as a place of sanctuary. Somewhere she could come for healing when she was in trouble. Now the practical reality came home to her. With only a few hundred residents, there was no doctor, no police officer. The only emergency service based on the island was the Coastguard and Rescue Service.

"He's almost certainly got concussion. He needs to be seen to."

At the back of her mind was still the thought that this head wound might not be an accident. If only James would come round enough to tell her.

"You could ring for an ambulance," Mrs Batley told her. "The causeway's open. Or drive him to Berwick Hospital yourself."

Her own responsibilities and the possible options were chasing themselves round Lucy's head. What were her priorities?

A firm voice spoke behind her: "You don't need all of us milling round. Why don't the rest of us go off and look for Rachel, as we planned?"

The warmth of gratitude flowed through Lucy as she raised her eyes to the red-haired photographer. Of course she had to stay with James now, however keenly she wanted to find Rachel. But that didn't alter the fact that the teenager had now been missing for – what? She looked at her watch with a start – nearly six hours.

"Thanks, Aidan. I'd be really grateful."

She turned to the pair of older women. "Do the best you can. There are only a few hours of daylight left. If nobody's seen her, I really think we'll have to turn out the coastguards before the light goes."

The others were moving off to begin their delayed search. David Cavendish hovered indecisively for a while, then took off after Aidan and Peter.

Lucy was conscious of the mobile in her pocket. Were her suspicions about James's wound strong enough to ring the police on the mainland, as well as to summon an ambulance?

James lurched suddenly forward in his chair. Lucy caught him.

"She was running away," he said thickly. "I tried to stop her."

He passed out.

Chapter Twelve

AIDAN THREW AN ANXIOUS LOOK over his shoulder at Melangell in the lounge doorway.

"I'll be back," he promised. "Before seven."

"Don't you worry about her. We'll be fine. Won't we, Mel?"

Aidan saw the curl of distaste in Melangell's face at Frances's shortening of her name. Oh well. He would just have to hope it went OK. The best thing he could do now was to take the search for Rachel off Lucy's hands.

He strode after Peter. The low sun of early evening was gleaming aslant along the puddled road. Beyond the houses, he could see a breeze was whipping up white curls on the crests of the waves.

He caught up with the solid figure of Peter, who was looking at the four cars parked in front of the house.

"Which one?" the student asked.

Before Aidan could answer, the raincoated figure of David walked towards a red Honda four-wheel drive.

"This is my little beauty. All aboard."

Aidan thought for a second time that the all-terrain vehicle looked out of keeping with the Cavendishes' urban clothes and polished shoes.

"Thanks. It'll give us a head start. We'll have enough ground to cover as it is."

They drove along the coast. Rain and tide had left pools beside the road, but the sea was still some way out. David stopped the car where the road bent round towards the causeway.

"Is this far enough?"

"Thanks, that'll do fine. We can cut across to the North Shore from here."

Peter and Aidan got out. David stayed where he was. His gloved hands still rested on the steering wheel.

"Aren't you coming?"

"Thought I'd drive a bit further round. Spread the net."

He lifted his hand in farewell and drove on.

Aidan stared after him. He shrugged his shoulders and turned to Peter. " You know Rachel better than any of us. What do *you* think has happened to her?"

Peter kicked a Coke tin into the blown sand at the side of the road. "You tell me. She's totally unpredictable. Chatting away like a magpie and blasting out grunge music one day. Next thing, she's curled up inside herself and as difficult to get through to as a hedgehog. I told Lucy she was taking on more than she could handle, bringing her up here. Not that Rachel doesn't deserve a break. If anyone needs one, she does. But Lucy's got all you lot to worry about as well."

"I know what you mean." He winced. *I wasn't exactly helping yesterday,* he thought. "And that was before James had what looks like an argument with a double-decker bus."

"You and Melangell were at the castle, weren't you? You said he and Sue were having a row. Was it, like, physical?"

Aidan tried to remember the approach to the castle entrance, the view from the roof, the voices of Sue and James somewhere below.

"I didn't exactly see them. There are steep grassy slopes around the rock. And there's a cobbled ramp. It was wet. He could have slipped."

Into his mind came the venom in Sue's normally conciliatory voice. He kept the possible implications of that to himself.

Peter and Aidan found a path that would take them across the narrow neck of the island to the northern shore. The traffic from the road to the causeway fell behind them, screened by tall dunes. The wind whipped harder as they approached the open North Sea.

"How shall we play this?" Peter asked. "Shall I take the beach, while you stay up on the dunes? You can see further from there, and I guess your eyesight's better than mine. Plus, there may be all sorts of hiding places in among the sand hills. That way, we'll cover as much ground as we can, though we can't look everywhere."

Aidan stood, poised on the higher ground, while Peter ploughed his ungainly way down to the shore.

The tide had turned. Further out, a channel carved across the sands was widening. The sea would come in fast over this gently shelving beach.

Could Melangell be right? Might Rachel have fled the island?

He looked back across the dunes towards the mainland. In the distance, he caught the stocky figure of David Cavendish beside his red car, gazing forlornly across the causeway.

Aidan watched him stand irresolute. Then, as Aidan had, he climbed the nearest dune.

The level light was grey under the clouds. It was high time to begin his search.

It was hard-going through soft sand. After a while, Aidan came across a trodden path between the grass-grown hummocks. It was easier walking now, but he was out of sight of the beach. There was a strange sense of disorientation. In every direction the dunes looked the same. There were no landmarks to give him a sense of distance. Only the poorly defined path told him he was going in the right direction, eastwards.

From time to time he left it to climb a dune. From there, Peter was a lone dark figure on the pale beach. No one else was out walking.

At other times, Aidan delved between the dunes, looking for one of those sandy hollows where Rachel might be curled up out of the wind, away from the world. He met only the mocking whistle of the tall grass.

At first he thought it was the distant scream of a gull. He trudged on through the clinging, rain-soaked sand. Time was slipping away. A glance at his watch told him it was nearly six. The sun had long since retreated into an ominous dusk. He had lost all sense of how far along the sandy isthmus he had come.

With an effort, he climbed another dune. The twilit water widened around him. Grey sea, ghostly sand, the hardly perceptible line of dusky mainland.

The cry came again, clearer and more human now. "Aidan!"

He could just make out the broad figure of Peter much further along the beach. It had been easier for him, walking along the compacted sand below the high-tide mark. The sea was swinging in a line of seaweed, marking the edge of the mounting tide. Aidan strained his eyes. Was that a clot of something larger, more solid than strands of weed, where Peter was standing?

Aidan gave an answering shout. He broke into a slithering run down the seaward side of the dune.

"No!" he was praying as he stumbled out onto the beach. "Please, no!"

Lucy put James's head between his knees. She dialled 999. This was only her second day on the island, and the situation was escalating out of hand. She had a sudden homesickness for her manse in Devon, and the comforting familiarity of her Sunday routine.

She asked for the ambulance service and outlined James's condition. A voice assured her that a paramedic car would be on its way as soon as possible to assess his condition. If necessary, they would transfer him to a hospital on the mainland.

"The tide will be over the causeway in two or three hours," Lucy warned them.

"That's all right, madam. We'll be with you long before then."

The call ended. Lucy stared at the open mobile in her hand. Should she make another call, to the police?

She was aware of Mrs Batley and Frances still watching her and listening for what she would do next. After a moment's indecision, she knew she did not have enough evidence to report James's injury as anything more than accidental. She would have to wait until he came round and hope that he could give more coherent answers to her questions.

The paramedics would surely want to know how it had happened – if James regained consciousness soon enough to tell them.

Still the phone lay in her hand. She had meant to ring Simon, hadn't she? He had been a rock of strength when she had fled to Lindisfarne seeking sanctuary five years ago. She had wanted to get him to help her search for Rachel around Snipe Point. It still wasn't too late, but the light would soon be fading. She should have called him sooner.

She made the call. There was only his voicemail.

James stirred. At once, Lucy's thoughts flew back to his injury.

She wished that Sue would come back. She might be able to explain his head wound.

"*She was running away. I tried to stop her.*"

That could only mean Sue, couldn't it? A scuffle? An accidental fall? But why would the infatuated Sue have left him alone and injured, to stagger back to St Colman's House on his own and bleeding?

"James? Can you hear me? How are you?"

"My… head… hurts."

"I'm sure it does. You've taken a nasty whack. Don't worry, I've called an ambulance car. We'll get you to hospital. Can you remember anything about what happened?"

"I… I was lying on the ground in this garden. It was wet. I couldn't find anybody to help me. So I started to walk back."

"Didn't you meet anyone?"

James tried to shake his head and cried out in pain.

"It's OK. Keep still."

"It was raining. I had my hood up. I just kept looking at the ground, putting one foot in front of the other."

If anyone had passed him, they would have seen a hunched figure, head down, his bloodied head hidden in the folds of his waterproof. No reason to stop and ask if he needed help.

"Could you manage a cup of tea?" Mrs Batley asked. "You've had a nasty shock."

"Yes… please," he said faintly. He was starting to shiver.

"Why don't you get him to lie down in his room?" Mrs Batley

suggested. "Get a duvet round him. It'll be a while before that ambulance car gets here. I'll bring his tea."

"Can you stand?" Lucy asked.

She helped him shakily upright. Mrs Batley had gone to put the kettle on. Lucy looked rather impatiently at Frances. "Could you give me a hand?"

"Well, I'm not sure if I'm strong enough. He's quite a big man."

Lucy got one of James's arms round her neck. Frances, unwillingly, did the same. Melangell ran ahead to open doors for them.

Together they got him to his room, beyond Lucy's.

"Key?"

James looked blank. Lucy patted the pockets of his anorak and found it.

They helped him to the bed and Lucy took off his shoes. Melangell had picked up the spare towels Mrs Batley had provided and laid one of them across the pillows with a self-important air. Lucy and Frances lowered James to rest on it. He sank back with a sigh, and they lifted his feet up.

Horizontal, and with the duvet over him, he looked more relaxed.

But there were bloodstains already on the protective towel.

Lucy looked around the room. Like hers and Rachel's, it was spacious. It contained a double bed and a single. She wondered again why James should think it necessary to book such a room just for himself, when Sue was upstairs in a single.

She ought not to be judging him. If he had the money from his successful pastorate, it was his to spend as he liked. Wasn't it?

She tried to put her personal animosity out of her head. James was one of her group. She had a duty of ministry to him, as to all the others.

"Please, Lord, bless James and make him whole," she murmured.

"Amen," came Melangell's unexpectedly clear voice.

Lucy's mobile rang. Simon calling back? The ambulance? She checked the screen. Her heart was suddenly beating painfully fast.

"Yes, Peter?" It was a cry of alarm more than a question. She could hardly bear to listen to the news he told her.

Chapter Thirteen

AS HE RAN, WILD THOUGHTS OF DENIAL were chasing through Aidan's mind.

Rachel had been taken ill and fallen on the beach. Peter had found her just before the tide reached her.

It wasn't a human body at all, just a pile of debris washed in by the surf.

The body wasn't Rachel's. Sue had gone from the castle towards the northern shore. She hadn't come back.

He almost tripped when he realized the implications of what he was thinking. Did he really want it to be Sue rather than Rachel? He hardly knew either of them. He had been moved to compassion for Rachel because of her hunted look, like a wounded animal. But what about plump, plain Sue, so admiring of James, who was almost certainly exploiting her?

Peter was tugging the figure clear of the advancing waves. A dark, three-quarter-length jacket obscured the head. There was a trail of long dark hair.

He had only to take one look at Peter's face to know the truth. Tears were trickling down the student's face beneath the horn-rimmed glasses.

"Is she dead?" Aidan panted.

"M-must be. The sea was washing her in."

Aidan bent down beside the sodden body. He turned her onto her side and ejected as much water from her slack mouth as he could. There was surprisingly little. Then he laid her on her back, breathed sharply into her mouth, and set to work with chest compressions.

He knew it was useless. Peter was right. But he had to try. He owed it to this unhappy girl. At the back of his mind was another thought: guilt. He had made things difficult for Lucy. And Lucy had cared for Rachel. She had done all she could to rescue the girl from whatever dark place she had been in.

At last, exhausted, he sat back on his heels.

"I phoned the police," Peter said. "And told Lucy."

Aidan thought back to the scene he had left. James, with a bloody head wound. He imagined Lucy, distracted from her mounting fear for the missing Rachel, having to cope with this new emergency.

She had struck him as calm and competent, whatever turmoil she was feeling inside. Her training in the police must have counted for something. He wracked his brains to think what he could do to help.

"What happens now? There aren't any police on the island."

"They said they'd send someone over from Berwick. But they're also alerting the coastguard service here."

Aidan remembered the coastguard hut near the harbour. He calculated the distance to this remote beach on the North Shore. Still, it shouldn't take long if they had a Land Rover.

"There feels something wrong about moving her body. But the tide's still coming in. If I had my camera with me, I could have photographed the position for the police."

"She could have died anywhere," Peter said. "You'd need to have someone who knows about tides and currents."

"You think she's been washed up from somewhere else? She didn't die here?"

Peter shrugged without speaking.

Aidan bent to examine the pale face, cleared now of its wet hair. The marks of her acne showed dark against the sallow skin. There seemed no obvious signs of trauma.

"Do you think it was suicide?"

Peter shrugged again. "What else?"

"I don't know. Some sort of seizure? We don't know her medical history."

"Does it matter?" Peter sighed. "She's dead, isn't she?"

Aidan got to his feet. The wind blew coldly in the grey light. He wanted someone to come and take the body away. To wipe what had happened out of existence. He had had too much of death. Losing Jenny… He wanted desperately for this grey world to turn over to spring again.

The call from Peter had hardly ended before Lucy's phone rang again.

"Lucy? Elspeth here. Bad news, I'm afraid. We're at the coastguard base. Someone's called the rescue service out. Word in the village is that there's been a casualty on the North Shore."

"I know." Lucy could hardly get the words out.

Elspeth's brusque voice softened somewhat. "I'm guessing you'd like to see her before the uniforms get there." When Lucy did not reply, she went on: "May be too late for that, I'm afraid. The coastguards are leaving now. They've got a Land Rover that can tackle the dunes. They'll cover the ground faster than you can. But they'll be going past St Colman's. I could ask them to stop by and pick you up… Hang on."

There was the sound of a man's voice in the background. Then Elspeth came back on the line.

"That's sorted. It's all happening here. I told them about James needing medical attention, but they say the ambulance paramedics will see to that."

"Yes," said Lucy, trying to hold her scattered thoughts together. "When he passed out, I dialled 999. He's come round now, but he doesn't look good."

She cast an anxious glance across to the bed. Was James listening to this?

"Right, then. You've got Frances there, and Mrs Batley. Has Sue come back yet? No? Anyway, Val and I will hotfoot it back after the coastguards. Should be enough of us to man the fort until the ambulance gets there. You go."

The call snapped off.

Lucy felt a surge of gratitude. She had been holding herself together since that terrible call, trying to balance her responsibilities to James, who, though injured, was still alive, with those to the dead Rachel, for whom she could do nothing more.

Dead. She found her mind would not accept the reality. Rachel could not be dead.

Lucy had seen her share of death in her few short years in the police force: traffic accidents; old people, only discovered when the milk bottles proliferated on the doorstep. And there had been the murder of a ten-year-old girl, for which Lucy had been the first officer on the scene.

She had thought this had toughened her; that she had learned how to cope. She even knew it might be some excuse for Bill's treatment of her in those days. The macho culture of the police station was partly a defence against scenes like those.

But Rachel? Dead on a beach on Lindisfarne – the island that was meant to be a place of healing for her? That broke through whatever professional defences she had managed to erect.

I brought her here.

She rose stiffly, as though she had been sitting for a long time.

"The coastguards are on their way. They're the first emergency service on the island."

"Is Rachel dead?" Melangell's innocent question cut through whatever evasions Lucy had planned to give the others.

"Yes, I'm afraid so," she said quietly.

The little girl ran across the room and hugged her.

Lucy made an effort to hold her voice steady. "The coastguards will deal with it until the police get here. I'm going to ask them for a lift out to where they found the… where she is."

"Is Daddy there?"

"Yes. And Peter. I expect they'll wait until the police arrive. You'll be all right with Frances?"

"You're not leaving us here alone?" Frances objected. "What if something happens to James? I know a bit about first aid, from the children's homes, but not this sort of thing. I wouldn't want to be responsible."

Lucy was saved by Mrs Batley coming in, bearing a tray with several mugs of tea.

"I guessed it's not just our casualty who could do with a hot drink." She put down the tray and looked round at their strained faces. "Has something else happened?"

"They've found Rachel," Melangell said. "She's dead."

"Oh, my goodness!" The mugs rattled suddenly on the tray. "The poor soul! I'm really sorry, Reverend. You must be having a terrible time."

Reverend. The word struck Lucy with unfamiliarity. It was hard to remember that Mrs Batley was talking about her. She had been back in that earlier life in the police she thought she had left behind.

"Yes, it's almost too much. Elspeth and Valerie are coming back as fast as they can. There'll be plenty of people to keep an eye on James until the ambulance service arrives. Elspeth suggested I could get a lift with the coastguards to the beach where they found Rachel. I'd like to… see her."

"Of course you would. Don't you worry about us. We'll look after him, won't we?" Mrs Batley smiled gallantly at Frances and Melangell. "Now, young lady, I think we ought to leave this poor gentleman in peace. I've no doubt he's got a nasty headache after a knock like that. You and Mrs Cavendish run along to the lounge. I'll wait here. I'm sure nobody's going to complain if supper's late for once."

"Thank you." Lucy smiled wanly. "I'll go out to the gate and see if they're coming."

She would have liked time to herself. Peace. A space for prayer. But she knew even as she opened the front door that there would be no room for that yet. Before she had taken a step towards the gate, the yellow and black Land Rover was heading down the road towards her.

A young man in blue overalls leaned over and opened the rear passenger door.

"I'm really sorry about this. I'm Dan, by the way. First aider. I hear you've got another casualty indoors."

"A head injury. He passed out and he's not really compos mentis yet. We made him lie down. We're just waiting for the ambulance."

Dan reached down a hand to help her aboard. The door slammed shut. The Land Rover sped off, the light on its roof flashing.

The Land Rover seemed crowded. There were a man and a woman in the front seats, the man driving, the woman talking into a radio. Two men shared the seat behind with Lucy. All wore dark blue overalls with gold insignia.

"How did it happen, this other injury?" Dan asked.

"Nobody knows. He came staggering back dripping blood. Nothing he's said makes much sense yet. He seems to have come to in the gardens of the castle, but he might be confused about that."

Her body was tense. She ought to be concerned about James, but all she could think of at the moment was Rachel's body, sodden with seawater, lying on a beach as the spring daylight faded. She could not put words to her grief. She had to be there.

A burly coastguard on the far side of the seat leaned over. His look was sympathetic. "It's a rotten do. I gather the girl they've found was a friend of yours. I'm John, by the way. Officer in charge of this crew." His large hand clasped hers.

"I'm the leader of the group she was with. But yes, she was a friend."

"Sven," said the younger, fair-haired man behind the wheel, turning a sharply angled profile. "We'll have you out there in a few shakes." The Land Rover was racing along the coast road now.

A friend? How accurate was that? Lucy had done her best to reach out the hand of friendship, of love. But could she honestly say that Rachel considered herself a friend to Lucy? At times, she had been more like a wounded and terrified animal, starting away at the slightest touch, back arched, spitting.

No. There had been other times, like yesterday, when Rachel had been laughing and singing with Peter in the car. They had been winning. Lucy was sure they had. Softening her, relaxing her, getting her to trust them.

So what had happened between one day and the next to make Rachel suddenly decide to take her own life? It must be suicide, mustn't it? It was too much of an irony that she could stumble to an accidental death here on this island of sanctuary.

But Lindisfarne was not a safe place, physically. It never had been. Every year the emergency services were called out for holidaymakers in trouble, forgetful of the treacherous tides. There were rocks that could prove dangerous to the unwary.

The Vikings had slaughtered the monks and left the sands red with their blood.

"Hold on," said the driver. "This is where we leave the road."

Lucy came to with a start. They had left the route that curved around the south shore towards the causeway. They were bucking over the dunes. The engine of the 4x4 roared, and then they crested the ridge.

The North Shore lay in front of them: a long expanse of sand glimmering in the pale light. Sven leaned forward and peered through the windscreen.

"Over there," said the woman at the radio. "To your left."

Lucy could just make out two small figures along the beach. The Land Rover rocked over the hillocks down on to gently shelving sand. Lucy could see them more clearly now, just above the high-tide line. Aidan and Peter. Waiting.

She tried not to look too hard at the dark thing that lay inert on the sand between them.

The Land Rover drew up in front of Aidan and Peter. Aidan watched a grey-haired man in blue overalls get out on one side. A taller, younger man followed. Lucy jumped down from the other side. The fair-haired driver stayed, with a middle-aged woman talking into a radio handset beside him.

He was startled to see how pale and tired Lucy looked. She had seemed so fresh-faced and fit when they met. He should not underestimate the depth of her shock.

She stood now, hands in pockets, looking down at Rachel's still face.

"May light perpetual shine upon her," she murmured.

Words Aidan remembered from Jenny's funeral service.

"Amen," he whispered.

The older of the coastguards held out a hand to Aidan. "John. I assume you've tried CPR?"

"As well as I know how."

The younger man knelt down. He held Rachel's nostrils and blew into her mouth several times. Then he began chest compressions, more strongly, even brutally, than Aidan had dared to. Mouth to mouth again. Then more compressions.

Time stretched out. Aidan felt that none of them really expected a miracle to happen.

At last the man sat back, exhausted. As Aidan had done earlier.

"No joy, I'm afraid. She's gone."

He got to his feet and turned to look along the coast, eastwards. There the sand flats ran out into a rocky headland.

"Funny, that. You could understand if she'd gone out on the rocks and slipped. Or got trapped when the tide turned. But how does she get to drown on the open beach?"

The grey-haired John turned his grave face to Lucy. "I'm sorry to ask this, love, but is there any reason to think she might have been suicidal?"

Lucy winced. Then she raised her eyes and looked steadily at him.

"She'd had a bad time. In care as a child. Mother a druggie. She'd been using drugs herself. But she was pulling herself out of it. Getting her life together."

"Still, it happens, doesn't it? They get a bad day. The black dog on their back. And suddenly it all seems too much to go on."

"Yes," Lucy almost whispered.

Dan, his hair whipping in the breeze, came back and knelt beside the body. He felt the pockets of her black coat.

"If they're set on drowning, they usually weight their pockets with stones, walk out into the sea and just keep going. Or throw themselves off a rock."

"She was in the water when we found her," Peter said. "At least, in the shallows. The waves were sort of rolling her up the beach."

"How long had she been missing?" John still had his eyes on Lucy.

"It was after half-past ten when any of us last saw her. At the priory."

The coastguards looked at each other thoughtfully.

"So, suppose she goes out to Snipe Point. Jumps off. How could the incoming tide carry her here?"

The older John shook his head. "No chance. She'd have been washed back onto the rocks. Or the current would have taken her east."

"So, she drowns on a flat sandy beach. And she's obviously not been swimming."

"I'm sorry, love," the senior officer said to Lucy. "It can't be very pleasant, listening to us discussing this. But the police will ask the same questions. We know this coast. They'll want our opinion."

"Yes, I know." Lucy's voice was firmer now. "Would you give me a moment with her?"

There was a brief hesitation before they understood her. Then, Dan flushing a little, the two coastguards stepped back. Aidan and Peter looked at each other. Then they too drew back, leaving a private space around Lucy and Rachel.

The young minister knelt on the sand and stroked the hair from the girl's face. She clasped her hands in prayer. From a distance, Aidan heard only the murmur of her voice.

Then Lucy stood. Aidan saw her straighten her shoulders in that familiar gesture. She was in charge of herself again.

The rush of the breeze was swallowed up in a louder roar. The senior coastguard shaded his eyes.

"Jean's done her stuff on the radio. They've sent in the cavalry, I see. Air ambulance."

Chapter Fourteen

JEAN, THE RADIO OPERATOR, leaned from her window. "Where do you want it?"

"Should be room in that little car park behind us. Not likely to be cars there this late in the day."

John leaped into the rear passenger seat and the Land Rover crested the dunes and disappeared. A few moments later, Lucy watched the helicopter settle out of sight, flattening the grass of the dunes as it passed.

She felt emotion draining away from her. She was becoming detached, distant from what was happening around her. She had done all she could, for James, for Rachel. It was out of her hands now. She could leave it to the professionals.

Professionals. Once that would have been her. PC Lucy Pargeter. In a way, she still was one. The dog collar she had worn this morning marked her out to the public as the Reverend Lucy Pargeter. The sort of person people expected to comfort them in grief.

Now she was the one who needed comforting. Or would do, when the reality came back to hit her with full force.

She recognized the detachment that was taking over, making everything seem small and far away, as a symptom of shock.

The professionals were coming back over the ridge. Besides the coastguard John, were a portly man in orange flying overalls and a younger one carrying a stretcher.

They had hardly descended the dunes when another man came striding after them. He wore a Nordic sweater and a waterproof jacket. Lucy flinched at the look of enthusiasm in his youthful face. She had already guessed who he must be.

He advanced towards the group, lifting a hand in acknowledgement to the younger coastguard, who seemed to know him.

"Hi, Len," Dan called to him. "Hope we're not spoiling your Sunday."

Len held out his ID to Aidan, assuming, Lucy thought wryly, that he would be their leader. "Detective Constable Leonard Chappell, Northumbria Police. Thought I might get here ahead of the air ambulance, but didn't quite make it. I'm sorry about this. Were you a friend of the deceased? A relative?"

"Detective?" Aidan sounded startled.

"Routine. Unexplained death."

Aidan motioned him towards Lucy. "This is the Reverend Lucy Pargeter. She's in charge of our group. She'll explain better."

"Sorry, Miss Pargeter. I mean, Rev." Her status seemed to embarrass the young detective.

"Lucy will do," she said, to put him at ease.

"You can identify the body?… Oh, by the way, this is Doctor Forbes." He waved at the portly man, who was now kneeling beside Rachel's body. "He'll deal with the medical formalities. We need him to pronounce her dead."

"Yes," said Lucy, marvelling at her expressionless voice. "Rachel Ince. I've known her for three years. I brought her to Holy Island." Just for a moment, her voice caught on the words. "I'm running a study holiday here."

"Who discovered the body?"

"I did." Peter shambled forward.

Lucy felt a pang of guilt that she had not given enough thought to Peter's grief. She did not think there had been anything sexual between him and Rachel, but he had been a firm and loyal friend to her through the roller-coaster of her struggles with drugs and lack of self-esteem.

"And it was here?"

"No." Peter waved a large hand towards the advancing sea. "Further down the beach. At the edge of the waves. Like the tide was bringing her in. We carried her up above the high-water line. I know you're supposed to leave a body where it is, but we didn't have a choice."

"We?"

"Aidan was with me. We were out looking for her."

The constable had his notebook out. "Why was that?"

"She'd been missing since this morning. We were worried about her."

The doctor was still kneeling over the body. "Hard to say the time of death. A couple of hours or more ago, I'd guess." He looked up at the group from St Colman's House. "There's some bruising on her arms. I'd say that's at least a day old. And a tear in her ear. Looks like an earring's been pulled through it."

DC Chappell raised his eyebrows at Lucy. "Can you explain that?"

It was Aidan who answered for her. "I think I can. As we were coming across the Pilgrims' Way yesterday – 'we' being me and my daughter – we saw a couple on the shore ahead of us. They seemed to be – I don't know – embracing, or fighting. In some sort of hold. I've got a shot of them on my camera, if you want to see it. And afterwards, when we reached the dry sand, Melangell found an earring. She gave it back to Rachel this morning. It was definitely hers."

"And the other guy? I take it we're talking about a man."

"Too far away. It was certainly large enough to make me think it was a man. But I can't swear it wasn't a big woman."

The figure of Elspeth in her hefty tweeds passed across Lucy's mind. She shook it away. "I think I can guess who it was. Another of our group, Sue, came to me yesterday afternoon. She was in some agitation. Her friend – boss – James was missing. She wanted to know if I knew where he was."

"And did you?"

"No, but I've reason to believe he may have taken Rachel off for a talk. Or seen her on her own and joined her."

"For a *talk*. And what sort of talk would that be? Would it involve some sort of getting close? A clinch? Or a struggle?"

"I don't know. I wasn't there. James is an evangelist. He feels a mission to convert sinners. He thought Rachel was one."

"I thought you were the Reverend."

"I am… but I don't work quite the way James does. Not so… in your face."

"I think we might need to talk to Mr James ...?"

"Denholme."

"Where will I find him?"

"Probably in Berwick Hospital. If the ambulance car's got here."

She saw Detective Constable Chappell do a double take. His eyes shot to the listening coastguards.

"Sounds like you've had a busy afternoon."

"Head injury," said John. "A fair bit of bleeding, by the sound it, and he passed out. The ambulance car was on its way, so we left it to the paramedics."

DC Chappell began taking photographs of Rachel's body. Doctor Forbes was on his feet again.

"What do you think?" he said to Chappell. "Do we need to leave her here for your scene of crime people to see, given this is not where the body was found, and the find site's underwater now?"

"Above my pay grade," Len Chappell answered. "I'll radio through and see what they say. I guess, under the circumstances, the body has to be the scene of crime."

Crime? Lucy's professional training told her he had to think like this. But she resented the enthusiasm she read in his eyes.

The coastguard Dan stood looking out to sea. He cupped his hands against the wind to light a cigarette. The breeze snatched a trail of smoke away. The helicopter blades had clattered to a halt. The beach was still.

Lucy made an effort to pull herself out of the stupor that was threatening to paralyse her.

"Somebody should tell her family."

"How old was she?" DC Chappell suddenly turned his attention back to her, notebook ready again.

"Eighteen. She wasn't close to her mother. She'd been in care. But Karen needs to know."

"You know her?"

Lucy sighed. "Slightly. Before Rachel came of age, I tried to get her to help. But she's in need of help herself. Not much of a mother, I'm afraid. And Rachel's father went off years back."

"Do you have a phone number? Address?"

"Not here, I'm afraid. But I can tell you the social worker who could put you in touch with her. Karen may know how to contact Rachel's father."

Len Chappell took the details down.

"And this James? The man with the hole in his head. Just how did that happen?"

"No one knows. He just came staggering back dripping blood."

"About the time your Rachel was washed up dead?"

"It seems so."

She saw that glint in the constable's eye. Not an accidental drowning. Not a suicide, as Lucy so often feared. She saw his professional hope that he might have landed himself a more interesting criminal case.

He looked at her thoughtfully. Then he snapped the notebook shut.

"Thank you. You've been very helpful, Reverend." To Aidan: "I'd like to see that photograph, if you've still got it."

"My camera's back at the house."

"I'll need to come back with you and take statements from everyone."

The young detective walked across to talk to the coastguards.

"You guys know the currents round here better than anyone. How do you think the body got here? Did she die here? Was she washed along from somewhere else?"

"That's what's been bothering us…"

They moved away as John and Dan pointed along the shore to the east, where the rocks of Snipe Point stood out as dark sentinels against the increasing twilight.

The beach fell silent. Doctor Forbes was standing beside Rachel's body waiting for a decision. Lucy, Peter and Aidan stood numbed.

Beside her, Aidan reached out and put a light hand on Lucy's shoulder.

"I think we've done all we can. They know where to find us."

Lucy looked up and saw DC Chappell talking into his radio. He came towards them.

"We're finished here. Permission to move the body to the mortuary.

You can go now. I'll catch up with you. You're not thinking of leaving the island, are you?"

"We're here for the week."

Lucy had a sudden awareness of the days stretching ahead of her. What should she do with that time now?

The air ambulance crew were lifting Rachel's inert form into a body bag.

Aidan touched Lucy's arm again. "Come on. Let's get you back."

Chapter Fifteen

"I FORGOT," AIDAN SAID. "We haven't got a car. David dropped us here and drove on down the road."

But when they climbed the dunes, there were two cars at the roadside: a silver Vauxhall that must be DC Chappell's and the Cavendishes' red CR-V.

They watched the helicopter lift off. The coastguard Land Rover rolled towards them, with its crew of four.

David was standing beside his vehicle. "I take it you found her, then? Is she all right?"

"She's dead," Peter told him abruptly.

"No! I'm so sorry! Terrible business." He looked flustered, not knowing what to do. He turned to Lucy. "Can I give you a lift back?"

"Thanks. Can you take Peter and Aidan too?"

"Anything to help."

Aidan turned to DC Chappell. "If you come back to the village now, the water will be over the causeway."

"Occupational hazard for Holy Island. Luckily there's not much crime here. I've got mates on the island. John will give me a bed if I'm stuck." He waved to the big coastguard as the Land Rover swung past them onto the road. "I need to take your statements. My bosses will expect me to have done my homework when they get here."

Aidan glared at him, with a glance at the back of Lucy's fair head. "You're treating it as a suspicious death?"

"That's not for me to decide. But the coastguards aren't too happy. Would you say she was a suicide risk?"

Peter's voice burst unexpectedly beside them. "Rachel was always on the edge of suicide."

The constable's face lit up. He turned from Aidan to the student who was about to clamber into David's car.

"You and Rachel go back... how long?"

"We went to school together," came Peter's muffled voice. "When she was there."

Aidan let the burden of the investigation pass from him. He heard snatches of their conversation. Peter, he noticed, seemed reluctant to give away any more about Rachel than he had to. Aidan remembered how the student had always been at her shoulder, as if silently protecting her. Was he protecting her still?

Fragments of the picture fell into place: Rachel at odds with her teachers; the growing absences.

"If she'd had a different mother, it wouldn't have happened!" Peter let out an uncharacteristic burst of emotion.

"What wouldn't?"

But the student lapsed back into generalities. "Moving around. Care homes. Fostering. Like she felt nobody cared about her."

"Was she ever in trouble with the police?"

Aidan knew the inevitability of the answer.

"A bit. Nothing serious," Peter muttered.

"Any associates we need to know about? That would be back in... Where did you say? Devon?"

Peter suddenly burst out, with a vehemence that made the others turn round: "You're wasting your time. She had a rotten life. And she couldn't take it any more. End of story. There's nothing suspicious about her death. Not even surprising. If anyone's to blame, it's all of us."

The listeners fell silent.

Yes, Aidan thought. There had been that first brief meeting, when her eyes had sparkled. But after that, from the little he had seen of Rachel behind that curtain of dark hair, she had looked deeply unhappy.

DC Chappell said uncomfortably, "I'll need to get all this down for you to sign."

Aidan climbed after Peter into David's car. They followed the Land Rover along the road, with the detective's car behind them.

Aidan was surprised at the weariness that came over him as they swung into the car park of St Colman's. The coastguard driver raised his hand in farewell and drove off into the lamplit village. Aidan, Peter, Lucy and David clambered out of the 4x4. DC Chappell drew up beside them.

The four of them walked up to the house that would always be empty now of one of its guests. Their search had ended in a result, but it felt like failure.

"I'll need to take statements from everyone who knew her," DC Chappell said.

Lucy nodded.

As they entered the hall, Aidan was assaulted by a slender figure that hurled itself from the lounge to wrap skinny arms around him and hug him tight.

"Whoa, there! I take it you're glad to see me back."

Melangell nodded vigorously and buried her face against his chest.

Elspeth was hoisting herself out of an armchair. Valerie was sitting upright, expectant. More guardedly, Frances Cavendish was on her feet, her mouth downturned in sympathy.

Mrs Batley appeared behind the new arrivals, her face tense and avid for news.

"Have they taken her away? That poor girl! And what with that gentleman coming in with blood all over his face. I've never had a thing like this happen to any of my folk at St Colman's. Never!"

"I'm sorry." Aidan watched Lucy turn a weary face to their landlady. "This must be upsetting for you. But it can't be helped."

Mrs Batley's face softened. "I'm not the one you should be sorry for. You look worn out."

Lucy turned with a visible effort to the police officer. "This is Detective Constable Chappell. He'll be wanting to ask us all some questions."

"I'm sure I can't tell him anything. I hardly saw the girl. She was missing more than she was here."

"Is there anywhere I could talk to these folk?" Len Chappell asked her. "One on one?"

"Well, there's the television room. Only I made it more of a chapel for Lucy." She pointed to a door the other side of the entrance. Then she turned back to Lucy. "It's seven o'clock. Do I serve supper? And where's Miss English got to?"

Aidan stiffened suddenly and scanned the lounge. Only then did he realize that there was still no sign of Sue.

Melangell wriggled out of Aidan's arms. "I'll go upstairs and see if she's in her room, shall I?"

She bolted away before he could answer.

DC Chappell was looking at his watch, aware of Mrs Batley's disapproving eye on him.

"I won't keep them very long. I just need a statement from everybody, saying anything they can help us with about the deceased."

He looked round the group, considering. "Reverend, perhaps I ought to begin with you."

Lucy was startled out of her private thoughts. "What? Oh, yes. If you like."

She started to move with him towards the chapel room when there were more footsteps on the stairs. Melangell came into sight, bright-eyed with self-importance. Behind her, with heavy steps, came Sue. Her broad face was blotched with tears.

"Sue!" Lucy started forward. "Are you all right? Where have you been?"

"Out." Sue seemed to realize suddenly that everyone was looking at her. She saw for the first time the sober looks on their faces, the stranger in the hall. Melangell must not have told her. Her hand flew to her mouth. "What's happened?" A frightened look round. "Where's James?"

Lucy said carefully, "We don't know what happened. That's what we'd like to find out. James came back about five o'clock. He's had a nasty bang on the head. We don't know whether he fell or whether something hit him. He looked as though he might have concussion, so we sent him across to the hospital to get checked out. We wanted to tell you, but nobody knew where you were."

Sue shifted uncomfortably. A closed look came down over her face. "I needed some time out. I went off and found some rocks on the beach. There was a little cove. I guessed the rain would keep people away."

"Did you see anyone else there? Rachel?"

"If you don't mind, Rev, I think that's my line of enquiry," DC Chappell objected.

Once more, Aidan saw Lucy start. *She's dropped into police mode,* he thought. *Where Rachel's concerned, this is her enquiry as much as his.* He sensed a battle within her.

Then she bowed her head in weary acknowledgement.

"Right. I'm sorry. I didn't mean to tread on your toes. It's just that they're my group. I feel responsible."

"Only natural."

The young detective was looking from Lucy to Sue, evidently unsure whether to go through with his plan of taking Lucy's statement first, or whether Sue might have new information. He reached his decision.

"Right, Reverend. If I could start with you."

The door of the television room closed behind them.

Sue was looking at the rest of them in alarm. "Did any of you see him? Was he badly hurt? What did he say?"

Aidan took charge of the situation. "We were all here. We were getting ready to go and look for Rachel when James came in looking the worse for wear – bleeding from his head wound. Groggy, but able to walk. It wasn't until we got him into a chair that he passed out."

"Then we put him to bed in his room," Melangell said eagerly. "I put some towels on the pillow because of the blood. And then the ambulance car came and took him away."

Sue looked at them blankly. "Why is that man here? Is he the police?"

An awkward silence fell over the group. Elspeth cleared her throat noisily. "Sorry. Has nobody got around to telling you? Rachel drowned."

The shock held them still, even those of them who had known it before. A little part of Aidan's mind was telling him, *We think she drowned. There'll have to be a post-mortem.*

Sue shook her head slowly, as if she could not take all this in.

"Did James…? Did she…?"

Aidan said firmly, "Last time I saw James he was on the slope below the castle. When he came back, he seemed to think he came round in the castle garden. We found Rachel's body on the North Shore. That's miles away."

He thought, but did not say, that the coves to which Sue had been heading lay considerably nearer the North Shore.

Chapter Sixteen

IT WAS A SUBDUED MEAL. Mrs Batley put smoked mackerel and salad in front of them. Aidan could have done with the comforting warmth of soup. Sue crumbled bread between her fingers and ate little.

"Why don't you ring the hospital?" Valerie suggested. "They may have news about him."

Would she do it? Aidan wondered. The words of their quarrel were echoing in his mind. Sue jealous about Rachel; about all James's female followers.

Mrs Batley was serving the second course when Lucy returned from the interview room. She nodded to Sue. "He'll see you next."

"Oh, good! It's toad in the hole," Melangell cried.

"I'm glad somebody's got an appetite," Mrs Batley retorted.

Aidan was drinking coffee in the lounge when he was called.

Mrs Batley had moved the large television screen into the corner. In its place she had set a table with a wooden Celtic cross and a bowl of spring flowers. DC Chappell had moved these to one side and was using the table for a writing desk.

Peter had been in before Aidan, and had presumably already told the constable the details of finding Rachel's body.

But Chappell wanted to take him further back.

"So, you saw Rachel in the priory this morning."

"We all did. It was part of Lucy's course. First we had a service, then she told us the story of St Aidan coming to Lindisfarne."

"And you didn't see Rachel leave?"

"No. I was listening to Lucy. And Rachel was... well, an unpredictable sort of person. The first time I saw her, she looked bright and bouncy.

But only a short time afterwards she turned into this shadowy sort of figure. From then on, she crept about with her head down, not saying very much. Almost as though…"

"Yes?"

"She was frightened."

"Frightened of what?"

"I've no idea."

He gave a careful account of his and Melangell's movements. Of Lucy's concern for the missing girl. Of his own offer to keep his eyes open for her. Their visit to the castle. He hesitated for a moment, then decided it was no time to keep information back.

"Just as we were about to come away, we heard voices from below us. Sue and James. They were quarrelling."

"Oh, yes? About what?" The policeman's hand gripped his pen, poised over his notebook.

"I got the impression that James has something of a track record with impressionable young females. Did you know he was the pastor of a church? Sue was accusing him of taking some of them off to the vestry for – I think she was being ironic – 'personal counselling'. She seemed to think he had his eye on Rachel."

Had Sue told DC Chappell this? Aidan wondered.

The constable gave nothing away.

"And that was it? No struggle? Nothing physical?"

"We couldn't actually see them. We were on the roof. There wasn't a sight line down to that slope below the wall. Sue seems to have stormed off, but James was still OK then. At least, he sounded as if he was. He called after her. Ordered her to come back."

"And did she?"

"No. When we got down to the foot of the castle we saw her walking away. She was heading for where she said she went: towards Emmanuel Head."

"And what about James?"

Aidan shrugged. "We never saw him. I suppose he went to the garden. That's where he said he came round."

"What time would this be?"

"Mm. About four? It looked as though there was heavy rain on its way, so Melangell and I legged it back to the house. Probably a bit before four, come to think of it. Mrs Batley was setting out afternoon tea in the lounge, and we were the first."

"And then?"

"Lucy and Peter came back really concerned. They'd been out looking for Rachel, and hadn't found her. Lucy had rung the police, and they'd tried to reassure her that Rachel was an adult and it was a bit early to start panicking. Anyway, we split up into pairs to search the rest of the island And then James came in."

"Thank you. Yes, I've got what happened then. Once the Reverend Pargeter had called the ambulance, you set off with Peter," he checked the surname, "Fathers, to search the dunes and the North Shore."

"That's right. It was Peter who found her. He was on the beach and I was up on the dunes. He phoned Lucy and the police. You know the rest."

"And at no time did you see this young woman with Mr Denholme?"

"James? No."

"Thank you. Would you send Miss Haccombe in?"

Aidan walked out into the hall. Did this policeman really think there was some connection between James's wound and Rachel's death?

He was making for the lounge when the front door opened. A man Aidan had never seen before strode in. He wore jeans, a black sweatshirt and a dog collar.

He held out a ready hand to Aidan.

"I'm terribly sorry to hear what happened. It's awful. Brother Simon. Fellowship of St Ebba and St Oswald. Could you tell me where I can find Lucy?"

Aidan showed Brother Simon into the lounge. He just had time to see the relieved delight that crossed Lucy's face before the newcomer strode across to her, arms wide, and crushed her to him in a hug.

"Lucy! Poor lamb! What a dreadful thing to happen." His wavy black hair overshadowed her lighter curls.

Aidan felt an unexpected jar. It had not occurred to him that Lucy would already know people on the island. Of course, now that he came to think of it, she had made it clear that Lindisfarne was one of her favourite places. She must have come here on many occasions. It was natural she would know some of its people too.

But not necessarily as well as this. There was no mistaking the note of intimacy in Brother Simon's voice. He and Lucy must go back some way.

As they separated, he caught the pleasure in Lucy's face. The priest's ready sympathy was sparking tears from her eyes, and yet his warmth was drawing a smile from her, even on a day like today.

A startling thought pierced the surface of Aidan's mind. He couldn't be *jealous*, could he?

He was shocked by the treachery that idea implied. Jenny had been dead less than six months. And he had shouted at Lucy when he thought she was invading his privacy. He turned away and discovered that his fist was curled in a tight ball. To calm himself, he stepped past Melangell, who had been playing Ludo with Peter on the floor, and retrieved his half-empty coffee cup. He took it to the table to see if the thermos jug was still hot.

"Look, this is a rotten business," Brother Simon was saying. "I gather the police are involved. Well, they would be, wouldn't they? A sudden, unexplained death. No, I'm not going to ask you what you think happened. You'll have had enough of that. I'm just offering a shoulder to cry on. Someone to talk to. Even," he swung his youthful smile around the rest of the group, "if these delightful people will let me, a share of this course you're running. I don't imagine you're feeling up to Celtic history just at the moment."

Lucy gave him a wan smile. "It's been a shock for all of us. Peter and Aidan found her. And the police still have to question Valerie and the Cavendishes. Not to mention James, who's in hospital."

The clergyman's eyebrows rose. "My! You *have* been having a difficult time. Tell me about it when you feel stronger."

Valerie Grayson and David and Frances were sitting rather stiffly in their chairs, still awaiting their turn. Peter was watching Lucy and her unexpected friend with a surprised look on his face. Sue was not in the room. Aidan guessed she would have followed Valerie's suggestion and gone to telephone the hospital for news of James.

Brother Simon now had his arm round Lucy's shoulders, possessively. He swung her to face the rest of the room.

"Look, this can't have been what any of you expected when you signed up for a holiday here. We can only pray for the poor girl. Rachel, isn't it? But I promise we'll make it up to you as best we can. If you don't mind, I'm going to take Lucy off on our own for a while. She's in need of some TLC. But if you stay around, I'll be back to talk to the rest of you."

He steered Lucy out of the room. When the door closed behind them, it was as though a boisterous wind had fallen silent.

After several moments, David Cavendish spoke, almost belligerently. "Who was *that*?"

"A clergyman, dear." Frances put a hand on his knee. "Didn't you see his dog collar?"

"He told me he was from the Fellowship of St Ebba and St Oswald," Aidan supplied. "I imagine that's some sort of religious community on the island."

"Yes," Peter agreed. "Lucy said she'd invite him over one day to talk to us. He and Lucy go back years. They were at theological college together."

"Well, it's all very well for him to talk about making it up to us," David protested. "He's not in our shoes. A thing like this can't help but spoil your holiday. No disrespect to the poor girl, of course. Don't want to speak ill of the dead. But it's not what we bargained for when we booked a week here. I'm thinking of asking for our money back. The balance, anyway. And take off somewhere else tomorrow. Put all this unpleasantness behind us."

There was stillness in the room.

Valerie steepled her fingertips together and said in a quiet voice, "That's understandable. It's been a shock for all of us. But personally, I shall stay and support Lucy. If it was just Rachel's death, it might have been kinder to leave her alone. Or at least with Peter, whom she knows. But there's all this business with James to be sorted out. I just hope it was a simple accident. I don't think we can just walk out on Lucy and leave her to cope."

Aidan felt a sense of gratitude for her calm good sense.

Elspeth strode into the room, filling it as usual with her larger-than-life personality.

"It's an old cliché, but really, that detective's still wet behind the ears. I've seen boys coming out of the school gates who look older. He wants you next, Val."

Valerie rose with a small smile. "I'm sorry, but you've just missed the latest drama. It appears Lucy has a… shall we say a very good friend here. A fellow clergyman. He's just swept her off for some tender loving care. Not that she doesn't need it, poor soul. But he says if we hang around he'll be back to talk to us."

"Hrmmph! Any more coffee in that jug?"

Frances had taken her turn with DC Chappell before Brother Simon returned. Sue had not reappeared. Aidan wondered what the news of the injured James was.

When Brother Simon came back, Lucy was not with him. Now that his first surprise had subsided, Aidan's keen eye assessed the priest more levelly. Younger than him, he guessed. A thick head of wavy black hair that fell forward over his brow. Keen blue eyes, quick and intelligent. It was not a handsome face, but the lively play of emotions over it caught the attention. He would probably be a hit with women.

In his presence, Aidan was conscious of his own smaller stature, his foxy red hair and beard. Not every woman's choice.

But Jenny had loved him. Jenny had borne his child.

Jenny was no longer here to affirm him.

What was it about clergymen and their relations with women? Sue had been jealous of James and his female congregation.

Aidan had not the slightest reason in the world to be jealous about Simon and Lucy.

The priest threw the warmth of his smile around them like an embrace. He looked about him and chose an armchair facing them.

"I'm Brother Simon. Call me Simon, if you like. Technically, ordination makes me Father, but that sounds a bit too patriarchal.

"Would it embarrass you if I led a prayer for Rachel? Feel free to tune out if it's not your thing. But I feel that for some of you it's the right and proper expression of our love. Rachel got up this morning, with most of her life in front of her. Now she's with her Maker. We ought to honour that rite of passage and sing her on her way into the arms of the angels."

Aidan put his arm around Melangell and drew her close. She sat curled up at his feet, resting her curly head on his knee.

Brother Simon had no book, but the words flowed from him. Simple words that were like a gentle closing of Rachel's eyes against a troubled world. Then the same Celtic cadences of blessing that Lucy had used in her prayers with them:

"Thou Father of the waifs,
Thou Father of the naked,
Draw me to the shelter-house
Of the saviour of the poor,
The saviour of the poor."

Aidan saw again the still pale face of Rachel, its blemishes shadowed by her wet dark hood. Her hair lank as seaweed.

He prayed for her peace.

Even Elspeth sat quietly, either hiding or softening her antagonism to organized worship. Perhaps for Valerie's sake. Perhaps for Rachel's.

Chapter Seventeen

FRANCES TIPTOED BACK INTO THE ROOM. "You next," she mouthed at her husband.

Her attempt at discretion was caught in the dazzling sunshine of Brother Simon's smile.

"Welcome back! And you're…?"

"Frances."

"Well, Frances, sit down. We've said a prayer for Rachel, God rest her soul. The police will take it from here. But I thought this might be an appropriate moment to tell you how Aidan died."

For a moment, Aidan, the saint's modern namesake, felt the shudder of his own mortality. Others, too, were looking his way. He wondered if Simon had picked up on Lucy's brief mention of his name.

"Not here on Holy Island," the young priest was saying, "but in sight of it."

"Sounds a bit ghoulish to me. Haven't we had enough of death for one day?" Elspeth objected.

"Believe me, it's relevant." Simon's smile was still steady as he turned it on the Oxford don, but Aidan sensed something steely behind it. As though he was not intimidated by her intellect, or her forthright manner.

"So, are we sitting comfortably?" He let his gaze play over the rest of them.

Aidan felt Melangell settle back, relaxed, against his legs.

"You've all passed the statue to St Aidan outside the church. I think it gives a good indication of the kind of man he was: lean, disciplined, idealistic.

"Put out of your mind all thoughts of fat, greedy monks of the later Middle Ages. The men of Iona and Holy Island were never like that. Money and gifts of jewels and gold flowed into the abbey here at Lindisfarne, but under Aidan, it flowed out just as readily, feeding the poor, ransoming slaves. Aidan beautified the altars to God's glory. But that was it. The church here was made of wood, with planks for the roof. It was such a poor affair that the rain came in. But Aidan didn't think that was the slightest bit important.

"As bishop of all Northumbria, he travelled huge distances over the hills to visit his people. And always on foot. He wanted to be down at the level of his flock, walking and talking with them, side by side.

"His first patron, King Oswald, who had called him from Iona, was killed by the Mercians at Oswestry, and his dismembered corpse hung on a cross. The Mercians split Northumbria in two. The north was ruled by Oswald's brother Oswy, the south by a cousin, Oswin... Sorry, Melangell. The Anglo-Saxons had this annoying habit of giving their children names that all began in the same way."

"I *know*."

Brother Simon's black eyebrows rose. "Young King Oswin in the south was a good man. He gave Aidan a splendid horse out of his own stable, trapped out in the finest jewel-trimmed leather suitable for a king or a great bishop. Aidan tried to back away. He didn't want to ride lifted up above the heads of his congregation. The king had to hoist him into the saddle himself.

"Well, anyone who knew Aidan could have told him what would happen."

"He gave it away!" cried Melangell.

"Dead right, he did." Simon beamed at her. "He'd hardly got round the first corner before he came across a beggar. So what does Aidan do? Give him a jewel out of his horse's harness, which would have fed him for months? No. He hands over the whole caboodle: horse, saddle, bridle, the lot. And he's back in his sandalled feet, walking the dirty roads and wading across rivers, just like always.

"But sooner or later he had to come back to the royal palace. And when King Oswin saw him come walking up the hill without the horse, he made him confess what he'd done. The king flew into a terrible temper. 'If I'd known you were going to give it away to a beggar, I'd have found you some broken-down nag, not the finest horse in my stable.'

"Aidan looked at him reproachfully. 'Sire, do you care more about a horse than about a child of God?'

"The king strode over to the fireplace. He stood there in a silent rage. The tables were laid, but the servants were too scared to serve dinner. After a terrible silence, they were even more scared when Oswin reached for his sword.

"He walked over to Aidan and laid the weapon at the saint's feet. He knelt before him. 'God forgive me if I ever question anything you do again.' And he led them all to the dinner table."

Out of the corner of his eye, the present-day Aidan saw David creep back into the room and join Frances. Simon threw him a quiet smile of greeting.

"But as Aidan sat eating little, a tear crept down his cheek. One of his monks whispered to him, 'What's wrong?' Aidan told him, 'He's too good a king for this world. He's not going to live long.'

"And sure enough, his cousin King Oswy, who ruled the north of Northumbria, got jealous of Oswin's rule in the south. He wanted the whole of Northumbria for himself, the way his dead brother King Oswald had reigned. So he went to war against him. Oswin would have surrendered, but Oswy's men chased him to the house where he was hiding and murdered him.

"When the news got back to Aidan on Holy Island, he was appalled. And remember, he was an Irishman. It was the custom there that if you committed a heinous crime, a holy man might turn up on your doorstep and begin a fast against you. It was supposed to be a public reproach until you repented of your crime and did penance.

"The Venerable Bede, when he writes the history of these times, doesn't tell us why Aidan camped out at Bamburgh church, in plain sight of the rock that bore Bamburgh Castle. But it's obvious to me. He was fasting against the murderer King Oswy. Bede tells us that Aidan fell sick. His monks wanted to take him back to Holy Island, but he wouldn't go. He was still sitting outside Bamburgh church, leaning against a buttress, when he died."

"They've got that blackened beam inside the church today!" Valerie exclaimed. "They say it's the wood he was leaning against. And when the church burned down, that beam alone was saved."

"Load of nonsense!" snorted Elspeth. "Just to rake in gifts off gullible pilgrims."

"Maybe it was, maybe it wasn't," Simon soothed her. "But there's a lot of truth in that beam, whether it's the right one or not. St Aidan's death was a reproach against the highest power in the land. Against the greed and power and callousness that led to the moment of King Oswin's murder. A cry for the innocent."

Aidan studied the storyteller's face. The bright eyes were still watching the group, willing them to understand.

At last Aidan said, picking his words with difficulty, "You told us that story tonight for a reason, didn't you? Are you saying that's what Rachel's death is? A reproach against someone? Against all of us, perhaps?"

For a moment, a spark of triumph flashed in Brother Simon's eyes.

Then he said carefully, "Interpret it as you wish. It may mean different things to different people here."

"Hmmph!" said Elspeth dismissively. "I hardly knew the girl."

Aidan summoned up a smile for Melangell's benefit. "Bedtime for you, young lady."

"Will you come with me?"

"Of course." He put a reassuring arm around her.

Outside in the hall, they found Sue sitting at the foot of the stairs. There were marks of tears on her face. Had she heard Brother Simon's story?

"Any news about James?"

"Nothing," she hiccupped. "They said to ring again in the morning."

Lucy sat in the chalet bedroom. The single bedside lamp she had lit cast shadows into the further reaches of the room. The shapes of Rachel's clothes, thrown on the other bed or dropped on the floor, could have contained a human form.

They never would now.

Her instincts longed to pick them up and tidy them away. To clear the bathroom of anything that was not her own. To confine these reminders of Rachel to the single bright pink holdall Lucy had bought her.

But something else in her forbade it. Her police training told her to leave the evidence untouched.

Evidence of what?

A girl too depressed and unsure of herself to cope any longer. A high point on a rock and the cold North Sea below. A jump that would end it all and bring her peace.

That was all it was, wasn't it? The sort of tragic ending Lucy had often feared as she tried to break through Rachel's defences and pour into her the healing she so needed. She had tried and failed. It was over.

Then why did she feel she must leave Rachel's things exactly as she found them, until the rest of the CID team arrived?

The words of the coastguard came back to her: *"She'd have been washed back onto the rocks. Or the current would have taken her east."*

Would there be enough in DC Chappell's report to classify this as a suspicious death? Not an accident, not suicide. But if not either of those, then what?

She was being ridiculous. Apart from herself and Peter, Rachel had never met any of the group before. It wasn't possible that in so short a time she could have formed a relationship with any one of them that might have ended in such a violent way.

Lucy got up with an effort and went to the bathroom. The merciless neon light illuminated more evidence of Rachel's all-too-recent presence: toothpaste, flannel, eye-liner, a packet of pills. Rachel had never had much money. She had not cared enough about herself to spend her meagre income on the array of lotions and make-up that most teenage girls regarded as indispensable. Except for the rare days when she hit a high, it was as though she had accepted that her lank hair and sallow skin were part of the burden she carried with her for life; that she had no right to be pretty and attractive like other girls.

Lucy touched the eye-liner sadly. Rachel's one concession to vanity. She sighed and went to bed. She turned out the bedside lamp and tried not to think about the crumpled clothes on the opposite bed.

Chapter Eighteen

LUCY RAN WITH THE COLD MORNING BREEZE whipping her face. To her right, the tide was rising. In another hour or two it would be over the causeway. Early sun glinted on the gently rippling waves.

"Father, make James well. Comfort Sue. May the police find the truth about this whole sorry story of Rachel's death. And help me to help everyone else."

She knew it was unconventional to say her prayers on her early morning run. Some people retired to their study with Bible and devotional notes. Some knelt before a cross or an icon. Others sat, spines erect, concentrating on their breathing, or reflected out of doors surrounded by flowers and birdsong.

Lucy's feet drove her body and her thoughts. She needed to be doing something.

She ran alternately on the hard surface of the south shore road and on the softer sand beside it. She swung round a bend and came in sight of the car park. A few more minutes and she would be back at St Colman's House. She tried not to be scared by the drop in her spirits. Yesterday had happened. She could not roll back the calendar to the time when Rachel was alive and Lucy had really thought she was getting better. Would the others want to leave? The Cavendishes, maybe.

Would James be released after his night in hospital?

Could whatever had happened between James and Sue have anything to do with Rachel's death?

DC Chappell would have made his report. There might be more CID arriving this morning. Would they all have to face another round of questioning?

There was a figure on top of a sand dune ahead of her. He was wearing khaki shorts and holding a camera to his eye. This, and the long lens, suggested a serious photographer, not just a holidaymaker staring down at the screen of his automatic.

As she came into sight, he swung the camera round towards her running figure, then swiftly dropped it to his chest. She saw the pointed foxy beard and ginger hair of Aidan Davison.

Lucy pulled up short. Her mind leaped back to that first evening, when she had made that crass remark about Jenny Davison running the course better than she could. She winced as she remembered Aidan's outburst. She had almost felt the sparks coming off him.

But yesterday he had shown real concern in his search for Rachel and for Lucy's grief.

She watched Aidan hesitate for a moment, and knew that he too was reluctant. Then he came down the side of the dune, slithering in the loose sand.

"Morning," he greeted her without smiling. "Do you always run before breakfast?"

"I pray better on my feet." The words were out before she realized. Had she wanted to share her secret with this man? "And you?"

He gave a forced laugh. "Trying to recover some sense of normality. Photography is what I do – choosing lenses and apertures and shutter speeds. It blots out all the other things I don't want to think about. And there's something about the early morning light. The quality of stillness on the water. The colours of wet mud. You'd never believe it had so many shades."

They both stood facing the strait between them and the mainland, drinking in its tranquillity. Lucy felt how hard they were both trying to hold on to that unspoiled magic. To use it as a defence against the reality that was closing in on them.

She began to breathe more easily. Could he have forgotten that clash between them?

By unspoken agreement they started to walk back together. The big car park ahead was almost empty. Though the causeway was open, it was too early for most day trippers to take advantage of it. Only the really keen and well-organized would get across this morning before the rising tide closed it again.

A single vehicle was coming down the road towards them from the village. Lucy recognized the black and yellow of the Coastguard and Rescue Land Rover.

"Not another shout for the rescue service?" Aidan asked.

"No," said Lucy as the Land Rover approached them. She had recognized John, the big coastguard driving it, but not the man beside him and the woman in the seat behind. As it rolled past, she saw DC Chappell, also in the back seat, turn round to watch them. He raised a hand. Lucy gave a small wave back.

"So the big shots from CID are here bright and early," she explained to Aidan. "Did you see our DC Chappell in the back? He'll be taking them out to see where you found Rachel." She shook herself briskly, casting the thought behind her. "Come on then. We'd better get some breakfast before they start questioning us again."

Aidan walked with her in silence for a while.

"Does it really need detective work? You're pretty sure it was suicide, aren't you?"

"Ever since I've known Rachel, it's what I've been dreading. I've been trying my best to convince her there's something worth living for – people who really care about her. But she's bipolar. She has... had... black moods when nothing got through. At times like that, she was always vulnerable."

"I thought... I know it sounds awful to say this... that Constable Chappell was almost hoping for something worse. Don't get me wrong, suicide's bad enough, but he seemed very keen to latch on to what the coastguards said about it not looking like a typical suicide by drowning."

"I know... I thought at first she might have thrown herself off Snipe Point."

"How high is it?"

"Well, it's not Beachy Head, if that's what you mean. But there are rocks below."

Aidan stirred the sand with his boot. "There was something else. Something that older coastguard said." He looked sideways at her with those keen, grey-blue eyes.

"I know," she said quietly. "A falling tide would have carried her eastwards quite quickly. An incoming one would have just washed her back onto the rocks. There's no way the current could have carried her west to that beach where you found her."

They walked on. Lucy felt the stillness of the island's beauty become one of chilling knowledge.

"So. She died there. On that beach… How? There were no stones in her pockets. She didn't just walk out into the sea to drown." She turned to Aidan in bewilderment.

He looked straight ahead of him, across the filling strait.

"You're the policewoman. Or you were. Is it possible she was already dead when she went into the water?"

Lucy stared at him with the blankness of horror.

"That would mean…"

"It doesn't make sense, does it? From what you say, Rachel had reason to kill herself. But why would anyone else want to kill her?"

The running waves were making Lucy feel giddy.

"I can't believe that. She didn't *know* anyone here, except me and Peter."

The wind shivered in the long grass.

Aidan seemed to shake himself back to the present. "I'm sorry. I probably shouldn't have bothered you with this. You've enough to cope with as it is."

"No." She heard her own voice, abrupt and breathless. "It's not just you. I've been thinking about it half the night."

"The police will handle it. The coastguard will tell them what he told us. Right now, I need to get back and see if Melangell's up yet."

"You didn't bring her with you?"

"I left her in bed. Lazy monkey. But she was awake. I told her I'd be back before breakfast and I'd better find her dressed."

"How is she taking this? She's awfully young to have a death like this thrust upon her."

"Melangell, sadly, is no stranger to death."

"I'm sorry."

Lucy held her tongue, waiting to see if he wanted to tell her more.

She looked sideways at him. He was staring down at the pavement ahead of him as he strode forward.

They turned into St Colman's House without Aidan explaining what he meant.

They were just in time to meet Elspeth and Valerie coming into the hall from the garden door.

"Well," Elspeth greeted them heartily, "you two have stolen a march on us. As far as I'm concerned, there's nothing like a good mystery for whipping up an appetite, never mind exercise."

"Elspeth!" Valerie said quietly. "I'm not sure that's appropriate, under the circumstances."

"Why not? Can't bring the poor girl back to life, can we? And I'd still love to know how Jamie boy got that nasty knock on the head. If that po-faced acolyte of his did it, she's got more gumption than I credited her with."

"Elspeth!"

Lucy watched Aidan circumnavigate the small group and bound upstairs to find Melangell.

She stood in the hall, overcome with the enormity of what they had just discussed.

Lucy forced herself to put the horror of how Rachel might have died behind her. CID were here. Surely she could leave it to them. Somehow she must fulfil her duty to the people she had brought here.

Still, she was more nervous than she would have been facing a drunken brawl on the city streets in the small hours of the morning. It needed courage of a different sort to think that she could lead a course on Celtic and Anglo-Saxon saints for a group of total strangers, in the face of what had happened. She wasn't a historian. All she had was a personal enthusiasm for the saints of Northumbria and a love of its islands and hilltop fortresses.

She had planned a trip to Bamburgh Castle for this afternoon. She'd been prepared to hire a minibus, but it looked as if there would be enough cars between them for so small a number. Now she was irresolute. How long would it take the detective inspector to ask all the questions he needed? Was it possible she was wrong? Would he ignore the coastguards and decide that Rachel's death was a simple human tragedy? Nothing more.

Meanwhile, what should she tell the others round the breakfast table?

She rapped her coffee cup to get their attention.

"Sorry, folks. This isn't what any of us expected when we came here. Detective Inspector Harland has rung me to say he'll want to interview us this morning, when he's back from where they found Rachel. I doubt if any of us can tell him more than we told DC Chappell yesterday, but he'll want to be sure. Meanwhile…" She swallowed an enormous lump in her throat and made herself continue. "We'll do our best to get back to normality. I spoke to some of you car drivers yesterday about a visit to Bamburgh, where the kings of northern Northumbria had their capital. Not the medieval castle you see today, of course, but you can get an idea of its splendid situation even in Anglo-Saxon times. And the church where St Aidan died. I'm hoping that CID will be through with us before lunch. The causeway's closed this morning, anyway. So I suggest you make yourselves available to DI Harland and then you're free till lunchtime. I'll save the story I was going to tell you this morning till a better time."

She was aware of a restiveness in the group around the table. She looked round at the faces she was beginning to know. Some, like Peter, of course, and Valerie, with her wise smile, and, she had to admit, Aidan Davison now, were looking at her with sympathy, anxious to be supportive. But the Cavendishes looked put out. It was almost as though it was Lucy's fault that such a dark cloud had been cast over their holiday. She would have to make an extra effort to see that the visit to Bamburgh Castle this afternoon lived up to their expectations.

Elspeth was a different problem. The older woman, with her air of dismissive superiority, made Lucy acutely conscious of how inferior her own education was to this scholar's. Sometimes she blushed with embarrassment to think that she was attempting to give the Oxford don lessons in history. Lucy had gone straight into the police force after A-levels. It was only ministerial training that had taken her to university. And even then, she had been no more than an average student as far as the academic part of the course went.

She couldn't read Elspeth's expression this morning. The big woman was leaning back in her chair. Her head was tilted, so that she seemed to be looking down her rather large nose at Lucy. There was a curl of her lip that could have been contempt.

Uneasily, Lucy's mind went back to their first evening. Elspeth had known, without being told, that Lucy was worried about Rachel's absence from their room. She had known, before Lucy did, that Rachel had returned. And there had been that strange, transient brightness about Rachel's mood, a flash of aggression, to be followed by black depression next morning. Was it remotely possible that Elspeth had anything to do with that?

The history lecturer's sharp blue eyes challenged her. Something defiant. Almost, though it was shocking to even think it in the circumstances, amused.

She tore her eyes away. James, of course, was absent. If anyone challenged Lucy's authority more than Elspeth, it was him. She tried to fight down a wave of exasperation. Why had he come here if he thought so little of her and her ability as a pastor?

It had been Sue's doing. A misunderstanding about the subject of the course.

Lucy told herself grimly, *James is hurt. He's in hospital. We don't even know if he's going to be OK. They've had him under observation overnight. It all depends how he wakes this morning. I should be praying for him, not seeing him as my enemy.*

Was he Rachel's enemy?

She shook that blacker thought away.

And what about Sue? Lucy just had time to register Sue's absence for the first time when the overweight young woman walked into the dining room.

Her broad plain face was sunny this morning. Lucy didn't need to wait to hear it from Sue to know that the news was good.

"I rang the hospital." Her eyes were alight with joy. "He's had a good night. I can go and fetch him this morning."

"Just one small problem." Aidan spoke up from the end of the table. "It's high tide. The causeway's closed till midday."

Sue's face fell. She turned to Lucy, almost as if she hoped the course leader could override the tides.

Lucy smiled sympathetically. "I'm sorry. Aidan's right. I've scheduled our trip to Bamburgh for this afternoon because nobody can get off the island till lunchtime. And anyway, we're all in for another round of questioning. The inspector in charge of Rachel's case came over early, before the causeway closed – Detective Inspector Harland."

"The CID are still on the case?" Elspeth leaned forward, suddenly interested. "Does that mean they think it's a suspicious death?"

"Not necessarily," Lucy said, more curtly than she intended. "But if a body is washed up on the beach, they can't take the cause of death for granted. There'll have to be a post-mortem. We don't know at this stage if Rachel died accidentally, or she took her own life. Or…" a catch in her breath.

"Or something worse?" Elspeth swung her heavy figure round slowly to look at all of them around the table. "Unless…" she focused on the woman in the doorway, "Sue can tell us more."

Sue's face went white, then flamed. "That's a ridiculous suggestion! I hardly knew the girl."

"Ah, but James did, didn't he? Or he was getting to know her pretty fast."

"What the hell…" The uncharacteristic expletive made Sue blush again. "What on earth do you mean by that?"

"I'm sure you don't need me to tell you that."

Lucy rang her spoon against her cup again. She needed to get control of the situation. "Look, folks, this isn't helping. We're all on edge. Let's just remember Rachel is dead and show some respect for her, shall we? I'll lead morning prayers in the lounge, since the police have taken over our chapel, at…" she looked at her watch, "quarter to nine. Then I suggest we all make ourselves available to DI Harland. And if there's anything you know, anything you remember at all, however insignificant it may seem, then for goodness' sake tell him."

"Like her earring?" Melangell's voice piped up. "The one I found in the sand."

"Yes." Lucy smiled at her, glad of the diversion. "That's just the sort of thing."

It was only as the others got up from the table and began to leave for their rooms that it occurred to Lucy to wonder just how significant Melangell's small find might seem to the detective inspector.

Chapter Nineteen

"I'LL NEED TO SEE THE YOUNG LADY'S BEDROOM. I take it I can get the key from Mrs Batley?"

Detective Inspector Harland rose from his chair in the television room, signalling that his interview with Lucy was over. She had told him, with a weary sense of hearing herself repeat her statement to DC Chappell, the same sad details of her past experience with Rachel and her movements during their two brief days on Holy Island.

The detective inspector was a lean and taciturn man, perhaps in his forties. Deep lines in his face had a weary downturn. Not a high flier, Lucy guessed. It was a relief to find that she had never worked with him on a murder team when she was in uniform. Probably from a different station. It kept her past at bay. He seemed to be going through the motions of an investigation, rather than keen on the scent of solving a mystery.

Was there really a mystery? Lucy asked herself. Surely what Aidan had suggested was unthinkable. Rachel was a suicide risk, with bipolar moods that could swing to black depression; a lack of self-worth.

Yet how could she have committed suicide on a flat, sandy beach?

DI Harland had talked to the coastguard. What was going through his mind? His face gave nothing away.

"No need to ask for a key," she said, getting to her feet as well. "We shared a bedroom. I'll take you."

Outside the interview room they met Detective Sergeant Malham. She was quizzing a harassed-looking Mrs Batley about tide times and transport links for getting on and off the island. She swung round and raised her eyebrows to the inspector. A large-boned woman, not much older than Lucy, but taller. A sensible waxed coat hung open over a polo-necked sweater and trousers. Like the detective inspector, she was a stranger to Lucy.

"We'll take her room next," DI Harland told her. "Lead on, Miss Pargeter."

"She's a Reverend," put in Mrs Batley in Lucy's defence.

"I beg your pardon."

"Don't worry," Lucy said, colouring. "Most people call me Lucy."

She led the way along the verandah and unlocked the bedroom door.

She had tidied her own half of the room meticulously, knowing this would happen. But the inner half was just as Rachel had left it. In daylight, the little heaps of discarded clothes looked less sinister than the night before. Just pathetic. The grey tee-shirt and black shorts Rachel slept in, tumbled on the pillow. Underwear she had pulled from her case and neither worn nor put away. A pair of dark jeans that Lucy knew she had bought from a charity shop. All sad-coloured, anonymous.

Perhaps it had been a mistake to buy her that bright pink holdall. It wasn't Rachel. She seemed not to believe she deserved anything cheerful and colourful.

But no. There had been other, rarer times, when those mood swings carried her to a high of frantic activity and too-brittle laughter.

She had fallen in love with the pair of earrings that Lucy had brought back from a previous trip to Lindisfarne, when she had been checking out the possibility of running this holiday. Red and gold enamel. A strange little beast with a scarlet tongue, its tail twisting in Celtic interlace.

And what about the red waterproof jacket she had been wearing the day they arrived? Before the day was over, Rachel had reverted to the shapeless black coat she had been wearing when Peter found her body on the beach. Lucy had found the jacket pushed to the back of the wardrobe.

She watched the two detectives professionally sorting through Rachel's meagre possessions, the empty bedside drawers, the holdall pushed into a corner.

Detective Sergeant Malham moved on to the bathroom.

"Excuse me." She put her head out of the connecting door. "Can you show me which things are hers?"

Lucy went to join her. She was acutely conscious that some details of her own private life were under scrutiny.

"There wasn't much of Rachel's. She had next to no money. On benefits. That's hers."

DS Malham picked up a foil sheet of tablets and examined them. "Do you know what these are?"

"Mood stabilizers. Lithium. Rachel had a rough time. Rehab, to get her off drugs. And she was bipolar. She could get really black moods."

"Did she ever mention suicide?"

"No. I've told your inspector that. But if I'm honest, it wouldn't really surprise me if she felt that way. Life's been pretty much stacked against her ever since she was a kid."

"Hmm." The detective sergeant put the tablets back on the glass shelf. She looked around. "Not a lot to go on, is there? I take it there wasn't a note."

"Nothing. She was there at the priory with the rest of us. Next moment, she'd gone. No reason. Or none that I know of. We never saw her again."

"No row with any of the others?"

"No."

She had said all she felt she needed to about Sue's outburst. And that had been directed against James, not Rachel.

"No undercurrents of feeling you picked up? Somewhere the vibes just didn't seem right?"

Lucy hesitated. The detective inspector hadn't asked her that. She had been as honest as she could about the possibility that Rachel might have gone off with, or met up with, James Denholme on Saturday afternoon. But there had been something else – too slight to form an answer to any of DI Harland's lacklustre questions.

"Just one thing. Saturday evening, something had upset Rachel. She wouldn't tell me what it was. She refused to come to supper. And when I brought a tray out for her, she wasn't here. I've no idea where she was. Then, when I was back at the house, Elspeth Haccombe came in. She told me I could stop worrying because Rachel was back in the bedroom."

"And?" prompted Malham.

"How did she know Rachel was missing? I hadn't told anyone. And when I came over here to check, Rachel was… I don't know… different."

"How?"

"Sort of high. Bright eyes. Tense. Quite aggressive to me when I tried to ask where she'd been. Of course, it could just have been the bipolar thing. A swing from a low to a high."

"But?"

Lucy sighed. "If you pressed me, I'd have to say it looked the sort of high you might get off drugs. Rachel had been clean for months. I'm as sure as I can be she didn't bring any with her."

"Hmm."

You may be only the sergeant, Lucy thought, *but you're taking this more seriously than your inspector is. To him, it's a simple case. Open and shut. He just needs to wrap up the formalities. You're prepared to consider something more alarming.*

"Well," said the detective sergeant briskly, "I guess we're done here. I'll need to write out a statement for you to sign. About the drugs – both the ones on the shelf and the ones she may or may not have got hold of here."

"I can't imagine how she could."

"No. But take a job lot of people, like the ones you've got here in St Colman's House, and you can bet at least some of them have got murky little secrets they wouldn't want everyone to know."

For a moment, Lucy was tempted to share her own secret: those years in the police force; a greater knowledge of the seamy world of drugs and crime than a young Methodist minister would normally be expected to have.

But something held her back. It was still too painful. DS Malham might be sympathetic, but she was bound to ask why Lucy left. And that was something she was not yet ready to share with anyone.

"You might as well eat your lunch here. I got in food for eleven."

Mrs Batley's invitation to the detectives was not exactly gracious, but she managed a smile. Sue had grabbed a sandwich before setting off to fetch James from hospital the moment the causeway opened.

Lucy could have wished the police officers had eaten somewhere else. It was hard enough to restore anything like an air of normality, to give those remaining at least a semblance of the holiday they had paid for. Valerie and Aidan had proved understanding, but it would not have surprised Lucy if the Cavendishes took off as soon as they could. She wondered if she should offer them a refund, to make it easier for them to go.

No, darn it, she thought, suddenly belligerent. *It's not my fault. I didn't plan any of this: Rachel's death, Sue and James having whatever row it was that ended with a dent in James's head.*

Detective Inspector Harland was saying something to her over the quiche and salad. "We'll wait for this young man – Mr Denholme? – to get back. Then we'll hear his side of the story. Miss English seems pretty clear. They had an argument and she walked away from the castle, leaving him OK. As likely as not, he was upset and didn't watch where he was putting his feet. Stone's treacherous stuff when it's wet. I don't see how it could have anything to do with Miss Ince's death."

"Then that's it?" Lucy wasn't sure whether her immediate reaction was relief or surprise. "You won't want the rest of us again?"

"My dear young lady... My dear *Reverend* lady," he gave her a patronizing smile, "it's a tragic affair, but I think we've taken enough of your time. It's not for me to pre-empt the coroner, but I'd be very surprised if she didn't come up with an open verdict: accident or suicide. I think we can be confident there are no indications of foul play."

He tucked into Mrs Batley's lunch with gusto.

Lucy was aware of Aidan watching her and the inspector intently.

She felt an air of desperation as she put her question. "Did you talk to the coastguard this morning?"

The inspector's thick eyebrows rose. "I am not obliged to give you the details of a police investigation."

Everyone around the table was listening now. The implications of what she was thinking could affect any one of them.

"The tides," she said, hearing how lame it must sound. "Where could she commit suicide? How did her body get on that particular beach?"

The detective sergeant's head shot up, but her inspector's face did not change.

"Death by drowning is hardly an uncommon method of suicide. Especially by young women."

If the coastguard had told him what he had said to Aidan, then the knowledge of the Holy Island currents had left the inspector unmoved.

"So? That's it? We've got the green light for Bamburgh Castle?" Elspeth had been listening with undisguised curiosity.

"We have your statements. I see no reason why you shouldn't resume your planned programme. Once we've heard Mr Denholme's version of what happened, we'll be off ourselves."

"And let poor Len Chappell get back to his long-suffering wife," Sergeant Malham laughed.

Lucy felt an unexpected sense of loss. It was what she wanted, wasn't it? The necessary enquiry gone through, the sad presumption that Rachel had taken her own life, or that she had slipped, as James had in the garden, and fallen to her death. But where?

What other possible explanation could there be?

She looked around the depleted group at the table. There were questions about some of their relationships with Rachel that would never now be answered. But it was overdramatic to suppose that one of them could possibly have had anything to do with Rachel's death.

She rearranged her face into a forced smile for DI Harland.

"You'll be relieved, I expect, police budgets being what they are. You'll probably have saved yourself a million or so by ruling out a suspicious death."

She saw the flash of surprise in his face. Immediately, she wished she'd kept her mouth shut. A Methodist minister probably wasn't supposed to know how much the decision to open a murder enquiry could cost.

A murder enquiry? It was the first time she had allowed herself to put a name to the doubt in her mind.

Too late now. By the time they got back from Bamburgh, the police would have gone. Case closed.

Chapter Twenty

"Are you sure it's going out?"

Melangell peered out of the side windows of Elspeth's car. The water was still lapping close to the causeway on either side.

"Yes," Aidan assured her. "The tide turned a couple of hours ago. And we'll still be able to get back for supper."

With only eight of them left, Lucy had decided that two cars would be enough. She was driving in front of them now, with Peter and the Cavendishes. Aidan and Melangell had hitched a ride with Elspeth and Valerie. Aidan decided he would rather watch the seascapes rolling away to left and right than Elspeth's cavalier driving across the narrow roadway.

He had thought of a causeway as a raised road above the sea, but the tarmac here was on the same level as the expanse of wet sand.

They passed the refuge on stilts, where the deep tide channel swung closer to the coast, and then the salt marshes were speeding towards them.

The mainland again. Melangell craned her neck to the car park where they had left their own vehicle for the week.

"Hello, car!" She waved. "Bye bye. See you on Saturday." She turned to Aidan. "Do you think it's lonely without us?"

"It's probably enjoying a week's rest. A seaside holiday."

He sensed they were all glad of the break this afternoon. A chance to get away from the island and its dark memories. Holy Island shouldn't have been like that. It was not what he had hoped for when he brought Melangell here.

But he knew the history of Lindisfarne better than most: conflict, betrayal, heartbreak, Viking massacre. Yet still the island kept its aura of sanctity. They would go back this evening, refreshed, and rediscover what they came for.

He wondered how Lucy was bearing the loss of the girl she had loved and done so much to try and help.

Would she take a possible suicide personally?

Suicide? He pushed away the thought that had closed its colder hand over his heart this morning. There must be a sad but unthreatening reason why they had found Rachel's body on that particular stretch of beach, mustn't there? The alternative was unthinkable.

"There!" he cried, suddenly seizing Melangell's arm. "That's Bamburgh church, where St Aidan was leaning when he died."

Valerie turned round from the front seat. "You really must go and look inside, Melangell. That half-burned beam I told you about. It's up in the roof now."

The road led down through the village to the foot of the castle crag. Melangell craned up in awe.

"It's *massive.*"

A long line of ramparts marched across the sky above them. Buildings rose within it, dominated by the sturdy square keep.

They drove up the ramp and parked the cars at the foot of the walls. Across the road, the way led uphill through the gateway. Fran, predictably, was complaining in a low voice to David. When they stood at last on the broad terrace of the middle ward, looking out to sea, the wind tugged at Aidan's hair. He turned to face the lively waves. Far below, beyond a wilderness of tumbled dunes, the beach ran long and level. Its pale gold sands threw back the light, even on a grey day. Instinctively he raised his camera. Through the long-range lens, the level slabs of rock that formed the Farne Islands sprang into view.

He lowered the Nikon and took deep breaths of salty air.

"There! Doesn't that make you feel great?"

Melangell was manning the cannons.

Lucy came towards them. Aidan was glad to see her face was brighter too. With a sweep of her arm she gathered the group around her.

"You're standing now where generations of Northumbrian kings stood. And queens too. Bamburgh is named after one of them: Bebba. She wasn't an Angle. She was a British princess who took the brave decision to marry an Anglian king, one of the leading invaders who was taking over her country. Her people had lost, but she could still put her own son on the throne.

"This is the place that King Oswald, who founded Holy Island abbey, took as his coastal capital after he marched south from Iona to drive the Mercians out. Forget the Norman castle, of course. Think of a great wooden hall with soaring gable ends, bright with painted carvings. Here Aidan came to talk to the king. And here, after the Mercians killed Oswald, his brother Oswy became ruler of northern Northumbria. He too married a British princess. But when she died, he took his second queen from Kent. She was a very special princess: Eanfled. I've told you how, years before, when King Edwin ruled in Northumbria, the Roman missionary Paulinus tried to convert him. Edwin resisted until one day he barely escaped assassination. He was wounded, and his Christian queen went into labour. After all that danger, little Princess Eanfled was born safely. Paulinus proclaimed the survival of all three as a miracle. King Edwin allowed his baby daughter to be baptized as a Christian with twelve Northumbrians to accompany her. And when the king himself was converted, thousands more Northumbrians followed him.

"When the Mercians invaded, King Edwin was killed, and little Eanfled was whisked away to Kent with her mother. Now she was coming back to her birthplace to marry King Oswy.

"But it wasn't an entirely happy marriage. Eanfled had been brought up in the Kentish court as a Roman Christian. Oswy had found his faith on Iona, among Celtic Christians. They had different ways of doing things – different dates for Easter, and that meant for Lent beforehand, and all the festivals after Easter. While the king was celebrating the greatest feast in the Christian year, the queen was still fasting for Lent.

"Into this divided royal household came a handsome teenage boy: Wilfrid."

Aidan's modern namesake heard the tightening in Lucy's voice at that controversial name. She evidently thought the same about Wilfrid as he did. He saw the wind tugging her short hair.

A pang of grief hit him. The image of Jenny's head after they had called a halt to her chemotherapy. The tiny hairs beginning to grow back in a golden fuzz.

The world rocked around him. Then he steadied himself to the sound of Lucy's voice.

"Wilfrid asked for the queen's help to make a career in the Church. Since there were no Roman monasteries in Northumbria, she sent him to Lindisfarne, to take care of a veteran warrior who was now disabled and was going to Holy Island as a monk.

"But Wilfrid had his eyes on more splendid things than Aidan's leaking church on Lindisfarne. As long as Aidan lived, Wilfrid held his tongue. Everyone loved St Aidan, whether their churchmanship was Celtic or Roman. But when he died, things fell apart. Wilfrid heard scholars disputing the two traditions. He spent his spare time studying in the library, and became fired by the dream of seeing Rome. He appealed to the queen again. She sent him to her brother, the king of Kent. He found Wilfrid a reliable escort, the former warrior Benedict Biscop, who went on to found the great monasteries of Wearmouth and Jarrow.

"The young men set out. They stopped at Lyon, and Wilfrid was so blown away by the magnificence of the Church there that he let Benedict Biscop go on without him. The archbishop of Lyon even offered to adopt him as his son. Eventually Wilfrid tore himself away and arrived in Rome.

"He got the pope's archdeacon to teach him. Then he set off to return to Britain, filled with the ambition to make the backward Northumbrian Church fall into line with the glory of Rome."

Lucy shrugged her shoulders in her windproof jacket.

"He was a brave young man. Passing back through Lyon, he was persuaded to stay with the archbishop again and took his vows as a monk. But the archbishop had fallen out with the local queen. He and eight of his bishops were sentenced to death. Wilfrid rashly jumped onto the scaffold to join them, until somebody spotted that he was an

Englishman and threw him off.

"So back he came to Northumbria. Here he began to plot with Oswy's son, Prince Alchfrith, the downfall of the Celtic Church."

Lucy stopped. Even Elspeth had held her tongue for the story. Now they were all looking at Lucy, their eyes demanding to know what happened next. Aidan knew, of course, but he had still been trapped in the magic of the story.

Lucy's blue eyes sparkled, as they had not since Rachel's death. The spell of Lindisfarne's story had held her too.

"Enough," she said. "It's only Monday. There's more to come. For now, try to enjoy yourselves. Of course, this isn't the early fortress of Oswald and Oswy, but once you're on the inside looking out, it could be. What better place to build a stronghold than on these cliffs, commanding the seashore and the Farne Islands and the coastal roads? Treasure the experience. Like the Celtic Church, the things we hold dear may not last forever."

The sadness returned to her eyes.

Aidan was glad to see the burst of energy with which Melangell raced through the castle rooms, chattering about the exhibits as she passed. Sometimes she would whirl around and dive for a particular display, to become enrapt with its details: a table made from oak scavenged from a bridge the emperor Hadrian built in AD 120; the gigantic chains hung either side of a doorway in the Keep Hall.

"That's what shire horses used to drag the shipwrecks ashore," the attendant told her.

"Did they have lots of wrecks, then?" Melangell demanded.

"Could be as many as four a week."

It was what she needed, a break away from the sadness of death, Rachel's drowning, the bloodstained figure of James, the ominous presence of the police.

"Look, Daddy! They must have umpteen million swords. They've made a star of them over the fireplace."

Everywhere Aidan looked there were weapons. Looking closely, he saw that they had been used.

He led her to the window. Bamburgh might have its own dark history, but here, today, the wind blew strong, the white foam streamed and horses galloped along the sands.

Aidan surveyed the seascape before them. Through the lens of his camera he could pick out the mêlée of seabirds on the stacks of Inner Farne, St Cuthbert's refuge.

He put his hands on Melangell's shoulders and turned her to look northwards.

"Can you see that smudge on the horizon? The bit on the right is Lindisfarne."

"That's funny." She screwed up her eyes. "When we're on Lindisfarne, we can see Bamburgh and it looks, like, really big."

"That's because it is. Remember how much smaller Lindisfarne Castle was? You can only just pick it out from here with the naked eye."

"But Bamburgh's huge, isn't it?"

"Would you like to live up here? I mean, would you have liked to be a princess in King Oswald's time?"

Melangell thought about it and pouted. "No. Because the Mercians killed him, didn't they? They put his head and his hands on a cross. I wouldn't want anyone to do that to you."

"Thanks!" He ruffled her hair.

"Well said, Melangell. Those were rough times in Northumbria."

Aidan turned at the sound of Lucy's voice.

Hers was not as expressive a face as Jenny's had been. She had a healthy outdoor look under her short-cropped hair. But still he noticed the lines of strain about her eyes. She was smiling for Melangell, but he sensed the cheerfulness was assumed now. A professional necessity. Today, she wore a black sweatshirt and jeans, with a dark blue windcheater. A white shirt collar showed at her neck. The austerity might well be mourning for Rachel, but it also made her look more like the minister of religion she was, even without her dog collar.

"Are you all right?" he said quietly, as Melangell scampered away to admire a suit of armour. He was still embarrassed by the way he had shouted at her.

"I'll manage." She gave him a brief, surface smile.

"You'll be glad the police enquiry is over. Or it will be by the time we get back. They should have finished with James by then."

"Yes." She sounded less sure.

"What's wrong?" he asked, after a moment's hesitation, though he knew.

"Probably nothing." She had her hands in her pockets, turning away from him into the wind.

"But?"

"Oh, I don't know. That hunch you learn to get in the police, that something's not quite right. You put your finger on it this morning. Those coastguards. They weren't too happy about it looking like a suicide, were they? And DC Chappell. He thought he was on to something more than an accidental drowning. Even the detective sergeant asked more questions than her boss. It's only DI Harland who seems ready to wrap it up."

"I think you touched a sore point about police budgets."

"Yes." She made a face. "I didn't mean to be hard on him. But if you know you may have a bill for a million pounds staring you in the face, you can't help feeling relieved if you see a way to close the book on it. I'm not saying the police would ever do that deliberately, but, well, things work on your subconscious."

Even indoors, the hollow sound of the wind haunted Aidan's ears.

"Then…" He looked at her sideways, suddenly anxious. The implications of what they were saying hovered on his lips. "We're thinking it wasn't an accident? Not even suicide?"

Lucy whipped round on him. He saw the alarm in her face. "I didn't say that! God knows she had reason enough to wish her life over. It's just…" The capable shoulders hunched now into her windcheater. "I wish he'd looked more as if he really wanted to find the truth. She deserved that."

Aidan thought for a while. He looked down over the battlements below. Members of their group were beginning to gather on the middle ward, where Lucy had asked them to meet. He struggled with the truth that was on both their minds. If Rachel's death wasn't suicide or an accident, then… Could someone else on Holy Island have had reason to want her dead?

Valerie Grayson? He watched her tall figure from above. Ridiculous. The somewhat irritating but otherwise inoffensive Cavendishes? Elspeth Haccombe was a more forceful character, but surely nothing could have happened between her and Rachel in just twenty-four hours to warrant such a startling assumption.

There was Peter, of course. He'd known her far longer than anyone else. Could his air of anxiety, his protective presence at Rachel's shoulder, be masking something more possessive?

And back on Holy Island, the more enigmatic and controversial figures of James and Sue. Did James remember now how he came by that head injury on the day of Rachel's death?

"There'll be a post-mortem, won't there? They'll find how Rachel died."

"It might not help. There's more than one way for someone to drown."

She straightened her shoulders in that characteristic way. The professional smile was back.

"I'm sorry. I didn't mean to spoil your afternoon away."

He was saved from the need to reply by Melangell bouncing back, curls whipped by the wind, eyes shining. "If I *was* a princess, I'd want to be like those girls down there, galloping my horse through the waves."

"You don't have to be a princess to do that," Lucy said. "Do you want to sit on an Anglo-Saxon throne?"

Outside in the inner ward stood a replica of the yellow sandstone throne, the remains of which they had seen in the museum. With a cry of glee, Melangell climbed up and threw herself onto it.

As she sat, gazing royally out to sea, a chill thought struck Aidan: *If Lucy is looking at every one of us, assessing if we might have anything to do with Rachel's death, what is she thinking when she looks at me?*

Chapter Twenty-one

LUCY FELT THE WIND BUFFETING THE CAR as she drove back across the causeway. She concentrated on holding a steady course along the roadway between the advancing sea. While they had been at Bamburgh Castle the tide had turned. It was flowing in again over the rose-tinged sands.

In the back seat, Frances was chattering about the treasures of Bamburgh Castle. She sounded more animated than at any time since the Cavendishes had arrived on Saturday. It was as if Rachel's death had not happened.

Beside Lucy, Peter seemed sunk in gloom.

She glanced briefly in the rear-view mirror and raised her voice to the couple behind. "You enjoyed it, then?"

"Oh, yes! The King's Hall was lovely. All those portraits, and the beautiful china, and the furniture and everything. You could tell by that gorgeous carved roof that it was centuries old."

"It's fake, you know," Peter said. "Nineteenth century. It's not as historic as it looks."

"Well… Still, I mean, looks like the real thing, doesn't it? And the family are living in it. You can imagine how it was. Not like those old things you keep telling us about. Everywhere we go, you say, 'Of course, this wasn't St Aidan's abbey. That was pulled down long before.' And, 'This isn't King Oswald's castle. The Normans built this one.' You can't show us anything that's real from back then."

"But I did!" Lucy protested. "We stopped at the church on the way back. I took you inside and showed you the black beam in the roof. The one that legend says St Aidan was leaning against when he died."

"Yes, well," Frances conceded grudgingly, "only that was so high up, you practically had to break your neck looking at it. Beats me how he could have been leaning against it."

Lucy sighed. She had explained to them how the ancient church had become a site of pilgrimage until it burned down, and how that post alone had survived the conflagration. When a new church had been built, the sacred beam had been installed, not in its original position on the outside wall, but inside as part of the roof over the baptistery.

She wondered how much more of what she had said had gone over Frances's head.

But Melangell had loved it. She had lain down on her back on the flagstones of the nave and gazed up at the blackened beam with eager wonder.

It must be great to be eight years old. To live for the moment. A pity she came from a broken family; that it had to be her father bringing her, not her mother Jenny Davison, who had written those books about Celtic saints. Lucy felt a sudden anger against Aidan. What had he done to bring that marriage to an end? She remembered that flash of temper and flinched.

The crossing was ending. She swung the car round, following the road that skirted the sandy southern shore of Holy Island.

A cold dismay was creeping over her. What had possessed her to revive her doubts to Aidan in the keep? There was no proof that there was anything more to Rachel's death than what Detective Inspector Harland clearly thought it was. It was her own evidence, more than anyone else's, that had convinced him suicide was the most likely verdict. There must be some logical explanation for why the body had been found on that beach.

So why was that insistent voice still telling her it was neither suicide nor a tragic accident?

The improbability that anyone Rachel had met in those fatal twenty-four hours on Lindisfarne could be implicated in her death struck home. It simply didn't bear thinking about. What if Aidan told the rest of the group? It was as good as accusing one of them of murder.

The word made her feel physically sick. Peter gave a startled cry and shot out a hand as the car swerved.

"Sorry," Lucy said, bringing them back on course.

She tried to imagine herself a young policewoman again. Just a uniformed constable, never a detective. What if she had gone to the senior investigating officer in a case like this and said, "I don't think this is suicide"?

Images were gathering in her memory. The frown on the older coastguard's face. Rachel's unexplained absence on Saturday evening. The bitterness of Sue's complaint about James's relations with his young female congregation.

No proof. Just a deep-down conviction that there were more questions to be answered than DI Harland appeared to be asking.

She turned the car in at the gates of St Colman's and parked in front of the house.

James and Sue's car was back. At last she might find out what really happened at Lindisfarne Castle yesterday afternoon. If it *was* there that James had met with his head injury.

She got out. The detectives' car had gone. They were on their own.

Lucy had hardly got inside the house before Mrs Batley accosted her.

"Reverend, I want a word with you."

Her heart sank at the landlady's accusing manner. She could understand that Rachel's death had been as shocking for Mrs Batley as for any of them. The reputation of St Colman's House was at stake. And she had rallied round with remarkable efficiency when James had come back dripping blood over her carpet.

But just now, Lucy had other things on her mind. Where were James and Sue?

"Could you give me a moment? Is James back? I really do need to talk to him."

Mrs Batley sniffed. "You needn't worry yourself about him. He's out in the garden, holding court with his young lady as usual. And looking not much the worse for that knock on the head. Not like that poor girl of yours. But I really need…"

"Thanks. Excuse me. I'll be right back."

She sped towards the door at the back of the hall. Whatever complaint Mrs Batley wanted to make, it could wait.

James was sitting at one of the wooden tables on the lawn. Glasses and bottles glinted in the sun. Sue jumped up and went to stand behind him. Her hand rested protectively on James's shoulder. Whatever tangled relationship linked these two, Sue had evidently swallowed her indignation towards James. In the face of the outside world, she was positioning herself on his side.

"James! You're back." Lucy's quick eyes took in the shaved hair, the considerable swathe of plaster on the right side of his head. James managed to make even this look dashing. She should have known.

"Like a bad penny." He flashed her a superior grin.

She fought down the temptation to jealousy that he could assume so easily that aura of charisma and authority that Lucy herself had to work at as an ordained minister.

She sat down on the bench opposite him. Elspeth and Valerie were making their way to their chalet room.

"The prodigal returns!" Elspeth boomed across the lawn.

The door closed behind the two of them. The Cavendishes made their quieter way to their own room, with only a curious stare at James.

Lucy leaned forward on her elbows. "I'm so glad it wasn't any worse. I take it they've given you a clean bill of health, if they've let you out. You're not going to pass out on us again?"

"Concussion. No permanent harm, thank the Lord."

"Can you remember what happened? Not surprisingly, you weren't exactly coherent yesterday."

The grin faded to a frostier look. "If you don't mind, I've been over all that with the police. I don't know what you told them, but from the way they questioned me, you'd have thought it had something to do with that poor girl's death. I told them, I'd barely met her. If she had troubled relationships with anyone, it would have to be you and Peter. You've been involved with her for years. Not like me."

How like him, Lucy thought, *to go on the offensive. All I've done is show the natural concern of a leader for a member of her group; of any decent human being. And he acts as if I've accused him of something and then throws it back in my face.*

"James," she said, trying to hold herself calm, "I'm not the police. Not these days. I'm a minister of religion. I'm running the course that brought you here. I can't help feeling a bit responsible if you get injured on my watch. I'd just like to understand what happened."

A glance passed between James and Sue.

"If you must know, we were in the garden near the castle. Have you seen it? The planting's supposed to have been planned by Gertrude Jekyll. Anyway, Sue was keen to go on to Emmanuel Head, but I could see the heavens were going to open before long. I opted to head back here. I slipped. That's all. Easy to do on wet stone. When I came round I was lying in a pool of blood and in danger of drowning in a rainstorm. The rest you know."

Lucy looked past him at the obstinate set of Sue's mouth.

He's lying, she thought. *Aidan and Melangell heard them quarrelling and then Sue stalked off. James would never take that kind of rebellion lying down. He'd have to go after her and try to dominate her again. They must both have been out among the rocks around the headland. I'm sure of it.*

But were they alone? Was it remotely possible they had come upon Rachel there? Much of Holy Island was bare of hiding places, but those coves and rock stacks were one place a wounded soul might hope to find privacy.

If James had come across her, alone and vulnerable, what would he have done? How would Rachel have reacted? What might have happened between the two of them?

And was there any way that Sue would ever tell?

The insistent voice murmured in her mind: *That wouldn't answer the question. How did her body get to a beach so far to the west?*

She got up from the bench. "Well, I'm glad you're back and no permanent damage done. I'm sorry you missed our outing to Bamburgh Castle. I'll see you both at supper."

She tried to make her parting smile as genuine as she could.

"And what romantic story did you spin them this time?"

"I told them about St Wilfrid, the worm in the rose of Celtic Christianity."

He raised his eyebrows, and winced as the movement puckered the skin around his wound.

"I sometimes wonder if your beloved Celtic Christians weren't a touch too close to heathenism."

She fought back the flash of anger.

"If you mean they had a love of God's creation and didn't think it sinful, that they gave positions of authority to women, then I think they were ahead of their time."

She was striding towards her room, all the refreshment of the afternoon at Bamburgh gone, when she remembered that Mrs Batley had wanted to talk to her urgently.

Chapter Twenty-two

LUCY FELT THE STONES OF THE WALKWAY pushing against the balls of her feet as she sped towards the house. The entrance hall was empty. There were sounds from the kitchen: a brisk chopping, the rattle of a pan. As she turned towards them, it struck her how much of the work Mrs Batley took on herself. Perhaps there had been a Mr Batley not long ago. Or maybe no woman from the village came up to her exacting standards.

She tapped on the half-open door. "Mrs Batley? It's me, Lucy. You wanted to speak to me."

As she spoke, she pushed the door wider. Mrs Batley stopped what she was doing. She stood, the sharp vegetable knife in her hand poised over the table. There was no smile of welcome. Her lips tightened as she looked straight at Lucy.

"And about time too, if you don't mind me saying so."

"I'm sorry. I was concerned about James. I needed to check how he was."

"Well enough, if you ask me." Mrs Batley sniffed. "Hardly got a foot in the house before he was ordering me about. 'Would you fetch this?' 'Mrs Batley, I'm sure you could find me a bottle of lager from somewhere.' I'm licensed to serve drinks with meals, but I'm not a barmaid."

"I'm really sorry. That was wrong of him. I'm afraid James does rather like to have women waiting on him."

"Went so far as to tell me women weren't too proud to follow Jesus and provide what he needed. That's blasphemy."

"Gosh! Did he really say that?" Lucy was genuinely alarmed that James's self-conceit could have gone that far. "Was that what you wanted to see me about?"

"No. I didn't need you to give him a flea in his ear. And he's not used to being spoken to straight, I could tell. Still, he'd sobered up by the time the police had finished with him."

Lucy's heart fell further still. That feeling of sickness again. What had emerged from DI Harland's final questioning? If only she could have been a fly on the wall. She desperately wanted something to come out of the investigation, and yet she increasingly feared what it might be.

"No," Mrs Batley was saying. She laid down the knife and advanced around the table. She grabbed up a wet cloth and wiped her hands with it. Anger was wrestling with concern in her face. "No, it's those women: Dr Haccombe and Miss Grayson. I'm not the fool they must think I am. If it had been Ellie doing out their rooms this morning, she'd probably never have noticed."

So there was a cleaner.

"But we were all at sixes and sevens, what with the police poking their noses into everywhere. You'd told me to leave your room for them to see, but I didn't trust her not to get the wrong one. It wasn't until this afternoon I got around to doing the chalet bedrooms myself." She paused dramatically.

"And what? You found something?"

Lucy's pulse was racing fast. What could Elspeth and Valerie possibly have left in their room that might incriminate them? Even as she thought this word, her brain caught up with the implication. Incriminate them in what? She had been surprised, angry even, about Elspeth's mysterious behaviour on Saturday evening. But Rachel had come back then, apparently unharmed.

She thought of Elspeth, prowling around the ruins of the priory on Sunday morning, while the others joined in Lucy's act of worship. Then she remembered. The history don had rejoined them for the story of Aidan's coming to Lindisfarne. She had still been with them when Rachel had silently disappeared from the group.

Her tumbling thoughts came to an abrupt halt. Mrs Batley was waiting with growing indignation. As soon as Lucy met her eyes, she gave an almost savage smile.

"This." She drew out from the pocket of her apron a plastic bag. She cleared a corner of the table and set out the meagre contents: a small folded piece of white paper, some crumpled silver foil, a cut-off straw. Lucy's police experience did not need the faint residue of powder to tell her exactly what she was looking at. Her eyes widened.

"Yes," said Mrs Batley triumphantly. "You know what that is, don't you? Cocaine. They may come over all posh, like she's some great scholar from Oxford, but that's a criminal offence. And what's more, I know the law. If I let that sort of thing go on in my house, I'm liable too. It's a disgrace."

Lucy struggled to make sense of this new drama. If Mrs Batley had found this while the police were still on the island, she would almost certainly have confronted them with it, whether it had anything to do with Rachel's death or not.

Had it? She remembered suddenly Rachel's mood shifts on Saturday. From the teenage girl singing songs in the back of the car, to the huddled silent figure who had refused to come to supper. And then the bright-eyed Rachel who had come back to their room on a high. Elspeth's enigmatic message to Lucy. She cursed herself for assuming it had simply been Rachel's bipolar mood swings. If Elspeth… She felt anger begin to consume her.

She tried to gather her wits to deal with Mrs Batley. "You were absolutely right to tell me. I'm really sorry they've abused your hospitality this way. I'm going to see Dr Haccombe and Miss Grayson right away."

She was out of the door and striding towards the chalets, blood pounding in her head.

She rapped on the women's door, but she hardly heeded the answering call from within before she threw it open.

She surprised the bulky figure of Elspeth Haccombe, peeling off her trousers, but with a lacy petticoat already pulled on over her upper half. Valerie, more completely dressed, stood rigid with alarm.

Lucy ignored the first flush of embarrassment she felt warming her cheeks.

"Sorry," she said, in a brisk tone that held little real apology. "I thought you said 'Come in'. I need to speak to you." She held up the plastic bag and opened it sufficiently to show the contents. "Mrs Batley found this while she was cleaning your room today. Fortunately, she recognized what it was. Her usual cleaner might not have done."

"Oh, dear," Valerie said quietly. "I've told you, Elspeth. You need to be more discreet."

"It's not a hanging offence, is it?" Elspeth countered, her voice as forcible as ever. "It's not my fault this country has some antiquated laws. What consenting adults do in their private space is their own affair."

"Consenting adults? It's bad enough that you abuse Mrs Batley's hospitality. She can be held responsible for what goes on on her premises. Have you thought of that? But there's worse, isn't there? On Saturday evening, Rachel was missing from her room. You knew that, when no one else did. And you knew when she came back. When I went to see, Rachel was on a high. Feverish. Aggressive. I put it down to her bipolar disorder, fool that I was. But it wasn't, was it? You'd given her cocaine."

Lucy glared at the older woman, expecting a blustering denial. It was not what she got.

"Well, poor little sod. She looked like something the cat brought in. A victim. I was doing her a favour. If there's one way to put all your troubles behind you, it's the blessed snow. I wouldn't have got through the challenges of my own career without it. Oxford can be a bloody cock fight."

"You idiot! Rachel had worked for months to get herself off drugs. Have you any idea how difficult that is? She was clean. And in a single evening you wrecked all of that."

"She was an adult. She knew the score."

"She may have been over eighteen, but she was a vulnerable adult, with an alcoholic mother, a childhood in care, drugs, theft. The last thing she needed was someone like you. And now she's dead."

Elspeth rose in all her majestic height. "Now look here, young lady. You be careful what you say. I've been honest with you. From the look on Valerie's face, I'd say she thinks too honest. I gave Rachel a snort. Right? That's all. An evening off from whatever hell she was inhabiting. I… did… not… kill her."

"Not intentionally, perhaps. But if the black dog got her next morning when she came down off her high, what then? She was always a suicide risk."

Valerie came towards them. Her grey eyes were troubled, her face tightly lined. "Lucy. This has all been very painful for everybody. Most of all you. I'm truly sorry if anything Elspeth has done contributed to that. But it's over now. Nothing is going to bring Rachel back. And you have it in your power to ruin Elspeth's career. How will that help anybody? You said yourself, Rachel was always a suicide risk. What she did could have happened any time, for any reason. It might have nothing to do with Elspeth."

Lucy was still seething. "And what about other vulnerable girls? Elspeth's students, perhaps?"

"She wouldn't. She doesn't." Valerie was visibly agitated. "I can assure you, Elspeth is responsible. Drugs are hardly a novelty among the Oxford staff, but most of them have enough sense to keep it to themselves. Elspeth wouldn't be so foolish as to lay herself open to a charge of pushing them to students."

Elspeth had stepped out of her trousers and was fastening herself into a skirt. "Thank you, Valerie. I think I'm capable of speaking in my own defence. Assuming there's anything I want to defend."

"Rachel wasn't your student," Lucy protested. "She was just a teenager you'd only just met, and wouldn't see again after this week. Not a gifted scholar. Not a bright graduate of the future. She didn't have pushy parents behind her. She was nobody important. She wasn't likely to complain, and who would listen to her if she did?"

"There, you see?" Triumph sparked in Elspeth's eyes. "You've said it yourself. She wasn't complaining. I did her a favour, for God's sake!"

Lucy stared at her for a long moment, unable to find the words to express what she felt. Then she turned on her heel and strode out of the room.

Chapter Twenty-three

THERE WERE ONLY TWENTY MINUTES to supper. Lucy really should be showering and changing. But the anger was pounding inside her. She needed to run. She looked at her watch. Ten minutes, she promised herself.

Some of the group were already gathering on the lawn: Aidan and Melangell, Peter, Sue and James. She lifted her hand in acknowledgement and jogged past them, heading for the road.

At the gate, she hesitated, then swung left, past the coach park and out towards Coombs Farm. The world fell quiet along the cart track beyond. Far ahead she saw the piled-up dunes that hid Cover Bay. The hedgerows on either side were breaking into new leaf. As she ran between level meadows, there were lambs frisking among the ewes. All around her, spring was rising. New life.

But not for Rachel. Only the chill of saturated clothing, a scrubbed slab in the mortuary, the pathologist's knife. Lucy shuddered. She wished she knew less than she did about post-mortems.

This wasn't helping. The feet that pounded the path were now expressing anger with herself. What sort of minister was she? Her group had been confronted with a death. She, more than anyone else at St Colman's, should be prepared to handle it; to say the words that would comfort others.

It was the week after Easter. Not just spring, but resurrection was in the air. She had to believe that Rachel was in the arms of mercy. It no longer mattered what was done to her body. That would be returned to them, outwardly at peace.

To whom? Her mother?

Lucy slowed her stride. She had given little thought to Karen Ince, other than to tell the police how to contact her. But, sooner or later, she would need to see Rachel's mother. She would have to find words of comfort.

She checked her watch. There had never been any chance that she would get to the rocky northern coast. She ought to turn back. Another supper, another story; trying to disguise her fury with Elspeth.

But the rush of energy, the pounding feet, had done their work. She felt calmer as she turned back to St Colman's House. She prayed for strength to get through the evening.

Lucy was coming out of the bathroom, towelling her hair, when there was a rap at the door.

"Who is it?" She grabbed a clean white shirt from the bed.

"Valerie."

Lucy quickly donned her shirt and trousers. "Come in," she called.

The grey-haired bookseller walked in and closed the door behind her. She stood stiffly in front of it.

"Hello," said Lucy. "It will need to be quick. Supper's in a few minutes."

"This won't take long." Valerie's face was grim. There was no sign of her usual sweet smile. "I know what you think about Elspeth. It was very wrong. But I need to have your word that this won't go any further. Elspeth…" She swallowed with difficulty. "Elspeth was not entirely honest with you. There *was* some business with a student. It was eight years ago. She got off with a reprimand. But I don't expect the Principal to be as lenient the second time around. Elspeth is brilliant, both as a scholar and a teacher. Some people find her abrasive, but her students adore her."

"All the more reason she needs a sense of responsibility towards them." Lucy tried to keep her voice level, not to snap.

"I know. I couldn't agree more. But you must see that if this became public, it could be the end for her. A vulnerable girl like Rachel, and then a suicide. I want you to promise that this will go no further. Elspeth would have difficulty in admitting it to anyone, but she's really contrite. It won't happen again."

Lucy straightened up. "That's not my decision to make. Or yours. I know you're trying to be a good friend to her, to protect her, but Rachel's death is under investigation. The police have to know the truth."

"They know it's suicide. That's all they need."

Lucy's mouth opened. But she caught back what she had been about to say. Instead she protested, "Valerie, I was in the police myself. I can't hold back relevant information."

The older woman took a step towards her. She was taller than Lucy. Still no hint of a smile softened her face. Her voice was harsher than Lucy had heard it yet.

"Reverend Pargeter, I need to make myself clear. If you were to say anything to anyone else about Saturday evening, I should regard that as a serious matter. I want your promise that it won't happen." Valerie's grey eyes looked at her steadily.

Lucy stared back with incredulity. "Are you threatening me?"

The eyes were steely. Still there was no answer. Then Valerie turned on her heel. The door closed behind her.

Lucy sat down on the bed. She felt shaken to the core. *Valerie?*

Aidan came down the stairs after a quick trip to the bathroom after supper. He paused on the landing. There were voices in the hall below. When he looked over the banister, he saw the fair head of Lucy and the dark bush of a man he did not immediately recognize. Then he heard a low cry, "Lucy! My poor lamb!" the voice struck a memory. Brother Simon was back. He sensed an intimacy about the pair. But he could not stay in the shadows, overhearing them. He came down the stairs.

Two heads turned swiftly towards him. Lucy's was tense, watchful. Her ready, open smile had gone. Brother Simon's gaze was more considering. He looked Aidan up and down, as if assessing where he stood in this tangle of events. Almost as if he was wondering whether Aidan was friend or foe.

"What have you got for us this evening?" Aidan asked Lucy as he joined them. He needed to break the inexplicable air of tension. "Is it time for Wilfrid and the Synod of Whitby? Or is Simon taking over again tonight?" He gave what he hoped was a casual smile to the priest.

"Neither," said Lucy. The smile was back, though he sensed it was forced. "You're stuck with me again, I'm afraid. And I don't think we can get to Whitby before I tell you about Hild."

"True," Aidan agreed. "I'd forgotten about Hild. Melangell will like her."

Lucy moved towards the door of the lounge. A low chatter told Aidan that most people were already there.

He was startled when Simon took Lucy in a bear hug. "Be careful," he said, and let her go.

Aidan followed Lucy into the room with that warning sounding in his head. What could Simon have meant? Rachel was dead. James had survived a nasty accident. Those had been shocks, one of them terrible, but they were over. The police had been and gone. All that was left for the rest of them was to pick up the threads and carry on.

Eight faces turned towards them. Melangell had saved him a place on her sofa, with Peter on her other side. The big student looked sunk in sorrow. Elspeth Haccombe sat hunched in an armchair, frowning. She looked more defensive than her usual confrontational self. Valerie gave Aidan a polite smile, more stiffly than usual. When Aidan looked at James, he had a sense that the young pastor was flaunting the conspicuous plaster that had replaced a sizeable area of his golden hair. Sue sat nervously beside him. She glanced at him anxiously from time to time, as if seeking his approval. Only the Cavendishes sat placidly. Fran was knitting. The white baby clothes of yesterday had been replaced by blue.

Simon tiptoed, with exaggerated discretion, to a far corner of the room and settled his substantial body on an upright chair.

Lucy took centre stage. Aidan saw the lines of strain on her face. But her voice, when she lifted it, was steady.

"Tonight, I want to take you back to the time when St Aidan was still alive. To a woman who stood in the opposite camp to Wilfrid; a woman for whom the Synod of Whitby, when it came, was a crucial turning point.

"Hild was a Northumbrian princess. Do you remember how Aethelfrith the Ferocious killed the males of the Anglian royal family to seize the throne? All except Prince Edwin, who fled to Wales. His nephew was Hild's father. He too thought he had found shelter in the little Christian kingdom of Elmet, around Leeds. But Aethelfrith's long arm reached even there. Prince Hereric was poisoned. But the night he died, his wife dreamed she had found a precious jewel under her skirts, which lit all Britain with its splendour. That jewel was her daughter Hild.

"Hild spent her childhood in exile. Then Edwin returned, killed Aethelfrith the Ferocious and took back the crown. Hild, her mother and her elder sister hurried to the court at York to pledge their loyalty. When he converted to Christianity, she was baptized too.

"Then tragedy struck again. This time, the Mercian invaders killed King Edwin. The rest of the court fled to Kent, but Hild stayed on. With the choirmaster James and a handful of others, they kept the faith alive.

"It was a scary time for her when the new king, Oswald, drove out the Mercians and set up his fortress at Bamburgh. Oswald was the son of Aethelfrith the Ferocious. Hild was the great-niece of King Edwin, who had killed his father. What was going through her mind as she bent her knee in homage to Oswald and pledged her loyalty? Imagine how astonished and overjoyed she must have felt when Oswald opened his arms and welcomed her like a sister.

"She watched Aidan setting up his monastery on Lindisfarne. She made friends with him, and the two of them talked when the abbot visited Bamburgh. She saw him found a school for English boys here on Holy Island. How she wished she could have been one of them. Hild was filled with the desire for a life of monastic service and scholarship, but there was no place for women on Lindisfarne.

"She made her decision. If there were no nuns in Northumbria, she would travel south. Her widowed sister, once queen of East Anglia, was now a nun in Gaul. Hild would follow her there.

"She got no further than East Anglia, where her nephew was king. A messenger caught up with her. Aidan had learned of her plans and was calling her back to Northumbria. He had seen the need for monasteries for women. In Hild's absence, he had consecrated the first Northumbrian nun and given her an abbey at Hartlepool.

"Hild went back and took the veil from Aidan's hands.

"Her great chance came when King Oswy, Oswald's brother, was on the throne. But the Mercians were their merciless overlords. Oswy made a brave bid for freedom. He gathered his warriors to ambush the great Penda of Mercia on the banks of the River Aire near Leeds. In the end, it wasn't the Northumbrians who beat the unconquerable Mercian army; it was the Northumbrian weather."

"I can imagine that!" exclaimed Elspeth.

"The heavens opened in the Pennines and the water swept down the river in a flash flood. Far more Mercian warriors were swept away and drowned than fell to Northumbrian spears. Mercia was routed. Penda was dead. Northumbria was free at last."

"Hooray!" cried Melangell, and clapped her hand over her mouth. Lucy smiled.

"In gratitude, Oswy fulfilled the vows he had made before the battle if God gave him success. He granted land and money for twelve new abbeys. The greatest of these was at a fishing port on the Northumbrian coast, which the Vikings later named Whitby. He gave it to Hild for her abbey. It became a famous house for both women and men. Whitby was renowned for its scholarship. Several of Hild's students became bishops. Her scriptorium produced illuminated manuscripts of the holy books. Among her cowmen, she discovered the brilliant English poet Caedmon. Hild herself preached rousing sermons."

"St Paul says women should keep silent in church." James's discordant voice broke into the story.

To Aidan's surprise, Lucy greeted his intervention with a delighted grin. "Thank you, James. I'm glad to see you're back on form. That's the question, isn't it? What did Jesus think about women? When Martha complained that her sister Mary's place was back in the kitchen, didn't Jesus defend her right to sit at his feet with the male disciples, like a rabbinical student?"

Her smile grew wider, challenging him.

Aidan let the discussion rise and eddy around him. He nudged Melangell. "Remind me to tell you about Caedmon later. You'll like him."

"I *know*," Melangell exclaimed. "He was too shy to take the harp when they passed it round the hall and everybody had to sing. So he went out to the cowshed. And in the night, an angel came to him and taught him to sing a great song about creation. And next day he went to the monks and they took him to Hild and he made up lots and lots of poems about God and the world and everything."

Fran leaned over her knitting. "She's a bright one, your Melangell. We had a lot of fun together, didn't we, duck?"

Aidan felt Melangell edge away.

"I suppose so."

Elspeth was giving her own loud-voiced opinion about the place of women in ecclesiastical and academic life. Aidan looked around the room, meditating. He could not see Brother Simon behind him, but the priest's words to Lucy came back enigmatically. "*Be careful.*"

Aidan studied his companions, one by one. Who was it Simon had thought she needed to be warned against? James? He had an uneasy feeling that there might have been more to James's dealings with Rachel than the pastor wanted to admit. What might that have led to? Was it enough to make him a danger to Lucy now? And if James was not the threat, who else?

And what...? He felt a sudden catch in his throat. What form did Brother Simon fear that danger to her might take?

He looked back at Lucy, in the centre of the room. For the moment, she had put her grief behind her. Her cheeks were flushed with animation, her eyes bright with argument. She looked like a woman who was not going to back down from her position. But he was suddenly aware that beneath that healthy body and lively mind there was a vulnerable human being.

He turned round to Brother Simon, wondering if he could ask what he meant. But the priest had got to his feet. With a lifted hand of farewell, he slipped out of the room.

Chapter Twenty-four

LUCY CLOSED THE DOOR and drew the curtains. She sank down on the bed. She had survived this long, difficult day, but she felt extremely tired.

The room looked different. At last she had been able to tidy away Rachel's things. She would have to dispose of them later. She supposed she ought to hand them over to Rachel's mother – not that Karen Ince had ever been much of a mother to the girl. Or should she simply take them to a charity shop?

The whole room now had Lucy's neatness. She swallowed as she remembered how Rachel's untidiness had irked her. Now the room looked big and bare without the girl's scattered clothes.

There were footsteps on the path outside the curtained windows. They went past and stopped. James, in the room beyond hers. On the nearer side was Elspeth and Valerie's room, and, closest to the house, the Cavendishes'.

Lucy looked at the door. Then she walked across and locked it.

She was uneasy with herself. Was she being melodramatic? Valerie's visit had been meant as a warning. But of what? It was hard to imagine the well-dressed, scrupulously polite and upright woman descending to violence. But there was no denying the fact that Valerie was intensely loyal to her friend Elspeth. That if Elspeth's wayward brilliance needed protecting, then Valerie would do anything in her power to safeguard her.

Lucy's hand strayed towards the mobile in her trouser pocket. She had confided the unsettling incident to Simon and he had been alarmed for her. Rather sweetly protective, really. He had told her she must report it to the police.

She hesitated, with the phone in her lap. She had wanted DI Harland to do more, but she was uncertain what. Just this frightening conviction that Rachel's death was not being given the importance it deserved.

But what had that to do with Valerie? Perhaps, more realistically, what had that to do with Elspeth? Or… She twisted the duvet cover in her fingers. New images were crowding in on her. Elspeth had admitted giving cocaine to Rachel. What if Lucy's unguarded outburst had been right, and that had contributed to, even caused, Rachel's death? But the all-too-obvious explanation of a depressive's suicide was becoming increasingly unlikely. What if Valerie had feared the consequences of Elspeth's rash offer to Rachel? What if she suspected Rachel might tell the ex-policewoman Lucy?

She felt the chill in her arms.

Elspeth herself lived for the moment, regardless of the consequences. But not Valerie. Valerie was thoughtful, a different sort of intelligence. She had proved herself as protective as a she-bear of her cub. Was it inconceivable that Valerie might take a pre-emptive step and silence the evidence only Rachel could give? A death all too easily explained as suicide?

A few hours ago, it would have seemed preposterous. But Lucy still remembered the ice in the air when Valerie had stood in that doorway, giving her grim-faced warning. There was more to Valerie than Lucy had guessed, behind that usually sweet smile.

Should she phone DI Harland? She checked her watch. Ten o'clock. Too late tonight for so tenuous a theory. She guessed it would be hard to convince the detective inspector to take her seriously, anyway. She wasn't sure if she believed it herself. Tomorrow morning would be better.

She was about to put the phone on charge and get ready for bed, when an idea struck her. She scrolled through her contacts list. Had she copied this one over when she changed her phone? Yes.

She speed-dialled the number. From what she remembered, Ian was unlikely to be in bed yet.

"Lucy! A blast from the past!"

"Yes. Sorry. You're not in bed, are you?… No, I know that's none of my business… Yes, I'm fine. How are you?… No, actually, I'm not. 'I'm fine' is something you say automatically, isn't it? I'm ringing you because I'm a pretty long way from fine right now. I need to call in a favour."

Lucy detailed the events of the last three days. "Yes, I know… Thank you. It's all been a bit of a shock. My first time running something like this… Well, we've had the police over, as you can guess. DI Harland and DS Malham… Yes, poor Len Chappell. You heard about that, did you? Got marooned on Holy Island overnight… No, I didn't know him. If he's local, he must have joined after I left the force. Still wet behind the ears."

"Do you and Bill…?"

Lucy's hand tightened around the phone. "No!… Sorry, Ian. I didn't mean to bark at you. It was… Let's just say it wasn't a good experience. I'm sure he's a great policeman, of the old school. But, well, I'm glad to be at the other end of the country. Except for now… Look, about that favour. Rachel's body has gone for the PM. I really need to know the cause of death. Ninety-nine to one it was drowning. Only… Yes, you're right. Let's say there's an element of doubt. In my mind, anyway. Possibly in Malham's. I think DI Harland just wants to wrap it up and put it in the archives. Case solved… Will you? Oh, thanks. You're a star. Right, Ian. Give my love to the guys. Only … I'd rather you didn't mention to Bill that you've talked to me. Or that I'm here. Cheers."

She closed the phone. She knew from the tenseness of her knuckles that she had done something dangerous. Was it interfering in a police investigation that was none of her professional business? Was she building Valerie's warning out of all proportion? Or was it stirring old and painful, even threatening, memories?

Aidan drew back the curtains and his heart gave a leap of joy. Today was just such a morning as he had imagined on Lindisfarne. The early sun was illuminating little white clouds in a lively blue sky. Across the fields, he could just make out the curling foam on the running waves. There was a touch of gold in the light.

His feet touched the floor, almost before he thought of getting out of bed. His hands were hungry for his camera while there was still this crystalline quality in the air. He splashed cold water over his face and pulled on his clothes. Shorts and sweatshirt.

Then the truth struck home. He was astonished and appalled that he had not thought about it until now.

Rachel was dead. An unhappy girl driven to death, for who knew what reason. It was terrible that she should come here, of all places, and not find peace.

Could she really have met something worse, on these light-filled sands?

Lucy was the only person he had confessed his fears to. He still sensed that she disapproved of him, after that stupid outburst of temper the first evening. He could have dispelled that in an instant by telling her the real reason why he and Melangell were here without Jenny. She was a minister of religion, used to dealing with death. It should have been possible to tell her, more than most, that his wife had died. But it was still too raw, too painful. He could not cope with the sympathy of strangers.

He opened Melangell's door softly. She was asleep on her side, small pointed features outlined against the pillow. Tousled curls made a halo round her head. He closed the door. He would be back in good time to get her up for breakfast.

The air outside felt wonderfully fresh. It was a perfect spring morning.

He started to walk towards the shore. As his feet found a sandy footpath, echoes of yesterday were coming back to him. Lucy in the hallway below him. Brother Simon warning her, "Be careful."

He pushed the thought away and got out his Nikon. The sparkling beauty of the morning around him was maddeningly elusive. Quartz flashed in the sand. Crushed fragments of seashells, in a rainbow palette of colour. The bending grass. The swing of gulls. Ripples curling over the stones of the beach on an incoming tide. How could he capture the dance of delight in a single static image? A slow shutter speed that would give him the blurred flutter of wings? Or the sharp clarity of white pinions feathered against the blue?

He focused on the beach towards Hobthrush Island.

Into the frame of his viewfinder a figure came jogging.

At once, Aidan let the camera fall to his chest. His face warmed with embarrassment. Had she seen him? Two days in a row. He had deliberately taken a different direction this morning. Yet so, apparently, had she. Would she think he had come down to this beach on purpose to photograph her morning run?

He remembered now that earlier meeting. Lucy had not just been jogging for exercise. She had confessed, almost shamefacedly, that this was the way she found it best to pray.

He tried to imagine it. The interaction of the balls of her feet with the earth beneath her. The lungfuls of God's good air. The energy that multiplied itself through physical exertion. The sense of exhilaration.

His mind flew back to Brother Simon's warning.

What could Lucy Pargeter have to fear here on Lindisfarne?

What did it have to do with Rachel?

He saw her check. She had spotted him. She must be resenting him for interrupting this precious private interlude before the day began and she had to assume the responsibilities of leader.

She came on, running steadily towards him. Navy blue tracksuit, white shirt.

"Hello," she panted. She leaned over, her hands on her thighs, while she caught her breath.

"Good morning." He gestured awkwardly at his camera. "I wasn't out here to snap you, honestly. I just thought this morning was too perfect to miss."

"I know. It should be paradise, shouldn't it?"

He hesitated. "Is it over? The police investigation, I mean. If the inspector's decided it's suicide, they won't be back, will they?"

"There's the post-mortem. We don't know the result yet."

"Could it be anything other than drowning?"

Lucy's clear blue eyes met his unflinchingly. "Let's wait and see."

Aidan stared back at her. This was his doing. He was the one who had told her about the coastguard's doubts. He could feel himself colouring, imagining how that must look against his ginger hair and beard. He took a step closer. "Yesterday, I was coming down the stairs. I didn't mean to listen in, but you were talking to Brother Simon. He told you to be careful."

She looked away. "Ah. You heard that, did you?"

"What did he mean?"

She turned her gaze back to him. She seemed to be considering whether it would be wise to confide in him. What was he to her, anyway? Just one of the people who had signed up for her history holiday. Someone she had known at a fairly superficial level for three days. Someone who had rebuffed her attempt at sympathy.

"I don't think I can discuss it. Not till I've told the police."

Alarm bells were ringing in Aidan's mind now. Told the police? So something *had* happened. Something that had given Simon reason to fear for her. Thoughts went tumbling through Aidan's mind. It had to do with Rachel's death; with the growing suspicion they shared that it might not be suicide. And if it was not... Someone here on the island was implicated, and Lucy knew who it was.

He felt the rush of fear for her that Simon must have felt.

"Tell me," he ordered. "Give me a name. If there's a possibility you may be in danger, someone else should be looking out for you."

Surprise at the vehemence of his demand widened her eyes.

"I can handle it. There may be nothing in it. Just something strange that happened, that's all. It wouldn't be fair to blacken someone's name if it turns out not to mean what I think it might."

You told Simon, he thought.

Simon's an old friend. You're not.

She started to move back towards the house, walking swiftly now. He fell into step beside her.

"I understand about confidentiality. But there's a word neither of us is saying, isn't there? If it's not suicide, and not an accident. Shall I spell it out to you? The only option we're left with is... murder."

The word fell between them, like a stone dropped from a great height.

"I've been trying not to say that to myself," she told him quietly.

"And does this person whose name you won't tell me know which way your thoughts are going? Is that why Simon thinks you're in danger?"

"You ask a lot of questions, don't you? As it happens, yes. I was given a warning to keep quiet."

Now Aidan felt the blood that had warmed his cheeks not long ago drain out of them.

"And you still won't tell me!"

She looked at him sideways, uncertain. "I don't think I can. Until I've told the police."

"Which this person presumably won't want you to do."

"I was given strict orders not to."

He saw the determined tilt of her chin.

"But you will?"

"What choice do I have? Even if I hadn't once been a police officer. I owe it to Rachel."

They were nearing the road in front of the house.

"Let me make one guess. You can tell me if I'm wrong."

"I don't think that it's for you to make the rules."

"James?"

He saw the start she gave. The flash of alarm in her eyes. Had he guessed right? Or was it surprise?

She pressed her lips tight. "I told you. I'm not saying. I've probably told you too much already."

She loped ahead of him, through the gates of St Colman's.

Chapter Twenty-five

LUCY PUT DOWN THE PHONE with a feeling of dissatisfaction. She had thought it would be easier to talk to the female detective sergeant. But DS Malham had listened non-committally to her tale of Elspeth's offering Rachel cocaine, of Lucy's scary visit from Valerie. She had asked a few basic questions, but she had not followed up this new revelation with the eagerness Lucy had anticipated. She had not even – and Lucy was aware of her own indignation – shown much concern for Lucy's safety. Did she not take her seriously? She had said, as she was bound to, that she would pass the information on to DI Harland.

It was professionalism, of course. DS Malham would feel obliged to hold her cards close to her chest. She wouldn't reveal operational confidences to a member of the public.

That's all Lucy was now. The Reverend Lucy Pargeter. No longer a police officer. Did Malham know she had been? If so, did she guess why Lucy had left the force?

Her words had vanished into thin air with no visible effect. Too late, she realized she could have asked Malham about the results of Rachel's post-mortem.

No, she sighed, *she wouldn't have told me.*

She stood up from the bed where she had been sitting and started to gather her things for the day. She hoisted the small knapsack onto her shoulder. Time to go out and meet her group at the front of the house.

The brightness of the April morning still held. Daffodils flaunted their trumpets in gardens along the road. Some of the group gathered by the front door were turning their faces up to the sun.

Not Peter. Her heart twisted as she saw him hunch his shoulders, still weighed down with grief. She ought to talk to him. To make a space where he could tell her how he was feeling.

She ran her eyes quickly over the group. Melangell, bless her, as eager as ever. Her bearded father. There had still been that prickly wariness this morning on the beach. Yet he had seemed chivalrously alarmed for her. Could she trust that?

Valerie and Elspeth. Her guts churned, remembering that visit last evening.

Sue and James. She sighed. Aidan might have guessed wrongly about James being the one who had threatened her, but that didn't mean the rival pastor was going to give her an easy ride.

Somebody still missing. The Cavendishes.

Lucy greeted them as brightly as she could. She jogged on the spot to get her adrenalin going. She would need the energy to put into her storytelling and hold the attention of her group in the face of everything else that had happened.

Her phone rang. She glanced down at the screen.

"Sorry, folks. I need to take this."

She loped away across the car park until her own VW partly hid her from view.

"Ian! That was quick."

"Yeah, well. The station's not been the same without you. The PM's in, and you're right. The pathologist reckons she didn't drown. She was dead before she went into the water. Asphyxia."

"Oh!" Lucy let out a long sigh. It was what an uneasy part of her had feared all along. But it was still like a blow to the stomach to have it confirmed. She could hardly begin to imagine the implications.

"You still there?"

"Yes. Sorry. Look, I'm really grateful to you, Ian. I don't think it's likely I'll be able to do anything in return, under the circumstances. But if ever…"

"Forget it. I owe you from the past. But don't, for God's sake, let Harland know you've heard this. Never mind who from."

"Of course not. Thanks a million."

"Oh, and there was something else you might want to know. Drugs in her system. Cocaine. Recent."

"Yes. I rather expected that."

"Take care of yourself. Just like you to leave the force and still land yourself with a murder enquiry."

There, that word. Not from her own teeming imagination this time, but from a serving police officer.

"I don't think I'll be putting the flags out. I've been trying not to believe that. She was a friend."

"Sorry! Me putting my big foot in it again. Are you OK?"

"Not really. But I'll cope. Not much point in being a minister of the Church if I can't handle death, is there?"

She closed the phone and looked across the top of the car at the assortment of people gathered waiting for her. While she had been talking, the Cavendishes had joined the group. She drew a deep breath. Did she have to face the thought that there might be a murderer somewhere among them?

She focused on the tall, dignified figure of Valerie Grayson. The neatly waved greying hair, the violet anorak, the steady eyes. Valerie had seemed the wise and serene member of the group. A loyal support. Until last night.

The house was old compared with most buildings on the island. Warm, red stone, the same colour as the stones of the priory Aidan had photographed. In close-up now, he focused on the pleasing irregularity of the masonry.

As Lucy led them to the door, he read the signboard on the wall: FELLOWSHIP OF ST EBBA AND ST OSWALD. So this was where Brother Simon led his semi-monastic life?

The door opened. Aidan expected to see Simon's burly, black-haired figure. Instead it was a spare-boned woman in a long calico apron, over a plain grey dress. Thin hair was scraped back behind her ears, but the radiant smile she gave outshone this initial severity.

"Lucy! Come in." She kissed her.

Again Aidan had that unsettling feeling that Lucy was not the stranger here that the rest of them were. Aidan's own brief visits to Lindisfarne had not engendered this closeness of friendship. He suspected that Lucy must have spent some time in this community. So why was this not just an interesting fact to add to his knowledge of her? Why did it make him feel shut out?

The tallest of them had to stoop their heads under the low beams. The woman in grey, Sister Agnes, led them down steps into a comfortable, if small, sitting room. The walls were lined with bookshelves. Aidan did not have to study them long to realize they were crammed with books about Celtic and Anglo-Saxon history, and especially of their churches. There were other books of local interest: flowers, birds, the geology of this shifting coastline. More books, particularly the lavishly illustrated ones, were spread out on tables for visitors to enjoy. He spotted a facsimile edition of the Lindisfarne Gospels, with their angular interlace and mythical creatures forming the decorated capitals and surrounding the magnificent title pages. And – it came as an almost physical shock – the whole collection of Jenny's books on the Celtic saints. He always thought of them as hers, even though it was his own photographs staring him in the face. It was Jenny's inspiration his camera had served.

Sister Agnes had turned back to Lucy. "My poor lamb. Simon told us all about it. What a tragedy for you! That poor girl." She swung her deep blue eyes round the rest of the group crowding into the small room. "It can't have been pleasant for you too, coming here for a holiday and expecting to go home rested and uplifted. But be assured. Rachel is at peace now, in the arms of mercy. It's us poor sinners who have to struggle on with the weight of bereavement and guilt."

Guilt. The word brought Aidan up short. It was an odd expression to use.

Agnes's radiant smile dwelt on each of them in turn. "But that peace which now embraces Rachel is available to you all."

Was it? Aidan's mind shot back to his encounter with Lucy on the beach this morning. Someone in this group had threatened Lucy. Surely that could only mean they knew something they ought not to about Rachel's drowning. If she *had* drowned.

He half-turned to find James behind him. The younger man was disconcertingly taller than Aidan at close quarters. And undeniably more handsome, he thought wryly. The shaved hair and plaster did nothing to minimize that. He thought again about Rachel's bright eyes the first time he had met her, on Saturday afternoon. There had been something almost flirtatious about her then. A total contrast from the fearful face, withdrawn behind her curtain of lank hair, that she had shown the next time he saw her, as she crept unwillingly into the introductory meeting. It had almost certainly been Rachel in her red jacket he had seen on the beach through his zoom lens as he and Melangell crossed the sands. Had it been James with her? And what had happened to turn those bright eyes into fear?

He found himself pulling Melangell away from James.

"Sit down, everyone," Lucy was saying. "There are just about enough seats for us."

He squeezed into a small battered sofa beside Peter. Melangell curled up at his feet.

He watched James cross the room, heading for another sofa. The Cavendishes got there first. James checked, with a look of outraged entitlement, and found the only other one occupied by Elspeth and Valerie. Elspeth's ample figure overflowed it. With an air of affront, James took the only other option. An upright chair behind the Cavendishes' sofa. Sue had slipped into an armchair just inside the door. She jumped up now, with a look of guilt.

"James! Sit here."

He waved her away with a martyred air. James, visibly wounded, only out of hospital yesterday. Was he really the victim? Or something worse?

Aidan watched Sue subside onto the armchair. She perched on the edge of it now, as if she did not deserve to be there. He could see by the way she was looking at James that she felt it was wrong to sit in comfort while her pastor did not.

A new thought crawled slowly through Aidan's mind. Sue was utterly devoted to James. Whatever he said was law to her. If James had some reason to get rid of Rachel, Sue was more than capable of doing it for him. Aidan had not the slightest doubt that she would risk life imprisonment for him.

Did that mean…? His eyes shot back to Lucy. She was the only one of the group still standing. She looked young today, in a pink clerical shirt showing a glimpse of a dog collar beneath the navy-blue tracksuit. An oddly heart-twisting blend. The authority of ministerial office with a youthful female vulnerability. Could it have been Sue, not James, who had threatened Lucy, and made Brother Simon fear for her safety?

Whoever it was, as long as they stayed on this island, Lucy could not help but be in close daily proximity to someone who knew more about Rachel's death than they should, and who saw Lucy as a threat.

Chapter Twenty-six

LUCY LOOKED OUTWARDLY UNCONCERNED. She had clearly decided to pick up the threads and carry on the week as she had planned. She raised her clear voice and the room settled. Sister Agnes gave her a reassuring smile and slipped out of the room.

"I've brought you here because it's one of the best places on the island to see the wealth of Celtic tradition on which Aidan's abbey was founded. Well, maybe the Priory Museum or the Lindisfarne Centre would have been better still, but they're not the places to tell you the story of the Synod of Whitby, with visitors coming and going all around us. But I'll take you on to the Centre after this. If you haven't seen it already, you're in for a treat.

"Look around you. You'll see evidence of the artefacts. The gorgeous manuscripts, the carved stone crosses, the island sanctuaries that became beacons of learning. All that came to us from Ireland, via St Columba's Iona on the west coast of Scotland. St Aidan was Irish, sent here from Iona. King Oswald and his sister Ebba, for whom this fellowship here is named, were English, but they grew up schooled on Iona, in Oswald's case, and the nearby Island of Women, for Ebba. The Celtic tradition was the wellspring of their Christianity.

"The Venerable Bede tells us that their difference from the Roman Church was about the date of Easter and the style of tonsure with which monks shaved their heads. But believe me, it was more than that. The Celtic Church was not a monolithic structure, ruled top-down from Rome. Each abbey was autonomous, adopting its own Rule after comparison with others. And the abbeys mattered. They were seats of learning and mission. Spiritual power in Celtic lands did not lie in the court of Christian kings. Lindisfarne's abbey is where it is, because it was separated from the palace at Bamburgh. Near enough for King Oswald and Aidan to talk whenever they needed to, but far enough for Aidan to keep his independence and speak truth to kings.

"These abbeys could be headed by women as well as men. Hild, as I told you, had a great company of men and women at Whitby. Monks and nuns alike became scholars and teachers.

"Then back came Wilfrid from Rome, fired with visions of the Roman Church's material wealth and glory, its claim to universal authority. His ambition was to bring Northumbria within that empire.

"He found an ally in King Oswy's son, Prince Alchfrith. Alchfrith ruled the southern part of Northumbria, roughly Yorkshire. He gave Wilfrid the abbey of Ripon. Wilfrid turned out the Celtic abbot and monks who refused to convert to Roman ways. Setting up his own brand of the Church in his father's Celtic Christian kingdom was just one act of Prince Alchfrith's bid for defiance against his father's power.

"King Oswy moved in. At all costs, he was determined to keep Northumbria one kingdom. He called the Synod of Whitby to decide the matter once and for all. Should Northumbria be Celtic or Roman? There's no doubt where his own heart lay. He had been brought up on Iona, like Oswald."

Lucy's eyes moved round the group. She was willing them to care about this outcome, more than thirteen hundred years later.

"It seemed luck was on his side. The Roman party chose as its leader Agilbert, a Frankish bishop. Bishops had foremost authority in the Roman Church, but Agilbert had been thrown out of Wessex because the king there couldn't stand his appalling English. Everything he said at the Synod would have to be translated.

"The Celtic party was led, as was only proper, by the abbot of Lindisfarne, St Colman."

"Is that the same as St Colman's House, where we're staying?" Frances asked.

"Yes, he's the one." Lucy beamed encouragement. It was not often Frances joined in their discussions. "Colman was another Irishman, but had served in Northumbria for many years. He was deeply versed in the tradition of St Columba and Iona. In the Celtic Church's favourite Gospel of St John, with its message of love.

"When Hild as host opened the Synod it must have looked like a foregone conclusion.

"Then the Romans sprang their trap. Since Bishop Agilbert struggled to speak English, Wilfrid would present their case. And Wilfrid was a passionate and clever orator. He ran rings round Colman. He baffled him with computations of the calendar that fixed the date of Easter. He derided Iona as a tiny island on the outermost edge of the world. He even poured scorn on the revered St Columba, whom the Celtic Christians held to be next to Christ. Poor old Colman was left shocked and speechless. Then Wilfrid played his trump card. Was it true, he asked Colman, that Jesus had entrusted to St Peter the keys of heaven? Honest scholar that he was, Colman could only say yes. Wilfrid appealed to the king."

Lucy's blue eyes held her audience.

"Remember, King Oswy of Northumbria had much on his conscience. There was that matter of the murder of a rival king that had caused St Aidan to fast to death outside his fortress. He saw himself as a sinner, approaching the gates of heaven and pleading with St Peter for admission. He made his choice. 'If St Peter holds the keys to heaven, then who am I to go against his Church?' The king ruled that henceforth the whole of Northumbria should go over to the authority of Rome.

"It was the death knell for women like Hild. No longer would spiritual leadership be in the hands of the abbeys. From now on, it would be the bishops who led the church. And bishops could only be male. Abbesses continued to attend councils, but no longer with the authority they had had. In time, they were pushed back behind convent walls, no longer out in the world influencing kings and peasants alike, the way they had done. At the Synod of Whitby, uniformity and male hierarchy won."

"And so it should." James's self-righteous voice cut across the room.

Lucy's phone rang. "Sorry!" She started guiltily. "I meant to turn it off." She snapped the button without looking at the screen. "Right. Any questions?"

Aidan watched the smile of triumph with which James was gazing at her. As though he had her where he wanted her. How far was he prepared to take male power?

The discussion ended.

"Before we leave for the Lindisfarne Centre, folks, I want to give you time to look at the books and artefacts here. It's a far better collection than the few things I brought for you to see at St Colman's House." Lucy gestured at the displays around them.

Aidan saw her slip her mobile out of her pocket and switch it on.

There was a general movement, as people rose from their seats and moved forward. Aidan found himself less concerned with the exhibitions of the Celtic Church than with the faces and body language of the people crowding the room. He moved deliberately to stand between James and Lucy. He knew he was being foolish. Whoever was threatening her would surely not do anything in a room full of people. On Lucy's other side, Valerie was talking to her. The tall figure of the older woman stooped forward over the minister's smaller body. She was asking something about King Oswy's baby daughter, who had been given to Hild's abbey at Whitby in fulfilment of his vow.

Nothing to worry about there, he told himself. Valerie had always seemed to be on Lucy's side.

Aidan turned away, his eye caught by a display of photographs of Holy Island. His eyes widened in admiration. Whoever had taken these pictures had captured the subtleties of colour in the flats of mud and sand at low tide. There was another of an oystercatcher with pink legs leaving a track of wedge-shaped prints across the beach, like Babylonian cuneiform. A haze of sea pinks turned the salt marshes into a rosy mist.

He heard Melangell's clear voice rise above the subdued murmur of voices. "They've got Mummy's book about St Chad."

Lucy swung round. "Yes. He was one of the first English boys at St Aidan's school on Holy Island. He went south to Lichfield, when one of King Oswy's daughters married the Prince of Mercia.

Together, they brought Christianity to the Midlands."

Melangell was holding the little book with Aidan's photograph of Chad's hermitage beside the lake at Lichfield on the cover.

"This was the last book Mummy wrote before she died."

The room fell still. Appalled, Aidan realized that everyone was looking from Melangell to him. He wished himself anywhere but here, under the unbearable gaze of so much sympathy.

Lucy turned to face him. She was so close their arms were touching. He saw two spots of colour burn on her cheekbones. There was the shock of guilt in her blue eyes.

"Aidan!" It was almost a whisper. "I didn't realize. I'm so sorry! I thought from the way you spoke…"

"That we were separated," he muttered. His face felt stiff with an illogical anger. "I meant you to. I didn't want to talk about it."

He felt her eyes read his face. She was too close, but he couldn't move away. The ample figure of Sue was close behind him, hemming him in.

Lucy's phone rang again. For a second more, her gaze held his. Then she extricated herself from the crowd and moved away to the door. She was lifting the phone to her ear as she left the sitting room for the quieter hall.

He was left with the rest of them, the murmured awkward condolences he could not bear. He longed to flee the room, to find the quiet outside, an empty beach.

He had only taken a step towards the door when Lucy reappeared. One look at her told him that something had happened. She was tense, her face alive with something between agitation and elation.

Her voice rang out across the room. "Folks, I'm sorry. There's been a change of plan. I've just had a call from Detective Inspector Harland. He's back on the island, at the village school. He wants to see all of us right away."

A wave of astonishment and apprehension ran through the group.

Elspeth was the first to put a name to the alarm surfacing in all their minds. "So he's decided she didn't throw herself off a rock. He thinks Rachel was murdered. And one of us here did it."

Chapter Twenty-seven

OUTSIDE, THE STREET HAD BEEN TRANSFORMED. In contrast to the leisurely passage of holidaymakers in colourful clothing, black-clad figures in police uniforms were working their way from house to house. Lucy checked, a constriction in her throat suddenly making it hard to breathe. It had happened. The sad, but low-key, enquiry into Rachel's suicide had become a murder investigation. It was what she had wanted, wasn't it?

The tourists scarcely gave them a glance, but Lucy was conscious of the locals looking at them long and inquisitively. In such a small community everybody would know, of course. That girl at St Colman's. Murdered. Must have been one of them. Which one?

But was that true? Who else? It was almost impossible to think that one of the small island community might have done it. But what about the hundreds of visitors who crossed to the island daily? Might one of them, perhaps with psychopathic tendencies, have found Rachel alone and vulnerable? Lucy's brief years in the police force told her this was not typical, but it could happen.

She led the way towards the small village school. She was aware of her group following her. Her thoughts kept turning back to that more disturbing possibility. Somewhere among them might be one who knew more than he or she should. Could it really be Valerie, grimly determined to protect Elspeth's reputation at all costs? Or Elspeth herself, for whom Valerie would undoubtedly cover up?

She glanced round at Peter, walking almost level with her. His head was down, staring at the pavement. The downward lines of his face were heavy with grief. She tried a quick, if forced, smile.

"At least we know how it happened now."

"Does that make it any better?" he muttered.

They had walked about a hundred yards before Lucy remembered that she had been interrupted in the middle of an embarrassing encounter with Aidan Davison. Why on earth had it not occurred to her that a breakdown of his marriage was not the only possible reason for him to be here alone with Melangell? She felt her cheeks hot with shame. She was an ordained minister, with two years' training in pastoral care. Surely she should be able to offer words of comfort? But she had fouled it up. She sent up a quick prayer for the wisdom to put it right. For the gift of peace she had failed to offer him.

Aidan's pain was raw. Melangell seemed to have survived the loss astonishingly well.

She turned to see the child's sombre face following her. What was Melangell making of all this? Lucy threw a reassuring smile at her. The grey-blue eyes met hers with a disconcertingly level stare.

The low school building came in sight. It must still be the school holidays for it to be available for a temporary incident room.

The group were stopped by a policewoman at the door. She checked their names.

"Reverend Pargeter? He'll see you first."

Lucy stepped forward into the glazed reception area. She was led inside, into the schoolroom. Suddenly she was on her own, separated from the rest of her group. She felt their eyes follow her.

Screens had been arranged to divide the schoolroom into smaller units. Officers were at work on computers. A shudder of fear ran through her. Could Bill be here, in this very room? Would anyone else recognize her? It had only been four years. She thought the backs of two of those heads looked familiar. But they had their eyes on their screens. She walked quickly past.

She was led round a screen to find two men seated behind a table. Another chair was set in front of it. She had expected to find Detective Inspector Harland and his sergeant Anne Malham. But she did not recognize the tall man beside Harland.

He spoke for the tape recorder on the table. "This is Detective

Superintendent Maurice Barry. The Reverend Lucy Pargeter has just entered the room."

"Am I under caution?" she said, a little too sharply.

"Not at all, Miss Pargeter. Sorry, *Reverend*. Please have a seat."

She was angrily aware how young she must look, even though she was wearing a dog collar. People still had difficulty taking her seriously as a minister of religion.

"Now, Reverend Pargeter, if you would just take us through your movements on Sunday the fourth of April."

She looked indignantly at DI Harland. "I've already been through that. First with DC Chappell, then with DI Harland and Sergeant Malham. I signed a statement."

Barry steepled his fingers and looked at her steadily over them. He had a clean-cut face with a prominent jawbone. Younger than DI Harland. Keener. His voice was surprisingly gentle.

"Forgive me, Reverend. As I understand it, the preliminary investigation was into the movements of the deceased. You told us," he glanced down at his notes, though she had a feeling he did not need to, "that you last saw her alive a little after ten, while you were talking to your group in the priory ruins. You then became concerned about her absence and spent the afternoon looking for her around the coves in the Emmanuel Head area. With Mr Fathers."

"Peter. That's right."

"So, let's go back, shall we, to the time when you finished your talk to your group. That would be…?"

"By the time they'd finished asking questions, about ten-thirty. I left them free to explore the priory and the museum, and meet up again back at the house for Sunday lunch at one."

"And meanwhile you were where?"

The reality was sinking in. This was no longer just about Rachel. She must account for every minute of her own time until the finding of Rachel's body, late that afternoon. She was a suspect. In the eyes of the two men across the table, she could have murdered Rachel.

She felt the prickling of her skin that told her the blood was leaving her face. She was all too conscious of the fact that the two detectives would be noticing this, even if DSI Barry did not say it aloud for the tape recording.

"I walked along the beach, and around noon, when the water was low enough, I crossed over to Hobthrush Island. That's the little bit that sticks out into the channel west of the priory."

DI Harland consulted the map spread out before him. "It says St Cuthbert's Island here."

"That's the same."

"Were you alone?"

"Yes. I'd told the others about it. I thought some of them might have walked across to explore while the tide was down. But no one did."

DSI Barry leaned across to look at the map. "It's a very small island. How long did you stay there?"

"An hour." She wrestled with a reluctance to tell them. "I was praying."

Barry raised his eyebrows briefly. "I suppose it goes with the territory. And you didn't see Rachel then?"

"No."

She was aware that, from their point of view, she was entering more dangerous ground when she began to describe how she and Peter had headed for the rocky north-east coast in the afternoon.

"There are coves there. And little caves tucked away among the rocks. I thought she might be sheltering in one of them."

"And was she?"

"I didn't see her. And nor did Peter. We'd split up. He went out towards Snipe Point and was going to work along from there. I took a stretch further east. We arranged to meet up at quarter to four. I needed to get back to the group."

"Did you see anyone else on your travels?"

Just as importantly, she thought, *did anyone else see me?*

"No. Aidan said he saw Sue setting off in that direction from the castle. But it's quite a walk. And she doesn't look very athletic. If she ever reached the rocks, I didn't see her."

"So. Just you. Until you met up with Mr Fathers again."

"Yes."

Barry leaned forward. "You were a friend of the deceased. You lived in the same small town. You'd been trying to help her out of drug addiction and petty crime. You offered to pay for her to join you on this holiday and brought her here in your car. You shared a room with her."

"Yes." Why should such acts of kindness sound like an accusation?

"Had there been any quarrel between you since you arrived?"

"No… At least…" She was angry with herself that the question made her feel guilty. "On Sunday night, Rachel missed supper. When I took some food back for her, she wasn't in our room. When she did get back, I asked her where she'd been. She shouted back at me that I wasn't her mother."

There was waiting silence. Then DSI Barry asked, "And where *had* she been?"

"I don't know." Lucy hesitated. Then she knew that only honesty would do. "You should ask Elspeth Haccombe. It was she who told me that Rachel was back. And…" she took a deep breath, "Elspeth admitted to me that she'd given Rachel cocaine. Valerie Grayson, her room-mate, came to me yesterday and threatened me not to tell anyone. It might ruin Elspeth's career."

She watched the detective's eyes widen. Had DI Harland not told him? She had their full attention now.

"Thank you, Miss… Reverend," said DSI Barry with heavy emphasis. "That's most interesting. We'll have your statement typed up for you to sign later."

She rose to leave.

"Oh, just one thing. What were you wearing?"

Lucy thought hard. "It wasn't a great day for weather. There were some squally showers. I think I had on some dark blue trousers, a navy sweatshirt and an anorak the same colour. Oh, and a white shirt underneath."

"Nothing in white wool?"

"No." She looked at the detective superintendent questioningly. Why did it matter? Had someone seen a figure in white in that area? Was that where they thought Rachel had been killed?

But DI Harland had talked to the coastguards. He must know that the body couldn't have got from those rocks to the beach where Peter found it.

"Thank you." His lean face rearranged itself in a half-smile. "That's all, Reverend. You can go."

She walked out, aware of feeling like a different person. No longer the Reverend Lucy Pargeter, ordained minister of the Methodist Church, leader of this group, but a possible murder suspect.

The rest of the group sat waiting on chairs, crammed into the small reception area. Lucy met Valerie's eyes and felt her cheeks burn. Was she safer or in greater danger, now that she had told the police about that threat?

Chapter Twenty-eight

AIDAN CAME OUT OF THE INTERVIEW ROOM and was met by a look of glad relief in Melangell's freckled face.

"Your turn next, poppet."

He had not expected them to interview Melangell. Neither Chappell nor Harland had questioned her earlier about Rachel's movements. *Perhaps,* he thought, swallowing suddenly, *Detective Superintendent Barry needs her to corroborate what I've just told him.*

It was odd how the presence of the police could make you feel guilty, even when you had nothing to hide.

At least he was allowed to sit in on the interview.

In front of the two detectives, Melangell was composed. She had even, Aidan noted with a wry smile, a touch of self-importance in the tilt of her chin. She took them clearly through the details of how she and Aidan had spent Sunday after they left the priory. He was relieved to find that her memory matched his. The walk to the castle. Running to escape the rain. The tour of the rooms that ended on the battlements.

"And the wind was so strong it nearly blew me backwards."

She told of their looking over the wall and hearing the quarrel between Sue and James below. Then hurrying back to St Colman's ahead of the rainstorm. James arriving with a head wound.

"And there was lots and *lots* of blood. And then Daddy left me with Mrs Cavendish, when he went to look for Rachel."

The pout was back. She wriggled uncomfortably in her chair. She had clearly not forgiven him for that.

"Thank you, Melangell. That's all very clear. You're an observant girl." DSI Barry checked his notes. "That's it, I think." He raised his eyes to her, still smiling his thanks, a shade patronizingly. "One more thing. Do you have a white wool jumper? Or a scarf?"

"No," she answered, surprised.

"Do you know anyone here who has?"

She thought, then shook her head. "No."

They had asked the same question of Aidan. The forensic examination of Rachel's body must have turned up some trace of white wool. But nothing in Aidan's memory matched it.

"Thank you both. We won't keep you from your lunch any longer."

With a start, Aidan realized that the morning had gone. No time now to take Melangell through the displays of the Lindisfarne Centre.

Outside, in the glazed entrance area, the Cavendishes were still waiting their turn. David pointed to his watch. "It's a disgrace! We're supposed to be here on holiday, and they don't even let us get our lunch. I've had enough." He got up and headed for the door. "I'm going. It's a free country. They can't keep us here against our will. It's what we should have done the moment this unpleasantness came up. I'm heading back over that causeway. We'll find ourselves a B and B somewhere else."

Frances tugged at his sleeve. "Sit down, David. You're making a spectacle of yourself. You can't leave now. They'll think we had something to do with it if you run away."

She took out the inevitable knitting. The little blue jacket. David glowered at her and sat down.

Being the last in the queue was, Aidan supposed with a flash of sympathy, the penalty of being the most innocuous of Lucy's group. It was hard to imagine this unimaginative couple having anything remotely to do with a drug-taking, petty criminal teenager like Rachel.

Hang on, an inner voice told him. *Don't underestimate them. They used to run a children's home. They will have seen their share of troubled teenagers.* He looked at them with a new respect.

In the fresh air outside the school, a breeze was chasing the clouds away. Aidan caught sight of Lucy ahead, on her way back to

St Colman's for lunch. She rounded the corner by a hotel.

As Aidan and Melangell came in sight of her again, a woman stumbled from the hotel garden across Lucy's path.

"Sorry!" She lifted an almost empty beer glass and waved it in front of Lucy's face. "Don't I know you? Well, I'll be jiggered! It's Lucy Pargeter." The voice came high, the words slurred.

Lucy halted, her body suddenly rigid. "Karen!"

The woman was blonde, hair permed but now dishevelled. She wore tight-fitting white jeans and a striped blue-and-white jersey. Make-up, more vivid than most younger women wore nowadays, slashed her face. She must be middle-aged, but she was trying to defy the years.

Lucy glanced round to see Aidan and Melangell approaching. She turned to them. Her face behind the smile seemed wary.

"This is Karen Ince. Rachel's mother."

Aidan registered shock. Lucy had told him about Rachel's inadequate parenting, but it was hard to associate that dark, brooding girl with the inebriated blonde in front of him.

Lucy struggled with the everyday formalities for Karen. "Aidan and Melangell. They're part of my group. When did you get here? Why didn't you tell me you were coming? ... Oh, I'm sorry, Karen. I shouldn't be talking like this. I'm so terribly sorry about Rachel. I feel responsible. I brought her here... Do the police know you've come?"

"Not bleeding likely. Some horse-faced WPC came round to the house to tell me. Bleeding shame. Poor little kid." Tears welled in the woman's mascara-smeared eyes. She staggered. Lucy caught her and helped her to a wooden bench beside a picnic table in the garden.

"I think," she said quietly, nodding to Aidan, "someone ought to tell CID she's here."

"Will do." He set off back towards the school.

Behind him, he heard a man's voice. "Making a spectacle of herself again, is she?"

Aidan turned his head to see a man come out of the hotel to join Karen and Lucy. Smartly dressed in blazer and pale trousers, with a cricket sweater. His fairish hair was carefully arranged, as Karen's too must have been when she started the morning. A yellow cravat at his throat.

Rachel's mother's latest boyfriend?

Aidan was rounding the corner to deliver his message to DSI Barry and DI Harland when a loud shout arrested him.

"Where the hell do you think you're going?"

He turned sharply. The man in the blazer was stalking towards him.

"Lucy thought I ought to let the police team know Rachel's mother is here."

"So she's told me. And what police team would that be?" He was standing close over Aidan now, breathing heavily. "The girl's dead, isn't she? Probably suicide, that WPC told Karen. What the blazes are they doing still asking questions?"

The enormity of today's developments sank home to Aidan. "Didn't Lucy explain? I'm truly sorry, but it's become a murder investigation now. There are police all over the place, questioning those of us who knew her… slightly… and possible witnesses from the village." A move of his hand indicated the street ahead. Uniformed officers were still visible making their house-to-house enquiries.

He glanced back at the man in time to see what he sensed was not just shock but fear in his eyes.

"Murder! I hope you're not bleeding well suggesting Karen and I had anything to do with that! They asked us to arrange about the body, and she just wanted to come and see where it happened. Ghoulish, I told her. You can leave us out of this. We only arrived last night."

"I'm sorry. I really think I should do what Lucy asked me." Aidan started to move on.

"And I say you bleeding well won't!"

A fist shot out and caught Aidan on the side of the chin. He staggered, off balance, and crashed down beside the garden wall. As he fell, his head caught a projecting stone.

He lay on his side, stunned by pain. His eyes found two crisp packets and a ground-out cigarette butt on a level with his face. They seemed to assume an inexplicable importance as he stared at them.

The wider world swung back into focus. Above his head, he was aware of Melangell flying at his attacker. Her small fists were pummelling him.

"Don't you dare do that to my dad! I hate you!"

Aidan tried to lever himself up from the pavement, but sank back with a groan. Then Lucy was there before him, in three quick strides. She caught hold of Melangell and put restraining arms around her. He heard the authority in her voice. This was PC Pargeter, not the Reverend Lucy.

"Easy now. Stop right there!"

A small crowd was gathering. The man's eyes flickered round at them. Karen was hobbling towards them at an unsteady run. Her feet were falling sideways on inappropriately high heels.

"Gerald! Are you OK?"

With difficulty, Aidan hauled himself to his feet. "I'm the one you should be asking."

Lucy's voice dropped lower, but still held a steely edge. "Just what do you think you're doing? Who are you?"

"What's that to you? I don't have to give an account of myself to some do-gooding lady parson."

"You've just knocked down a man who did nothing to you… Aidan! You're bleeding."

Aidan lowered himself again to rest on the wall. He put up a hand to the side of his head and found it sticky with blood. He felt more sick than he wanted to admit.

"It's all right," he managed. "I'm not going to pass out on you like James."

He hoped it was true.

As Lucy's arms relaxed their hold, Melangell ran to him and hugged him tightly. "He's not allowed to do that. He shouldn't have, should he?"

"No, love. Definitely not."

Karen's hand was gripping Gerald's arm. She was looking up at him, her lipsticked face distraught.

"It's all right, Gerry. They can't say this has anything to do with you. You weren't here when it happened."

Lucy's level voice cut through hers. "You still haven't told me who you are, or why you found it necessary to attack Aidan just because he was going to tell the police that Rachel's mother is here."

"He's Gerald Morrison, if you must know." Karen was still clutching his arm possessively. "We go back a long way, him and me. He's Rachel's father."

She gave her partner an uncertain smile.

The world was spinning slowly around Aidan. He grabbed the edge of the wall for support.

Gerald Morrison spoke over Karen's dishevelled hair-do. "Let's just say I didn't come here to be questioned by the police. Nobody warned me this was a murder enquiry. I'm getting out."

Karen's eyes grew round. "Rachel? Murder? You never said! The police didn't tell us."

"I'm really sorry, Karen. I didn't have time. It's a new development. I was trying to break it to you gently, but Gerald jumped the gun."

"Oh, yes! So it's my fault now, is it? I'll have you know I'm a bereaved father."

Lucy threw him an unsympathetic glance. "I don't recall that you showed any concern for Rachel all the time I knew her. I'd be surprised if your behaviour just now was caused by grief."

"That's a lie!" Gerald was coming towards her now belligerently. Aidan wondered if he would have the strength to fight him off. "She was my kid. You're to blame for her death. You brought her up here. If you hadn't done that, she'd be alive today. She was my kid, and somebody's going to pay me for her death. I want compensation."

"Compensation! Rachel's dead, and all you can think about is money?" Lucy retorted. Yet at the same time she took a step back from the angry man. She was standing close to Aidan now. He heard her breath come fast. This wasn't like her.

Nevertheless, her voice steadied. "If anyone's talking about compensation, it should be Aidan. Look at him. He certainly didn't cut himself shaving."

He thought he saw the ghost of a smile in her blue eyes as she looked into his bloodied, bearded face.

Gerald Morrison glared at them both. "I'll get someone for this!"

Chapter Twenty-nine

AIDAN STEADIED HIMSELF AGAINST THE WALL. "I'll get the police," he said thickly. His jaw was throbbing. He had forgotten about it until now, because of the violent pain in his skull. He wondered if he could walk in a straight line. But there was no way he was going to be yet another burden on Lucy's leadership.

"I'll go," she said in concern. "Are you sure you'll be all right alone?" She cast a meaningful look at Gerald Morrison.

"I'll do it," Melangell cried. "I know what to say."

Before anyone could stop her, she set off at a long-legged run, back towards the school.

"Are you sure?" Lucy took a step after her. "Let me come too."

"Leave her. She's a bright kid. She'll get it right."

"She is rather special, isn't she?"

Karen had collapsed on to one of the picnic benches outside the hotel. Gerald gave a last scowl at Lucy and Aidan, then went to console her.

"Have you met him before?" Aidan murmured.

"No, never."

Almost immediately, Melangell reappeared with a woman police constable in tow. The officer stopped when she saw the blood on Aidan's head.

"Are you all right, sir?"

"No. But I'll do."

"Do you want to press charges? I take it that's the gentleman over there?"

Aidan shook his head, then wished he hadn't. "No. There are more important things right now. They're Rachel's parents."

The police officer strode briskly towards the pair.

"Let's get you back to the house," Lucy said. "I should probably drive you to the hospital. The causeway's open."

"I'll be OK."

As they moved away, he saw the officer cross the hotel lawn to Karen. A sharp shout from Gerald Morrison rang out.

"Now look here, young woman. I haven't come all this way to be treated like a criminal. Do you know who I am?"

The policewoman's reply was lost behind them.

"Who do you think he is?" Aidan asked. "Somebody important?"

"No idea. As I said, as far as I'm concerned, he never featured in Rachel's life till now."

"Do you think that's really what brought him up here? The fact that he might be able to sue somebody for her death?"

Lucy stopped dead on the road. "I've had a sudden terrible thought. All this time I've been telling myself that murder victims are usually killed by somebody they know. To read the tabloids, you'd think the greatest danger was from strangers, but it's really not true. Ever since we found it wasn't suicide, I've been puzzling my brain to think who on Holy Island could possibly want her dead, or had got her into a position which ended up with killing her accidentally. What if it wasn't one of our group? What if Gerald Morrison was already on Holy Island on Sunday? Is it possible *he* could have killed Rachel?"

"For the chance of compensation? It sounds a bit far-fetched. And why wait till she's in Northumbria? Wouldn't it have been easier to do it in Devon?"

Lucy persisted. "It's just the unlikelihood of it happening here that would be his best cover."

Aidan was relieved to find he was walking steadily now. They were almost at St Colman's House. He glanced down into Melangell's anxious face and managed an uncertain smile. But the face he turned to Lucy was more sombre.

"Could there be another reason? Something in his career that would make the discovery of an illegitimate daughter with a criminal record a blot on his prospects?"

"I would have thought it was hardly unusual enough for that to matter nowadays. And killing her wouldn't destroy the record. It would be more likely to draw attention to him. But I still think there's a darker reason for him to be here."

Aidan realized he would be glad to get indoors and sit down. But an insistent thought would not be silenced. "Are you sure you're not latching on to him because you don't want to think it's someone from our group?"

"That would be a relief. But look at the way he hit you. He's obviously got a violent streak if he's crossed. And it's almost a carbon copy of James's injury. James still can't remember what happened, or he says he can't. But don't you think it's too much of a coincidence? Two of you falling and sustaining head wounds? It looks very much to me like the same modus operandi. What if he found Rachel and James together? Knocked James out and... disposed of Rachel?"

Aidan turned his head cautiously as they crossed the guesthouse car park. Lucy was striding towards the door with renewed animation.

He called after her, "There's one name you haven't mentioned. One person besides yourself who's known Rachel a long time. Who's been sunk in depression ever since she died. Hasn't it occurred to you that if Rachel knew her killer, then the most likely person is Peter?"

"No!" Melangell cried out.

Lucy spun round to face him. "That's impossible! Peter cared about her. He would no more have killed her than I would."

If blue eyes could be said to blaze, hers did.

Aidan held up placating hands. "I'm only following your logic. That most murders are committed by someone the victim knows. And nobody here knew her better than Peter, except you. How do we know what went on between them?"

He had a sudden picture of the day of their arrival. Meeting Rachel running down the stairs, her eyes bright and provocative. She had been coming from the top floor where Peter had his room.

Lucy's face in front of him was very still now, as she thought about his words. Then she shook herself, slowly. "I can't believe it's Peter.

Especially now that I've seen how violent her father can be. Believe me, I've had experience of that kind of man." He saw her shudder.

"When you were in the police?"

There was something more to it than that.

She looked at him guardedly, as if wondering how much to say. Then she turned away. She spoke so quietly he hardly heard her.

"Yes and no. My partner was in the police force too. Don't get me wrong. He was a good officer in his way. But not a good human being. If I did the slightest thing wrong, he hit me."

Aidan held his breath, waiting for her to go on.

"If I'd stayed in that relationship, I think he might have killed me."

Lucy stood in the hall, still shivering with remembered shock, while Melangell bounded upstairs to get ready for lunch and Aidan followed more slowly. What on earth had possessed her to share that most painful secret of her past with this foxy-bearded man she had only known for three days?

All the same, she had been very glad to have him with her when she met the violent anger of Rachel's father. She winced. Aidan had come out of that encounter with a bruised jaw and a bloody head. At least he was not playing the martyr, like James.

Should she really take him to the hospital, in spite of his protests?

But the thought came crowding back of the appalling suggestion he had made.

Not Peter.

She sat at the lunch table, struggling for once to find conversation with her guests. She was alarmingly conscious that Valerie was glaring at her malevolently. Did she know, or guess, that Lucy had told the police about that threatening visit and Elspeth's luring Rachel to take cocaine?

"Pass the mayonnaise," Elspeth barked.

Lucy jumped. It was ridiculous to react as if the most normal request was filled with menace.

Across the table, she caught Aidan's eye. He gave her a small smile, and she immediately felt better.

But she hadn't told him everything. Aidan had heard Simon warning her to take care, but she had refused to tell him where that threat had come from.

Her eyes fell on Peter at the foot of the table. Aidan was right about one thing. Peter's large form was slumped in his chair, a picture of depression. A pang of guilt seized her. Had she done enough to try and comfort him? He had taken Rachel's death hard.

A treacherous worm of thought was boring its way in. She hadn't picked up the impression that relations between Peter and Rachel had gone that far. She had never thought of Peter as being in love with the troubled teenager. Just a loyal friend, doing all he could to help Rachel out of the mess she had made of her life.

So why this depth of grief? Could Aidan possibly be right? Was it not only grief but guilt?

She watched his dark, shaggy head bent over the table. He was hardly eating.

Lucy looked around the remainder of her group. Would they stay, now that the island was overrun with police? James and Sue looked mutinous. They had never really wanted to be part of her course. James had made his anger at Sue's mistake abundantly clear. She could hardly blame them if they cut their stay short.

But the people she most expected to leave were the Cavendishes. She sat up with a start. There were still two empty places. Where were they? Then she relaxed a little. They must be the last ones being questioned at the village school. That was hardly going to improve David's temper when they returned late for lunch.

Almost as she thought this, he came storming in. Frances followed him more apologetically.

"I'm lodging a complaint! A law-abiding citizen's got a right to go about his business and enjoy a holiday, without being marched before the police every day. Three times they've questioned us. Three times!"

He slammed his fist on the table as he sat down. "I'm not standing for it! If they try to question me tomorrow, they'll have another think coming. I'm off."

"Now then, dear," Frances tried to soothe him. "They were only doing their job. The poor girl's been murdered, by the sound of it. They have to ask these questions. But it's not very pleasant, is it?" She turned to Lucy, appealing. "I mean, it's not what you expect when you come to a holy sort of place like this."

"No," Lucy told her. "It's not what any of us expected."

Calculations were chasing through her mind. Ought she to refund some of their money if they left now? Where would that leave her budget for the course? Could she carry the drain on her own income?

How could she be thinking about money at a time like this?

She laid down her knife and fork. "I'm sorry about all this. You've still got some free time this afternoon. You might like to visit the Lindisfarne Centre, since we didn't get there this morning. They have a good exhibition about the history of the island, and a video about the Vikings attacking Lindisfarne." She threw a smile in Melangell's direction.

"Just what we need," boomed Elspeth, with forced heartiness. "A set of Norse thugs bloodying their battleaxes on the necks of a load of religious fanatics. Murder and mayhem."

The table fell still. Nobody laughed.

Lucy found her voice. "I'll see you all again at St Mary's church at half-past three."

Back in her room, Lucy took out her phone.

"Ian? Sorry to trouble you at work. It's just that something's come up… Yes, to do with Rachel's murder. The place has been swarming with police this morning. I did wonder if I'd see your ugly face." She tried to keep her voice light.

"DSI Barry's heading up the enquiry now… Yes, of course you'd know. It's just that he's been asking everyone the same question. 'Were you, or did you see anyone else, wearing a white wool sweater or scarf?' They've got evidence, haven't they? Forensics from the post-mortem."

The voice at the other end hardened. No longer the easy banter between friends. "Look, Lucy. I did you a favour. I told you the cause of death. I stepped way over the mark for you. You're under investigation in a murder case. You know that, don't you? Your whole group is. I'm sorry, Lucy, but that includes you. I can't give you critical evidence."

She felt, not just her face but her whole body, flame. "I'm sorry, Ian! I should have thought… No, I quite understand. I should never have asked you."

She was about to snap the call off when a dreadful thought struck her.

"Ian! If this is all over the station, do they know names? Does Bill know I'm here?"

There was silence at the other end of the phone. Then a short laugh. "Don't blame me, but you're never going to believe this. The local press has got hold of the story. Well, they would, wouldn't they? It's not the sort of thing which happens on Holy Island. And what with you being a vicar. There's a photo of you in today's online edition. Some joker's done a print and stuck it up on the wall here, along with the 'wanted' mug shots."

"So… Bill…?"

"Sorry, love. There was no way to keep you out of this."

Lucy sat back, the phone idle in her hand. She felt cold fear stalk through her.

Chapter Thirty

LUCY WAS NOT SURE HOW MUCH time had passed when she found herself sitting on the bed, still stunned. She was astonished at how scared Ian's news had made her feel. The knowledge that her ex knew she was back on his patch woke old terrors. When she had realized she must break free from him for her own safety, she had fled first to Lindisfarne, to the Community of St Ebba and St Oswald, to sort herself out. Then she had taken herself as far away as possible and made a new life for herself. There was no police force on Holy Island. She had thought she could slip back here from time to time, incognito.

But now her photograph was on the noticeboard at Berwick police station. There was no way Bill wouldn't see it. And Bill was the sort of man who thought his partner was his personal possession, to do with as he liked. He would not have forgiven her, even after four years. Leaving him had been defiance of his authority, theft of his property. He would surely come after her, now he knew she was so close.

He might even… she thought of the streets of Holy Island thick with uniformed police officers going house to house… be on the island now.

She felt very naked and alone.

Still, she couldn't sit here all afternoon. She needed to be up and doing something. But did she dare show her face on the street, when she might come face to face with Bill around any corner?

Through the open window, she heard Elspeth's loud voice next door. So she and Valerie were still in their room. Did that mean that any time Valerie might come to her door, demanding in that steely voice to know what Lucy had told the police? With a sinking heart, she knew the detective superintendent must have questioned Elspeth about giving a Class A drug to Rachel. It could have had a bearing on Rachel's death. Valerie was not going to forgive Lucy for that.

And on the other side, James. Was he also in his room? James, whose movements that Sunday afternoon were still a mystery.

She needed to get out.

She was on her feet, still uncertain where to go. She felt an urge to get away, but nowhere felt safe any more.

The Community of St Ebba and St Oswald?

She ran a comb through her hair, picked up her fleece and stepped outside.

The brilliant morning had clouded over. The air was grey.

Just for a moment, as she was crossing the hall, she wondered what the red-haired Aidan and his bright-eyed daughter were doing this afternoon. With a start of surprise, she realized she would feel happier in their company.

But Aidan Davison had suffered enough this week from all that had happened. She could not burden him with her new fears.

All the same… her eyes went up the stairs. Peter's room was on the top floor. She could not go around much longer, weighed down with the thought Aidan had forced upon her. If Peter had anything on his conscience, it was her job as his minister to give him the chance to unburden himself.

She straightened her shoulders and started up the stairs.

She tapped at Peter's door. There was a murmur from within, too low for her to distinguish the words. She opened the door a little and looked in.

Peter was sitting on his bed with his back to her. His shoulders were hunched. Beyond him, the window gave a view of fields, and past the castle, the grey North Sea. He did not turn his head.

"Peter? Are you all right?"

He swung round with a sudden fierceness. His shaggy hair overshadowed his spectacled eyes. "Of course I'm not all right! What did you think?"

Lucy came further into the room and closed the door. The space seemed suddenly small for the two of them. She tried to keep her voice gentle, reassuring.

"I know it's terrible what's happened to Rachel. But she's at peace now. Not like whoever did it."

She waited, breath held.

"I'd like to kill them!"

"Peter! That doesn't help. You'll only destroy yourself."

Relief was flooding through her. She could believe him, couldn't she?

"Would you like me to pray with you?"

"I've tried that," he muttered, avoiding her eyes. "It doesn't help."

Doubts were creeping in again.

"There are times when grief gets such a hold of us, we can't. But other people can do it for us. A raft to hold us up."

Since he did not answer, she sat on the bed beside him and spoke the words for both of them.

One part of her mind went out in compassion to the bulky student close beside her. The other wondered what he might be keeping back.

Lucy closed the door softly behind her. She paused on the landing. There was no sound from Aidan and Melangell's rooms. They must have gone out for the afternoon.

She felt an unexpected disappointment.

It took courage to step out onto the open street. To her relief, the pavements were almost empty. There were no police in sight. They must have moved on to the other end of the village and the outlying farms. The population of Lindisfarne was under two hundred, plus visitors. It should not take them long.

She would keep away from the school, where the detectives had set up their headquarters. Her feet took her down the lane to the church, almost without her conscious decision. She stepped inside and felt the peace of centuries enfold her.

At once she was drawn to the massive sculpture in the south aisle. Six craggy-faced monks bore on their shoulders the coffin of St Cuthbert. He had died a hermit on the nearby island of Inner Farne and been buried here on Lindisfarne. But the ravages of Viking raids had made the monks of later years dig up his remains and take them inland for greater safety. He lay at rest now in the great spiritual fortress of Durham Cathedral. But his much-loved memory remained on this holy island where he had served as prior and bishop.

Lucy sat down and gazed at the rugged elm wood, carved deeply by a chainsaw. She felt humbled by its powerful presence and strangely comforted.

It was too easy to think of Holy Island as a place of peace and sanctuary. It had known its share of death and violence. Rachel's was one more sacrifice to add to that litany.

The latch of the door clanged behind her. Lucy whipped round, suddenly reminded of her scarcely buried fears.

Brother Simon, with dark eyes smiling, was coming towards her.

Aidan groaned as he levered himself up on one elbow. His head still hurt. He would have been glad to spend the afternoon resting. But it was not fair to Melangell.

He leaned over the edge of the bed. She was stretched out on the bedroom rug in her favourite position, reading a book. She lay on her stomach, chin propped in cupped hands, heels kicked up behind her.

He could tell, from the alacrity with which she sprang round when she heard him stirring, that she was getting impatient.

He managed a grin for her and straightened up. "OK. You win. It would be a pity to waste the afternoon. I suppose you want to go and see the Vikings. Bloodthirsty little horror."

"Yes, please!"

The video in the Lindisfarne Centre exhibition was more suggestive than explicit. But he had been right that it would fire Melangell's imagination.

"Did they really do that here? Chop off their heads and steal their treasures?"

"Not just here, but all around the coasts of Britain and Ireland. The monks were sitting ducks. Communities of peaceful men and women, with churches full of gold and jewels. Lindisfarne suffered like all the others."

Why, a sudden insistent voice in his mind asked, had Rachel been killed? She would have had nothing worth robbing her for. No rich inheritance.

Sex, perhaps? But then he remembered her sodden body on the beach. Her clothing did not appear to have been violated.

He shook the thought away and led Melangell out onto the street.

"I haven't shown you the church yet, have I?"

"Yes, you did. That great big ruin, where Lucy said prayers on Sunday morning."

And Rachel slipped away, never to be seen alive again.

"Not that one. The parish church they still use today. It's right next to the priory."

He led her past the statue of St Aidan and opened the church door. The latch clattered. Two figures started as he stepped inside.

"Sorry," he said automatically though he had done nothing wrong.

Lucy was on her feet before the great carving of the six tall monks shouldering St Cuthbert's coffin down the south aisle. He saw alarm, even fear, in her face.

It was a second before he transferred his gaze to the figure close in front of her. Brother Simon, from the Fellowship of St Ebba and St Oswald. Aidan read a wary tension there that matched Lucy's.

He was unsettled by the way they were looking at him. As though he might be the object of their alarm.

Thoughts raced through his mind. The evident close friendship between these two. Simon warning Lucy to be careful, the day after Rachel's death.

He had raked his mind to think who, in that small group, might be a source of danger to Lucy. And why. Because that person had already killed Rachel?

Cold fingers stalked up his spine. Was it remotely possible that they could suspect *him*?

Lucy's face relaxed somewhat into a smile.

"Hello, Melangell. Have you come to see the monks? They're pretty impressive, aren't they?"

Melangell came forward, past Aidan. Her fingers stroked the roughly hewn wood. The gaunt faces of the cowled monks stared straight ahead.

"They're big," she said. "And... sort of like rocks, even though they're really wood."

"Yes. Really powerful. They won't give up until they've taken Cuthbert's body to a place of safety."

"Right, Lucy. I'll see you again." Simon spoke almost as if Aidan and Melangell were not there. Aidan thought he detected an emphasis in his voice, for a reason that was not clear. Then his tone lightened. "Are you sure you'll be all right?"

"Yes, I think so." Lucy's low answer was not as confident as Aidan would have liked. It had been a revelation to him this morning to hear how much Lucy still feared her ex-partner.

Bill! That was it. If he really did still work in the local police, then there was just a chance that he might be among the squad of uniformed officers making enquiries on the island.

Some of the shock began to fade from Aidan. It was not him she was afraid of. Was it?

But one way or another, fear stalked Lindisfarne now. Rachel's killer, probably still on the island. And now perhaps too the man Lucy had feared might kill her if she stayed with him.

He heard the church door close behind Simon.

Aidan was suddenly aware how vigilant he needed to be. This was more than an intellectual puzzle about who the murderer might be. He must make very sure that Rachel's was not the only death.

Chapter Thirty-one

L UCY LOOKED ROUND AT THE SMALL GROUP gathered in the
church with dismay. It was twenty to four. Aidan and Melangell
were there, Melangell's face as eager as ever. Elspeth had stridden
determinedly up the aisle, with Valerie in her wake.

Lucy fought to control a tremor of disquiet. Surely she should feel
glad they were still on board enough to keep attending her course? But
she sensed the undercurrent of resentment in the two women.

Peter had come last. Somehow he had prised himself out of his
depression and managed the short distance from the guesthouse to the
church. He sat now in a back pew, his shoulders still hunched. Peter,
whom she had relied upon as her stay and support. Now she knew that
he was wounded and needed her to support him.

Looking at his bowed head, she chided herself that she could ever
have allowed herself to be possessed by Aidan's doubts that Peter might
be responsible for Rachel's murder.

Murder. The word still shocked. How far had the police got with
today's enquiries? Most murders had a pretty obvious suspect. An angry
or desperate parent. A rejected partner.

She winced. That was too close. It was probably foolish to think
that Bill would be on Lindisfarne this very moment. That she might
meet him face to face for the first time since she fled their flat four
years ago. But her head, as well as her heart, told her it was possible.
The uniformed officers she had seen on the streets today would have
come from a fairly local area. Ian had confirmed that Bill was still at
the station where she and he had served together. And he knew she
was here.

She tore her eyes away from the closed church door and her thoughts back to the task in front of her. It should have been easy. St Cuthbert, probably the most loved of all the Northumbrian saints. Behind her, the wood-carved monks carried his coffin on their shoulders.

But there were too many fears snatching at her thoughts. She scanned the few in front of her. Aidan, in his shorts, regarding her attentively. Melangell waiting, as if for a treat. Elspeth, in her tweeds. Valerie, her face inscrutable.

The Cavendishes weren't coming. Lucy felt a heavy sense of inevitability. They had never been wholeheartedly committed to the subject of this holiday. The seventh century, which for Lucy was a source of delight, was too far back for David and Frances to grasp with their imagination. Rachel's death had hit them hard. But now the shadow of murder lay over the island. They must have done what they had threatened so many times, and left Lindisfarne.

Sue and James were missing too. Had James decided not to waste any more of his valuable time on a woman minister too obsessed with the past to get to grips with the present-day need for a mission to the north? She had always meant to bring the story up to date in the last session of the week.

It seemed impossible to believe that it was only Tuesday.

She must make this afternoon count for those who had stayed with her. She cleared her throat and began.

"Today, we're standing in front of a statue which celebrates what happened to Cuthbert after his death. But it's his life I want to show you. Cuthbert was a well-built lad, the son of a family with horses and servants. He did his military service. He was Christian enough to berate the locals who failed to pray when they saw the monks of Wearmouth being swept out to sea on their rafts.

"But his life changed one night when he was out on the hills with the sheep. He saw angels carrying a brilliant soul up a ladder to heaven. Next day, he heard that the beloved Father Aidan had died on Lindisfarne. He left the sheep, took his horse and spear, and set out for Melrose to become a monk."

For once, Lucy was struggling to remember what came next. Her eyes kept going to that closed door.

She took her hearers, as best she could, through Cuthbert's missionary rides to hill communities others were afraid to go near, to his appointment as guest-master at Ripon.

"One snowy day a young man appeared in the guesthouse. Cuthbert washed his feet and held them to his chest to thaw them. He asked the visitor to wait, while he went to the bakery for fresh bread. When he returned, he found only three new-baked loaves, smelling deliciously. There were no footprints in the snow outside."

"Superstitious piffle!" Elspeth snorted to Valerie, none to quietly.

"A story doesn't have to be literally true for it to have meaning," Lucy retorted, more sharply than she normally would.

She led them on, through Cuthbert's eviction by Wilfrid from Ripon, with the other Celtic monks. His patient work on Lindisfarne in the wake of the Synod of Whitby. The Irish monks had gone off, broken-hearted, to Ireland, and the English monks who remained bitterly resented the changes. Cuthbert would leave them quarrelling in the chapter house, and take long walks around the island, talking to farmers, returning only when they were ready to conform. But increasingly he was drawn to his hermitage on the distant island of Inner Farne.

"You forgot the otters," came an accusing voice.

Lucy blinked. Melangell's pointed face was staring up at her, demanding a favourite story. Suddenly it hit Lucy. The eight-year-old was like a younger child who wants the same bedtime story over and over again. And not a word must be out of place in the telling. She knew, piercingly, that Jenny Davison must have told these stories to her daughter, time after time. And now she never would again.

Lucy's eyes strayed to Aidan. He was sitting in the pew, looking down at his feet. Months had passed but the hurt was still raw. Could either she or Peter feel that deeply about Rachel?

"Why don't you tell us about them, Melangell?"

Delight shone in Melangell's face. She stood up and turned to face the others.

"Cuthbert was visiting another monastery. St Ebba was in charge. But the nuns and monks hadn't been behaving themselves and Cuthbert was upset. He went out onto the beach to pray. He used to do that standing up to his waist in the water, in the middle of the night. And when he paddled back to the shore, he was cold and wet. But the otters came frolicking along the beach. And they wrapped their furry bodies all round his feet and legs, and they dried him and warmed him up."

This time, Elspeth led the group in a round of applause.

"You should take my job," Lucy smiled.

Somehow she managed to get to the end. The hermit happy on his windswept island, with a wind-eye in his cell looking up to the sky. Growing crops in the crevices of the rock. Scolding the ravens who stole the corn from him. "The king himself had to row out to Inner Farne and drag him away to become bishop of Northumbria. But the bishop of Lindisfarne took pity on his unhappiness and changed places with him, so that he could stay.

"The old hermit fell sick on Inner Farne. At first he struggled on alone, eating only onions. At the end, he was nursed by monks in his cell. One night, a flame across the water told the monks of Lindisfarne St Cuthbert had died. They buried him in the abbey, perhaps right where we stand. They left him for years, for the flesh to fall from his bones. But when they dug him up to reinter the bones before the altar, they found the body miraculously undecayed. They dressed this humble man in Byzantine silk, with a precious cross on his breast and his episcopal ring on his finger. A gifted scribe penned the Lindisfarne Gospels in his honour. A labour of love."

She let the church fall silent. Let there be one happy story in the midst of this gloom. Time enough later for the Viking massacres and the restless journey of Cuthbert's coffin from place to place.

There were few questions. They were not in the mood.

Lucy stood up with a sense of unfinished business. "There'll be tea back at the guesthouse."

It took courage to step out into the open. It was only four o'clock. If Bill was really here, the meeting she dreaded was still possible. She welcomed the closeness of the little group around her.

They reached the corner of the road to St Colman's. There was the usual procession of visitors beginning to head back to the main car park.

But other vehicles were coming round the corner from the school. Police cars. A black van. Lucy stood back against the wall, hoping Aidan's lean figure would shield her. She lowered her head, so that any curious faces looking out would not see her face.

It was nerve-wracking moments before the last car passed.

Yet now her heart was lifting. Whatever information DSI Barry had hoped to get from the people on the island, he must have gathered it. The police were leaving. She watched the convoy of vehicles dwindling down the road. The causeway would still be open this evening, but the police would be across it long before it closed.

She took a deep breath. She had got away with it. If Bill had been drafted over here today, he had gone.

Chapter Thirty-two

A CLATTER OF RUNNING FOOTSTEPS startled Lucy. Someone clutched her arm from behind.

Still tense, Lucy turned swiftly.

Karen Ince's pinched face was staring up at her. Her eyes were scared.

"Lucy! Thank God I've found you. I had to tell you." Her eyes swept round the small group listening. Then she seemed to decide. "They're here. On the island. I thought there was something familiar about their faces. And then I heard that policewoman call their names."

"Who, Karen?"

An angry shout rang down the street. "Karen! You come back here at once!"

Fear twisted Karen's features. Lucy felt the grip of the woman's fingers fall away from her arm. Karen turned towards Gerald's commanding approach, then back to Lucy. There was a desperate look on her face.

"I've told you though, haven't I? I never trusted them. But nobody would believe me."

She was gone, half-running up the street on her high heels towards the man advancing upon her. He caught hold of her arm, twisted her round, then shouted back at Lucy.

"You leave her alone, do you hear me? If it wasn't for you, we'd never have got mixed up with the police."

He started to haul Rachel's mother away.

"Mr Morrison." Lucy strode after them. "If Karen has any information about Rachel's death…"

"There's nothing that concerns *you*. You leave her alone. You've done enough damage already."

"If you assault Karen, you'll be in worse trouble."

He whirled around, his face scarlet. "Oh, so you're threatening me, are you? Two can play at that game. I'm warning you, back off."

Lucy heard Aidan's quiet voice at her elbow. "Go easy, Lucy. He may be threatening you, but he'll take it out on Karen."

She pulled herself to a halt, trembling with frustrated anger. She knew he was right. What could she do? Suddenly she regretted her first reaction of joy that the police were leaving the island. Was it too late to dash for the school and see if any officers were still there? She could only watch helplessly as Gerald took the stumbling Karen back to their hotel.

"I didn't handle that very well, did I?" she said, as she and Aidan walked back down the street.

The others were waiting for them in a silent group: Melangell, looking worried, Elspeth and Valerie, Peter.

"I don't think there *is* a good way to handle bullies like that," Aidan comforted her.

"I should have known. More than anybody. It's my fault. There was something she wanted to tell me."

"About Rachel's death? Someone she'd met. Somebody she already knew?"

Lucy shook her head and sighed. "I can't think what she was talking about. And to be honest, she's always been a bit muddle-headed. If it's not drink, it's drugs. Sometimes both. You can't always believe what she says."

Lucy entered the sitting room at St Colman's and checked in surprise. David and Frances Cavendish were sitting on one of the sofas, drinking tea and eating Mrs Batley's fruit cake.

"Hello! I was beginning to think you'd left us, when you didn't show up at the church."

"I'm ever so sorry." Frances put down her teacup and licked the cake crumbs from her fingers. "But we found this marvellous shop. It was full of all sorts of lovely things. Jewellery and food and tee-shirts for the kiddies. And they make their own wine."

"Mead," her husband corrected her.

"I said to David, we could do half our Christmas shopping here. And the time just flew. By the time we finished, it was nearly four o'clock. But we got some beautiful things, didn't we, David?"

"Quality stuff," he agreed. "Not just your tourist tat."

Lucy poured herself a cup of tea and sank down in a chair. The tension of the day was ebbing out of her, leaving a deep exhaustion. She drank in silence, no longer trying to play the leader's part of chatting to the members of her group.

Still, she was counting them over. Everyone was here now, except Sue and James. Should she ask Mrs Batley if they had left? She glanced out of the window at the guesthouse car park. Their car was not there. There were very few roads on the island. Not many places where you could park a car. The Cavendishes had stayed today, but if James and Sue had left, would the older couple follow?

She got up and found Mrs Batley in the kitchen, preparing supper.

"James and Sue aren't in for tea, and they weren't in the church with me this afternoon. They haven't left, have they?"

Mrs Batley sniffed. "If they have, they haven't returned their keys to me." Then she managed a warmer smile. "You're having a bad week of it, love."

"I know. I don't know what the police found out today, but I hope they get to the bottom of it soon."

Her mind was still moving over the faces in the sitting room. Was it really possible that one of them was guilty of Rachel's death? Or James and Sue? And now Karen and Gerald had suddenly been thrown into the mix. Had Rachel's dysfunctional parents really only arrived for the first time yesterday? It might be none of these. Just the tabloid stereotype of a psychopathic stranger who had found Rachel alone on the beach.

"Am I supposed to keep supper for them?" Mrs Batley wanted to know.

Sue and James had still not returned.

"No. Go ahead. It's their responsibility if they want to stay out," Lucy said.

She looked down the depleted table. She felt more keenly than ever that she was losing her grip on this course.

The pair arrived as Mrs Batley was serving the main course. James strode into the room unapologetically and took his seat. Sue sidled in after him.

"I've cleared the soup," Mrs Batley told them pointedly.

"That's OK," said Sue hastily. "The liver and bacon looks lovely."

James's voice overrode hers. "I'm sure you still have some in the kitchen."

There was a clatter of plates, louder than necessary, as Mrs Batley stalked off to get it.

"Some people have the manners of a pig."

"Did you have a nice afternoon?" Valerie asked politely.

"We've been doing the work of God. Which is clearly not what's been happening here."

"We went to Alnwick Castle," Sue said enthusiastically. She turned to Frances. "You'd love it. The gardens are gorgeous."

"Sue!" James thundered.

A painful blush mottled Sue's cheeks.

"I'm sorry, James," she whispered.

"Work of God be blowed," Elspeth snorted. "You missed some excitement here. Karen Ince, Rachel's mother. Stoned, by the look of her. But grabbing Lucy's arm like there was no tomorrow and telling her she'd recognized somebody from her past."

The cutlery stilled. All eyes were on Elspeth. Those who had not been there when it happened stared at her avidly. The Cavendishes, James and Sue, Mrs Batley in the doorway.

"Go on, then," Frances urged. "Who was it?"

"Search me."

Lucy saw their eyes turn to her. She shook her head. "She didn't manage to tell me before Rachel's father hauled her away."

Elspeth's bark of laughter held no real amusement. "He certainly put a stop to it. That cad in his cricket togs. By the way he dragged her off, I'd say we'll have another murder on our hands."

Lucy felt the weight of the silence around the table.

She had her own reasons to know how dangerously close to the truth Elspeth might be.

Aidan woke in darkness. He was not sure what had disturbed him. Had Melangell cried out? He listened, but there was nothing now. His hand reached for the familiar bedside lamp switch, and found only the wall.

Memory came belatedly. He was not at home, but in St Colman's guesthouse. Ought he to check whether Melangell was all right?

He swung his feet out of bed, and stood at the window in his shorts and singlet. Cool air flowed over him. Starlight bathed the garden. The lights along the verandah were out.

Then he heard it again. The sound that must have woken him. The crash of broken glass.

A faint light sprang to life in one of the chalet bedrooms. Lucy's.

Without stopping to think, he went running down the stairs. The garden door resisted him, but he found a bolt. Past the Cavendishes' room, then Elspeth and Valerie's.

The lamplight from the curtained bedroom showed him the jagged hole in the glass pane. His heart lurched as he saw the door stood open. Then he heard Lucy's smothered cry from within.

There was a crash as the lamp went over onto the floor. Aidan hurled himself into the room.

Shadows of two figures struggling were thrown grotesquely over the walls and ceiling by the fallen lamp. Lucy was almost lost to sight beneath a huge Batman-like figure clad entirely in black. There was a muffled cry, but for the most part she was fighting in silence for her life.

Aidan cast around frantically for a weapon. He seized the dressing-table stool and threw it with all his strength at the black shape grappling with Lucy on the bed. It caught the middle of his spine.

There was a dreadful groan. The wildly wrestling shadows on the ceiling collapsed. For a terrible moment, Aidan could not tell where Lucy was. Then he saw the edge of a white nightdress beneath the sprawled weight of her attacker.

As he dashed forward, the inert form over her began to shift. There was a snarl of rage. At any moment he would turn his wrath on Aidan. He knew his slight figure would be no match for the giant who had loomed supernaturally tall. There was a flash of memory. He darted out onto the verandah and slammed his fist against the glass of the fire alarm. Then he was back inside, scared to death, but knowing that he had to defend Lucy.

As he flung himself at the bed, a clanging of bells shattered the night air. The black-clad stranger reared in shock. The shaded light showed the balaclava that hid his face. Through holes, eyes glared fury at Aidan. Long legs crossed the room in two strides. Aidan braced himself, desperate to know how to defend himself against such an opponent.

Lights snapped on from the verandah outside. Elspeth's deep voice rang out. "What's going on?"

Aidan saw the panicked eyes in those slits. They flicked sideways. Then long arms reached out and seized him. He was hurled across the room. He landed jarringly against a coffee table. He heard the television set smash beneath him.

The door flew wide as the dark giant fled into the night.

Chapter Thirty-three

ELSPETH APPEARED IN THE DOORWAY, a green dressing gown wrapped round her voluminous figure. "Are you all right in there? Where's the fire?"

"There is no fire." Aidan picked himself up off the floor. There would be more bruises to add to the ones Gerald had given him. "I needed to create a diversion."

Lucy sat on the bed in her nightdress. He could see she was shaking. He picked her fleece off a peg and wrapped it round her.

"Hot tea. Or maybe something stronger."

She had seemed such a fit, physical young woman. Now, with his hands on her shoulders, he felt her vulnerability. A tremor of surprise ran through him. He drew her closer.

"I've rung the police," Elspeth declared. "Though goodness knows how they'll get here if that causeway's shut."

"They'll call out the lifeboat to bring them, if it is," Mrs Batley said over her shoulder. "They'd have to do that for the fire crew, anyway. But it'll be far too late to catch him. He'll have made himself scarce before any police get here."

"He *was* the police," Lucy managed in a small voice.

"It was him?" Aidan asked her.

She nodded against his shoulder. "They won't be able to prove it, though. He'll have seen to that. No DNA traces." A long shudder ran through her. "He would have killed me if you hadn't come when you did. I'm only thankful he hates me enough to want to do it with his own hands. If he'd had a gun…"

Aidan stroked the hair from her face.

A sudden thought made him start. "Melangell!"

He took his hands away and dashed outside, past Elspeth and Mrs Batley.

The occupants of St Colman's were gathered on the lawn. Melangell rushed towards him.

"Daddy! Where *were* you? I couldn't find you."

"Sorry, poppet." He picked her up and held her close. "There was a nasty man in Lucy's room. I had to see to him."

"Peter told me not to wait for you. He brought me downstairs. But there isn't a fire, is there?"

"No, honey. Thank you, Peter."

The big archaeology student nodded silently.

"Somebody had better cancel the fire brigade callout."

"Goodness me! It went right out of my head," Mrs Batley cried. "We'll have that lifeboat out from Seahouses if we're not careful!" She hurried off to the house.

The others were subdued, still shocked by the sight of Lucy's attacker dashing past them into the dark. Gradually, they began to stir, but there was too much unexplained for them to start back for their bedrooms.

James's voice came out of the shadows on the lawn. "We should have known earlier what sort of person is leading this group."

"What's that supposed to mean?" Peter rounded on him.

Aidan put Melangell down. He stepped forward, stiff with fury. "Lucy's got enough to put up with, without this."

They were interrupted by David Cavendish's voice from further down the verandah. "Well, I suppose we know now who killed that poor girl."

Aidan turned towards him with a sense of shock. He had not for a moment connected what had happened tonight with the murder that hung over them all. Was it possible? Could Lucy's rejected partner have hated her so much he would kill the girl she cared for? Anything to get his own back on her?

He saw again the eyes glaring through the slits of the balaclava and shivered.

It was four o'clock in the morning before Lucy and Aidan had told their stories to the police sergeant and his female constable who came in answer to Elspeth's call.

"Lucky the tide was going out when we got the call," the sergeant said. "It's always touch and go on Holy Island. Just as well we don't often get trouble here. They're a law-abiding lot. But on the downside, your man will have got clean away. If the causeway had been shut, we might have cornered him."

"You're really sure it was Constable Parkinson?" the PC asked Lucy. "I mean, it was the middle of the night. You were asleep when he broke in, and you said he had a mask on. You never saw his face."

"It was him." Lucy shuddered. "But you're right. I can't prove it. He won't have left any evidence. And Aidan can't identify him."

She fingered the bruises on her neck. "If Aidan hadn't come when he did…"

"We'll take him in for questioning, of course," Sergeant Meldon said. "If we can get hold of the clothes he was wearing, there might be something. A hair of yours, if we're lucky."

"You won't find the clothes. He'll have ditched them. He knows too much about how you work."

"Then there's nothing more we can do here, I'm afraid. No chance of anyone seeing his car in the dark."

"Was he here yesterday?" she asked quietly. "Making enquiries about Rachel's death?"

"We'll check that out. But if he's clever, he won't have stayed behind. Someone would have noticed. Easy to come back after dark, when the causeway opened again."

He had come once. He could come again.

Aidan sat across the room from Lucy. He was disturbed by how much he wanted to cross that space and put his arms around her.

Suddenly his tired brain sprang to life. "Ask him to show you his back!"

"I beg your pardon, sir?"

"If it was him, then he should have a massive bruise across the small of his back. I threw a stool at him."

Lucy turned to him. He was rewarded by the first flash of hope in her pale face.

Something was bouncing up and down on Aidan's chest. His eyes flew open. Melangell was shaking him.

He winced as pain caught him in the ribs. He struggled to sit up.

The memory hit him. Lucy struggling for her life under that almost obliterating shadow. The venom of the eyes that had turned on him beneath the black mask. His own helplessness against the hands that had seized him and hurled him aside.

"What time is it?" he said thickly.

"Quarter to nine. I'm hungry."

Aidan groaned again as he shot his feet to the floor.

"Give me ten minutes. I need to shower."

He let cold water flow over him, shocking him awake.

No time now for that early morning walk with his camera, drinking in the beauty of the island.

Would Lucy have been out on the run that was part exercise, part prayer time? His mouth twisted in a painful smile at her eccentricity.

No. The shock was sinking in as he towelled himself. A man she had once loved had tried to kill her. If Aidan had not woken up, their little community might be reeling now with the horror of another murder. He did not think Lucy would be running on the dunes alone.

There was a lesser shock as Aidan and Melangell came downstairs to breakfast. James and Sue were handing over their keys at the reception desk. Their bags stood packed by the door.

Words like "rat" and "sinking ship" flew through Aidan's mind.

"You're leaving early?"

James swung round on him. Aidan was struck again by the plaster on the side of his head, in the very same place as Aidan's own lump where Gerald had knocked him against the wall.

"I should never have allowed Sue to talk me into coming if I'd known the sort of sentimental twaddle this was all about. Next door to paganism. I'm going back to where the real Lord's work is."

"It was my fault," Sue said humbly. "'Mission to Northumbria.' I thought it would be about planting churches in northern towns. Unemployed. Broken families. You know."

"Do you think Lucy doesn't know that too? This is where she gets her strength to go back and do that." Aidan was surprised at the vehemence in his own voice.

"She has some very strange friends for a minister of religion."

"He tried to murder her! Is that her fault?"

"It was hardly a Christian relationship, was it? By the sound of it, they weren't married."

Aidan turned on his heel and strode into the breakfast room.

Lucy raised her eyes to Aidan momentarily, then lowered them again. She had wrapped a white silk scarf around the bruises on her neck.

"Are you all right?"

She nodded.

He could have kicked himself for the inanity of the question. Of course she wasn't all right. The shock of the attempted murder was only hours away. The horror of it would haunt her all her life.

There was a moment's hesitation. Then he laid a hand gently on her shoulder. His grip tightened.

"Thank you," she said in a husky voice.

He fetched a glass of orange juice and sat down beside her.

"Look. I don't know what you were planning, but you're not fit to be running a course for us this morning. Don't even think about it. Everyone will understand."

"I was planning to do the Lindisfarne Gospels. How the book was made in St Cuthbert's honour."

"Why don't I do it?" The thought took him by surprise. "I could. There's that great story about the monks putting it in his coffin when they carried his body away for safety. But a storm washed over their ship and the Gospel book was lost overboard. One of the monks had a dream. St Cuthbert had appeared to him and told him where it had been washed up. When the tide went out, they found it lying there on the sands."

She managed a smile. "You know so many of the stories already, I don't know why you bothered to come."

He took his eyes away from hers. He found the words hard to speak. "Let's say it's a family pilgrimage. Bringing Melangell to the places Jenny loved." His voice brightened, and he lifted his head. "Honestly, I probably know more than you think about how these illuminated Gospels were made. The way they prepared the vellum from calf skin. The inks from lampblack, or red from insects living on Mediterranean oak trees. Lapis lazuli from Afghanistan. Did you know that the left wing of a wild goose provides a better quill for a right-handed scribe?"

She gave a shaky laugh. "I think you've got the job. I've even brought some sheets of the designs for people to colour in with felt-tip pens."

"Great. Melangell will enjoy that, won't you?"

"Yes, please."

Lucy moved a teaspoon in a slow circle. "I've been worrying about something else. Karen was trying to tell me something yesterday. Something important enough to make her slip away from Gerald and find me. She knew he didn't want her to talk to me. I hate to think what she's suffered for that."

"It was someone she recognized, wasn't it? Someone here."

Aidan glanced along the table. Elspeth was engaged in a booming conversation with Valerie. The Cavendishes were pushing back their chairs.

Lucy's voice came low. "I need to know who that was. It may very well have been Rachel's murderer."

There was a sudden silence. Elspeth had finished what she was saying and turned to them, her dark eyes suddenly sharp. Valerie stared inscrutably. The Cavendishes halted on their way to the door. All eyes were on Lucy.

"Sorry," she said huskily. "It's not a nice thought."

Chapter Thirty-four

AIDAN LOOKED ROUND THE SITTING ROOM with a feeling of satisfaction. He had got through the story of the Lindisfarne Gospels creditably. The details of the vellum, the inks, the precious cover of gold and jewels. The single scribe, Bishop Eadfrith of Lindisfarne. The craftsmen who bound and ornamented it. The scholar who added an Anglo-Saxon translation.

"I could take you to the ruins of the farm where they raised the calves for the vellum. It's on the other side of the island."

Not far from where Rachel met her death, he reminded himself.

The monks had left Lindisfarne to escape the marauding Vikings. The precious manuscript had been swept overboard and miraculously found. Seven years they wandered through Northumbria, until they found a resting place at Chester-le-Street. And then the final translation of Cuthbert's body to lie before the high altar in Durham Cathedral.

"That stone in the floor bears a single word: CUTHBERTUS. If you're a Northumbrian, you don't need to be told anything else about Northumbria's favourite saint. The Lindisfarne Gospels themselves are in the British Museum."

He had distributed Lucy's photocopied sheets, showing the outline of the initial page of St Luke's Gospel. The curious bird which poked its beak from the finial of the great capital letter reminded him of Rachel's earring, which Melangell had found in the sand.

He showed them how the scribe had ruled faint lines and pricked the vellum to guide the flowing interlace in a series of red dots. But the overall impression of the great illuminated page was not only of mathematical order but of riotous spontaneity.

He had a feeling of self-consciousness as he handed out the felt-tip pens.

The morning's group was startlingly depleted. Rachel was heartbreakingly dead. James and Sue had driven off the island. Lucy was recovering from the shock of being nearly murdered. Peter was nowhere to be seen.

Only Elspeth and Valerie and the Cavendishes were here. And Melangell, of course. She grabbed a fistful of pens with enthusiasm and set to work in the position she liked best, flat on her stomach on the floor.

Elspeth inspected the choice of colours. "Haven't done this since I was in kindergarten." She sounded oddly uninsulted for an Oxford don. She seized on the scarlet.

Valerie chose more delicate colours, mauve and pale green.

Only David Cavendish looked as though he might be going to protest that this was beneath his dignity. But Frances held out the packet of pens to him with an encouraging smile.

"We used to do this with the kiddies, didn't we?"

The room fell silent, except for the whisper of felt pens across the paper. Aidan looked out of the sitting room window behind him. The air was grey. Fingers of mist were beginning to creep under the trees that lined the road.

He saw a figure in a navy-blue tracksuit striding across the car park, almost at a run. Lucy turned to the left, towards the village centre. He went to stand in the bay window and watched her lope away up the road.

She was probably going to the Fellowship of St Ebba and St Oswald, to Brother Simon. No doubt she would pour her heart out to him about what had happened and seek his consolation.

Spiritual comfort, or something more?

Aidan felt something sharp twist inside him. He remembered the shudder of Lucy's body against his own last night.

Don't be ridiculous. They're old friends. It was here that Lucy fled when she ran away from Bill. What possible reason could you have to feel jealous of Simon?

Then memory overwhelmed him. Jenny was only six months dead. The pain hit him again, and swept away all thought of Lucy.

It was minutes before he turned back to the room and today's reality. There was a low buzz of chatter in the room. Lucy had guessed right. Adults four of them might be, but three of them seemed to be enjoying themselves as much as Melangell. David alone had done very little of his. He had filled in a few of the spaces a dull brown. Melangell's was already a riot of colour. David seemed to be watching her work more than his own.

"That's great," Aidan told her. "We'll show Lucy at lunchtime."

Something stirred at the back of his mind. That memory of Lucy's loping figure. Like someone running for a purpose. In haste.

Suddenly he knew this was not the gait of someone on her way to her spiritual counsellor. Something had overridden the shock of Bill's attack which had made her so subdued at breakfast time. Something had galvanized her into action.

In a flash of revelation, Aidan knew now where she was going. The last thing she had said to him at the table.

"I need to know who that was. It may very well have been Rachel's murderer."

Lucy must be making a last attempt to contact Karen, before Rachel's mother left the island.

What would the volatile Gerald do if he found them together?

Another thought came thundering in behind that.

Had Lucy guessed what Karen knew?

A hand seemed to grip his heart. If Lucy, or Karen, knew who the murderer was... If the murderer realized that... Lucy's life might be in danger twice over.

He threw a swift glance around the five absorbed in their tasks.

"Excuse me, folks. I'll be back."

He made for the door. Melangell scrambled to her feet.

"I'm coming too."

"No, love. Not this time. You'll be fine. Go on with your colouring." He was striding across the hall as he spoke.

"I don't *want* to stay."

Frances appeared in the doorway behind her. She put a capable hand on Melangell's shoulder.

"Don't you worry about her. She'll be safe with me. Won't you, Mel?"

Melangell's panicked eyes cut Aidan to the quick. But he couldn't waste time talking sense to her.

"Do what she says, love."

He had a last glimpse of her stricken face as he shot out of the front door.

Lucy reached the small hotel on the corner and swung into its car park at a run. She was desperately afraid she had come too late. After yesterday's encounter, when Gerald had ordered Karen away, he might have swept her straight off the island. What would there have been to keep him another night?

It was both a relief and a shock when the first thing she saw was Gerald loading a suitcase into the boot of his car. No, not *his*. Lucy recognized one of a fleet of local hire cars. A man like Gerald Morrison could have given a false identity to the company to hide his tracks. His own car would be something more flashy than this. Too easily recognized and remembered.

When had he really come to Holy Island?

Yesterday, she had feared his violence. But nothing could compare with the terror of the man who had loomed over her last night.

It was on the tip of her tongue to say, "Where's Karen?" But she checked herself. For reasons she dared not explore too deeply, Gerald had not wanted her to talk to Rachel's mother.

Cold fear of another sort was beginning to crawl through her stomach. The doubts were coming back. She looked at the clean-cut face, the handsomely trimmed fair hair, as his gaze swung round to meet hers.

That cricket sweater. Hadn't the police been asking about someone wearing white wool?

Fool! She should never have dashed off like this without telling someone where she was going.

"Can I help you?" The words were icy. The last thing in the world Gerald Morrison wanted to do was help a friend of Karen's.

Where *was* she?

"You're checking out?"

"I can't think how I let Karen persuade me to stay another night in this God-forsaken spot. If you'll pardon the phrase. Nothing here but sand. And not even a golf links. Just a religious tourist trap. Not my scene. There isn't a decent cocktail bar in sight."

He slammed the boot and opened the driver's door.

Lucy could restrain herself no longer. "Where's Karen? Isn't she coming with you?"

"I have not the faintest idea where she is. And frankly, my dear, I don't care."

His hand reached out to shut the door.

"Just a minute." A wiry figure shot past Lucy and grabbed the door before it fully closed. Aidan was suddenly between them. He was panting from the run. "You can't just drive off like that. There's a murder investigation. Karen's daughter is dead. Was Karen in the hotel last night? When did you last see her?"

Gerald kept his supercilious smile with difficulty. He looked around him with exaggerated care. "I see no police. They seem to have finished their enquiries here. I gave them my contact details. I'm free to go. If you wouldn't mind removing your hand, before we have a regrettable accident with your fingers. Don't forget, I'm a grieving father. Don't I deserve some sympathy?" He got into the car.

Lucy stepped up beside Aidan and put her own restraining hand on the door. "You haven't answered Aidan's questions."

The terror of last night was receding a little. It felt better to have the fiery-bearded photographer at her side.

Next moment, the car shot backwards, almost flinging Lucy and Aidan to the ground. It swung in a vicious turn. Then it headed straight towards them, door swinging wide. Aidan grabbed her arm and hurled her sideways. Grit showered her as the car slewed out of the gate and accelerated down the road towards the causeway.

"Are you OK?" Aidan asked. He was breathing hard himself.

She rubbed the flaming marks on her arm where he had grabbed her. "Yes, thank you… But Aidan, I'm scared. What has he done with Karen?"

"When I caught you up, he was sounding as though he had no idea where she was."

"That could be a bluff." She set off for the hotel entrance.

A couple was checking out at the reception desk.

"You'll want to be quick," the receptionist was saying. "The causeway closes in fifteen minutes. Don't try and cross after then."

Lucy could barely contain her impatience until the visitors had settled their bill.

"Please! Can you tell me if Karen Ince has checked out?"

"Ince?" The girl seemed not to recognize the name. She thumbed down the register.

"She was with Gerald Morrison. I've just seen him leaving."

"Yes… yes, he's settled his bill. Bit of a looker, isn't he?"

"Mrs Ince wasn't with him. Did you see her leaving? Blonde, middle-aged." It was on the tip of her tongue to say, "*And usually stoned.*"

"Not while I've been on duty this morning."

Lucy turned away in frustration.

Aidan drew her aside. "What is it you're frightened of, Lucy?"

"That he knows more about Rachel's death than he's saying. And if he does, then he might want to silence Karen."

"But that's not what Karen was saying yesterday. She'd met somebody else… Hang on! No. Didn't she say *them*?"

Lucy stepped out into the gathering mist. She looked slowly round at the half-familiar landmarks of the village, now blurred and indistinct.

"You're right. That's why I came here. I had to talk to Karen before she left. Meeting Gerald drove it out of my mind." She shivered.

Something plucked at the edges of her memory.

"I've been trying to think – once I got over last night. Who could there possibly be on Lindisfarne that Karen would remember?"

"Has she been here before?"

"I've no idea. But I shouldn't think so. It's hardly her sort of place."

"A visitor, then. Or visitors, rather."

Lucy's memory strayed over the only visitors whose names she knew. Peter was too well known to Karen to make meeting him a surprise. Elspeth and Valerie had been with Lucy when Karen overtook her. But she had shown no reluctance to speak in front of them. James and Sue? James had had an unhealthy influence over Rachel, and his head wound was still unexplained. The pallid figures of David and Frances Cavendish, more banal than sinister?…

"Aidan!" She spun round and clutched his arm. "I know who Karen recognized! I could kick myself! Even when they told me they'd run a children's home, it never occurred to me…"

It was a moment before Aidan's mind connected.

"The Cavendishes? But surely…?"

"Karen told me once that when Rachel was a child she'd complained about something that happened in the children's home she was sent to. Karen told Rachel's social worker, but no one would take her seriously. I mean, you can understand why. Drink, drugs. She's hardly in her right mind most of the time. But what if, all along, she was right? What if Rachel did suffer abuse from the very people who were supposed to be protecting her? And what if she met them again here?"

She could see Aidan thinking furiously. "When we met Rachel on the stairs that first day, she was bright-eyed and bushy-tailed. Then she came into that meeting where we introduced ourselves, and she was a different girl. Eyes down. Hiding behind a curtain of hair. As if someone had switched off the light inside her."

"I've been an idiot! I put that down to her bipolar disorder. It never occurred to me that she might have come face to face with the very people who abused her. No wonder she ran away that evening!"

"And if she recognized them, they probably recognized *her*. She must have changed, but the name was still the same. They would have had every reason to silence her, before she told anyone what they did."

Aidan gave a great start. She saw the horror in his eyes.

"God forgive me! I've left Melangell with them!"

Chapter Thirty-five

LUCY WAS THE MORE NATURAL RUNNER, but fear drove Aidan's feet. They were nearing the house when Lucy drew level with his shoulder and panted, "It's all right. They won't do anything to her. They'll want to stay inconspicuous."

But all Aidan could see was the pleading look on Melangell's face, Frances's restraining hand clamped on her shoulder.

How old had Rachel been in that children's home, when no one but Karen would believe what had been done to her?

Foolishly, he clutched in his mind the image of the sitting room at St Colman's just before he had left it. Melangell stretched out on the floor. Elspeth attacking her task with hilarity. Valerie choosing her colours carefully. Frances filling in the outlines with exaggerated care. David more truculent.

He burst in. The sitting room was empty. Someone had tidied away the felt-tip pens and the colouring sheets, and stacked them neatly on a coffee table. There was no sign of Melangell.

Lucy held his arm firmly. "There's no need to panic yet. Maybe they're in the garden. Or they've gone for a walk."

Aidan dashed upstairs. Melangell was not in her room. Peter emerged from his bedroom next door.

"Have you seen Melangell?"

"Sorry."

He flew downstairs. His feet sped him through the garden door. Tendrils of mist dampened the wooden tables and chairs. Lucy was already there, looking around her. Her face was graver now.

He saw a light on through a gap in the curtains of Elspeth and Valerie's room and pounded on the door.

It was Valerie who answered. She looked, tight-lipped, over his shoulder at Lucy. "Yes?"

"Where's Melangell? Have you seen her? Or the Cavendishes?"

Elspeth strode forward to stand behind her friend. "You missed the excitement."

Blood seemed to crawl through Aidan's body, as though time had been slowed down. He could hardly get the words out. "What happened?"

"That Ince woman. Rachel's mother. After we'd packed up the kiddie colouring stuff, we found her lurking in the garden, Val and I. She grabbed my arm and asked for Lucy. Kept looking round her, as if she was terrified of something. Then out came the Cavendishes, with your Melangell in tow. The woman gave one look at them, let out a sort of scream and fled."

"What did the Cavendishes do? Do they still have Melangell?" He was almost dancing on his feet, with a desperate urge to run after them. To find them somehow.

Elspeth shrugged. "Search me. You left her with them."

Valerie said more kindly, "They stopped dead when they saw Rachel's mother. You could tell from their faces it was a shock. Why? Was there something between them? I didn't see what happened after Karen ran. We went into our room."

Aidan dashed to the next chalet bedroom and hammered on the Cavendishes' door. There was no reply.

When he turned, Lucy was already on her mobile. She was recounting the details crisply to someone. He assumed it must be the police.

She looked up as Aidan met her eyes. "I've called out the coastguards. They'll start a missing person search. I hope to goodness they don't find the Cavendishes doing a bit of harmless shopping, or I'll have egg on my face. No, sorry, Aidan! I *do* hope that's what they'll find. But I've warned them what we suspect: that they could be dealing with a pair of murderers. They just need to locate them and hold back. I'm going to call in the police to make the arrest."

She was back on her phone.

He felt an enormous thankfulness for her capability. It was incredible that she could be so strong and decisive only hours after an attack on her life. His own heart was pounding.

"What's up?" Peter had suddenly materialized behind them.

"It's Karen," Lucy said briefly. "I'm pretty sure she believes the Cavendishes killed Rachel."

She turned her attention back to her mobile. "…Yes, the causeway's closing any time now… Aidan!" She swung round on him. "Was the Cavendishes' 4x4 still outside?"

She must have seen the alarm in his face as he sped back through the house.

There were only three cars left: Lucy's VW, Mrs Batley's Ford, and the elderly Bentley Elspeth and Valerie had arrived in. For the first time, Aidan cursed his last-minute impulse to walk across the sands and leave himself on the island without a car.

When he got back to the garden with his news, the other four were consulting earnestly.

"The police are on their way," Lucy assured him. "They'll have to use the lifeboat. The helicopter can't operate until this fog clears."

"But if the Cavendishes' car has gone, they could already be off the island!" Aidan was almost bursting with impatience.

"Why would they take Melangell?" Valerie asked. "It would only make things more difficult for them."

"I don't think it's Melangell they're after," said Lucy. "It's Karen. They'll think she's the only one who knows what this is all about. They don't know she's already told me what Rachel said about them as a child. That they were abusing the children in their care."

"Then where's Melangell?" Aidan protested. "What's happened to her?"

Lucy took command of the situation. "Show me," she ordered Elspeth and Valerie. "Where did you see Karen go?"

The two women looked at each other.

"She'd come out of those bushes at the back of the garden," Elspeth said. "And dived back in there when she saw the Cavendishes."

"Did they go after her? Are you sure you didn't see anything before you went indoors?"

"As far as I remember, they stood stock still, as if they'd had a shock," Valerie volunteered. "They sort of looked at each other, as though they didn't know what to do. I'm sorry. That's really all I saw. It seemed too rude to stand and stare at them."

"Right," Lucy decided. "Show me where Karen went."

The five of them plunged into the thick screen of bushes at the back of Mrs Batley's garden. Aidan, not surprisingly, was ahead of the others.

He gave a sudden cry.

Lucy's heart pounded in alarm. She was at his side in seconds.

"Here," he showed her. "Someone's broken through the hedge into the field."

A horizontal branch of the beech hedge had been snapped. Smaller twigs were bent aside. The ground was littered with fallen leaves.

She squeezed through after Aidan. The meadow beyond sloped gently down towards the big car park on the outskirts of the village. The further edges of the field were lost in fog. Nothing moved on it in the gloom but sheep.

"Look here!" Aidan cried.

Not far from the gap, two high-heeled white shoes lay thrown on the grass.

Lucy thought rapidly. "If they came after her, Karen might still have got away. Without those ridiculous shoes, she's probably quicker on her feet than the Cavendishes."

"Would she have realized she was in that much danger?"

"I'm sure now she believed they killed Rachel to keep her quiet. That's what she was trying to tell me. So yes, she's intelligent enough to know she's almost as much a danger to them as her daughter was."

"But if they chased after Karen, why take Melangell? Why not just leave her behind?"

She saw the anguish in his face.

"I'm sorry. I've got no answer to that."

The others had pushed through the hedge behind them. Lucy turned to them.

"Elspeth and Valerie. Go back to the village. Find out if Karen's there. Or if anyone's seen her or the Cavendishes and Melangell. Peter, there's a footpath that goes across the middle of the island. Check that. Aidan – " she read in his eyes the desperate need to do something active – "I've asked the police to put out a check on the mainland for the Cavendishes' car."

"We don't know the number. Unless it's in Mrs Batley's register."

"Trust me, I memorized it. Old habits die hard. A red Honda CR-V. But if they lost time chasing Karen, they'll still be on the island. The causeway's closed now. It's my belief their first priority will be to silence Karen if they can. We need to find them."

He was already breaking into a run back towards the garden. "They'll almost certainly have seen her running away. If they couldn't catch her up, all they had to do was get in their car and overtake her at the end of this field. We have to find that Honda."

"My car," Lucy panted. "You're right. They have to be here. There's no way off now."

They raced back through the bushes, across the lawn, into St Colman's small car park at the front of the house. Lucy clicked her key and lights flashed from her car. Aidan leaped into the passenger seat. Lucy swung the car out onto the road.

She sped down the slight slope to the public car park. There were more vehicles than she had expected. People had crossed the causeway earlier that morning, to spend the day on Holy Island. The tide would be down again mid-afternoon.

No figures moved among the parked cars.

Her heart wrenched at the look on Aidan's face. She swung her gaze around, searching for the bulk of the red 4x4.

She reeled off the registration number. "It's a pretty distinctive car. I always wondered why a couple like them would want an off-road vehicle. But it means they could have driven across the dunes to that beach where you found Rachel's body. Anyway, it shouldn't take us long to find, if it's here."

Aidan sped away. Lucy checked in the opposite direction. In a couple of minutes they were back at Lucy's car. She knew the answer by Aidan's face.

"You said they could drive over the dunes. Could they have chased her that way? Do you think they took Melangell with them?"

A grim picture was forming in Lucy's mind. If Melangell knew now what the Cavendishes had done to Rachel, and might, even now, be doing to Karen, what about the child? Might they devise a scenario that would make it look as if Karen was responsible for her own death and Melangell's?

She dared not say this to Aidan.

"There's only one way to find out. We'll drive as far down the road as the tide will let us."

Below the car park, the road swung abruptly seawards. They reached the corner at Chare Ends, where the Pilgrims' Way across the sands made landfall. All Aidan could see now was the beginning of the line of posts that marked the route, looming up out of the grey water, until they were lost in the mist.

"Blow!" Lucy said as she rounded the corner. "I'd forgotten this next bit of road was below the high tide mark. But we can make it a bit further, if you're game. It's not over the tarmac yet."

Aidan was leaning forward. His eyes were groping through the patchy fog ahead. There was no sign of another vehicle.

"Why would they come this way? Wouldn't Karen be safer running back to the village?"

"We'd have met them on our way back to St Colman's if she had. Their car's gone. There are only two choices. There's just this one road. It has to be this way."

Aidan tore his eyes away from the water lapping ever closer to the surface of the road. He looked at the sandy flats on the inland side, pooled with water after last night's tide. To their right, beyond a fence, rough grass faded into the mist.

"They might just have made a run for it, before the causeway closed. Taken a risk on Karen. After all, you said nobody believed her the first time."

"It wasn't a murder enquiry then."

They drove on. Lucy's phone rang. She fished it out of her pocket and handed it to Aidan. "Take that, would you?"

A male voice spoke in his ear. "Miss Pargeter? Northumbria Police."

Aidan's grip tightened on the phone. "She's driving. Can I take a message? I'm Aidan Davison. Is this to do with Rachel Ince and the Cavendishes?"

A hesitation. A thought raced through Aidan's mind. This could be nothing to do with Rachel's death. What about that murderous attack on Lucy last night?

The voice identified itself. "Detective Inspector Harland. Miss Pargeter called us a little while ago. She was concerned about Rachel's mother. I just wanted her to know that we've received a call from Mrs Ince."

"*What?*" Aidan strained forward and met the sharp resistance of the seat belt. Lucy shot a startled look sideways.

"She was reporting the whereabouts of Mr and Mrs Cavendish. We've got our people coming in as fast as we can, given the weather. And we've put the coastguards on alert."

"Did she say anything about Melangell? Where are they?"

"I'm sorry. I'm not at liberty to say. I recommend that you and Miss Pargeter stay out of this."

Lucy swung the car onto a stretch of short grass at the roadside.

"What's going on? Give it to me."

"Karen's rung the police. She knows where the Cavendishes are."

Lucy grabbed the phone. "This is Lucy Pargeter. Where's Karen?"

She pulled a face and handed the phone back to Aidan. "He's rung off."

They looked around them at the shrouded scene. The road, Aidan was relieved to see, had swung marginally away from the sea. Rough grass separated them now from the advancing tide. The ground on their right was beginning to rise. There were glimpses of hummocks of sand dunes beyond the fence.

Would Karen really have run this far in her bare feet, fleeing from her daughter's killers? Or tracking them?

He peered at the damp tarmac ahead. But the road stretched away into nothingness.

"I'm getting out to see what I can." Lucy switched off the engine and stepped out into the grey silence.

Aidan fought back an instinct to grab the steering wheel and drive on in pursuit. He watched Lucy climb the fence and wade through the long grass to stand on a low mound. A pall of denser fog crept in. He could no longer see her.

His eyes struggled to probe the road in front of him. He was willing the Cavendishes' Honda to appear out of the mist, even momentarily. For some reassurance that they were still on the island. That he might get to Melangell before it was too late.

Then Lucy was beside the car again.

"Nothing. Visibility's terrible."

"I keep thinking I can hear the police helicopter. But it's just my imagination. You can't even hear the waves lapping now. We might be in the middle of nowhere."

Lucy settled into her seat and switched the engine on. "They won't be able to bring the helicopter in this weather. It'll have to be a lift in the lifeboat from Seahouses."

Aidan tried to remember how far down the coast that was. Past Bamburgh Castle. How long would the sea crossing take? His knuckles tensed.

Lucy drove on. Like Aidan, her head was bent forward, peering ahead.

"There!" he cried.

Out of the gloom, a red vehicle loomed at the side of the road. Lucy accelerated, then swung in beside it. They both jumped out. Lucy checked the numberplate.

"It's them."

The Honda was empty. Heart hammering with fear, Aidan pulled the rear door open. The Cavendishes' luggage was thrown in the back. His whole body gave an enormous lurch of relief. There was no sign of Melangell. He closed his eyes with a prayer of thankfulness. He had been denying to himself the fear of finding her bound and gagged. Or worse. Was that how the Cavendishes had brought Rachel along this road, to drive over the narrow neck of dunes and leave her body on that deserted beach at the edge of the rising tide?

A new fear almost paralysed him. Had they carried Melangell from here?

Suddenly urgency galvanized him. He raced up the grass-grown dunes. The fog was patchier here. As it lifted momentarily, he thought he could glimpse the sea, not more than a few hundred metres on the other side of the island.

Then he turned and saw them. Two figures widely spaced, stumbling through the sand. One in a beige raincoat, the other in green.

Even at this distance he knew them.

David and Frances Cavendish.

The wind changed. The mist came rolling back to cover them.

Chapter Thirty-six

"MELANGELL!" AIDAN'S SHOUT WAS SWALLOWED up in the fog. "Melangell!" he cried again.

He started to run towards where he thought he had seen those figures. He was stumbling in shifting sand.

"Be quiet, Daddy! They'll hear you." The voice was startlingly close.

The blood seemed to leave Aidan's face as he spun round. Had he wanted to find her so much it was her ghost he was hearing?

A tousled, and very real, curly head emerged from a hollow in the dunes. Bright grey-blue eyes rebuked him. Mist beaded the tips of her hair. There were bits of broken grass on her tee-shirt.

Behind her, Karen was struggling up the slope of sand, hauling herself on tussocks of grass. Sand and fragments of vegetation clung to her striped sweater. Her feet were bare and scratched.

But Aidan gave Rachel's mother only a second's glance. He was plunging over the top of the dune to take Melangell in a hug. His arms went round her tightly. Only now did the full horror of his fears declare itself. He had hidden from himself the depth of the devastation he would feel if he had lost not only Jenny but Melangell as well. For the moment, the realization of that pain eclipsed his joy.

Melangell wriggled free.

"Silly Daddy. You're crying."

"I'm not. It's just the wind making my eyes water."

"There isn't any wind."

But there was. A breeze was strengthening, tugging at the strands of mist. As it streamed them out, he had a clear view of the sea below him. Next moment, it was lost again. Patches of blue were beginning to appear overhead.

He raked the uneven dunes for the beige- and green-coated figures of the Cavendishes. The tumbled landscape and the lingering fog still hid them.

"They heard you," Lucy called. "They were making for their car."

Aidan was already sprinting after them.

Her voice arrested him. "Leave them. They can't get off the island. The police are on their way." She had her phone out.

Still Aidan ran. He crested the next ridge and looked down. Below him was the road and the two parked cars. The Cavendishes were getting into their 4x4.

He realized he was still holding Melangell's hand. He did not think he would ever let go of her.

Then shifting trails of mist hid the scene below. He heard the engine roar.

Lucy had come up behind him. "Where do they think they're going?" he asked her.

As if in answer, the fog was torn apart. The red Honda reversed, then shot forward. It was startled seconds before Aidan realized it was heading straight up the bank towards them. He leaped back, pulling Melangell with him. The four-wheel drive came lurching up the sandy slope, slithering sometimes on the flattened grass. Aidan, Melangell and Lucy woke up to their danger and fled.

Aidan turned his head. The Honda was tottering on the ridge of the dunes. It came plunging down towards them. He scrambled aside, and threw Melangell behind him.

But the vehicle was not aimed at them. When he looked down, he saw a flash of white, spreadeagled in the hollow. White jeans, blue-and-white striped jersey, blonde hair. Karen lay sprawled where she had fallen. The Honda swerved and plummeted towards her.

He heard Lucy cry out, and clutched Melangell to him.

Suddenly, above the roar of the straining engine, he heard the clatter of another, larger, machine approaching. He looked round in bewilderment. A black helicopter, yellow-topped, came swooping in low over the shoreline.

When he looked back, the Cavendishes' vehicle hid Karen's

prostrate body from view. He let go of Melangell and raced down the slope towards it.

The rotors of the helicopter flattened the grass on the top of the dunes and whipped up the sand around him. He crouched and covered his face.

The Honda skidded to a halt. David Cavendish was wrestling the wheel, changing direction. It was climbing the dunes now, heading back towards the road.

Lucy sprinted past Aidan into the hollow. As Melangell ran after her, Aidan caught the child and held her back.

Karen was on her knees, head hanging. Aidan let out a long-held breath. There was no visible blood.

Lucy shouted up at him. "Get the ambulance. Quick. I think they hit her."

The helicopter wheeled around. Aidan had to shout into his mobile above the roar of its engine.

By the time he scrambled back on to the ridge and looked down, the Honda was speeding off down the road.

"It's all right," he said, squeezing Melangell's hand. "They can't get away. The tide's too far up on the causeway."

"What are they going to do?" Melangell asked. "Will they get out and hide among all these sand dunes?"

"Search me."

The police helicopter was hovering low in the Cavendishes' wake. Would it be able to put down on the road?

Yet still the red vehicle sped on round the bend in the shore road. It was heading straight for the tip of the island and the wide channel between Lindisfarne and the mainland.

"It'll have to stop soon."

"Is Karen going to be all right?"

"I hope so."

He looked behind him. To his relief, Karen was sitting up, supported by Lucy. But he was too far away to know how badly she had been hurt.

"What happened?" he asked Melangell. "How did you get away from them?"

"I wasn't *with* them, silly. It's a long story. Look, Daddy! You were wrong. They aren't stopping, are they?"

He followed her eyes. The breeze had blown the last shreds of mist away. Morning sunlight gleamed on the strait, turning the steel grey to silver. And out in that water, the red vehicle was still moving forward. Slower now. The waves were mounting around it.

"Idiots!" Aidan murmured under his breath. "There are always some people who think the laws of nature don't apply to them."

The helicopter had landed on the road. Two police officers jumped out.

Along the road below Aidan and Melangell there came speeding a dark blue and yellow Land Rover. The Holy Island coastguards. It shot past, circled the stationary helicopter, and stopped where the water lapped up over the causeway.

Far out in the channel, the Honda had come to a stop. The refuge box on stilts was still a long way off.

There was nothing anyone on the island could do.

A figure was crawling out of the window onto the roof. They watched him, sprawled out, leaning over to the open window on the other side. The water was mounting. The vehicle shifted. The current was tugging it sideways. Still Frances had not appeared through the window.

"Dear God," Lucy murmured.

Aidan struggled to know how he felt. One part of him knew a terrible anger that would be satisfied only to see the couple disappear beneath the tide. Yet still his heart wrenched at the human drama being played out before his eyes.

It seemed an eternity before the orange inshore rescue boat of the RNLI came scudding across the waves from the south. He watched the lifeboatmen haul the Cavendishes on board from their flooded vehicle.

The inflatable veered sharply. It came shooting in to where the police were waiting on the causeway.

Aidan let go of Melangell's hand and breathed again.

Chapter Thirty-seven

"SO TELL ME," LUCY PLEADED with Melangell. "How did you get away from the Cavendishes?"

"I've just told those policemen."

"I know. But I wasn't there. Humour me. Please!"

Melangell made a show of buttoning up her lips, but her eyes were dancing with mischief.

They were sitting on a bench overlooking the harbour, eating ice creams. Almost, Aidan thought, with a wrench that was part pain, part pleasure, as though they were a family. The ice creams had been Lucy's idea.

To one side of the sheltered bay, Lindisfarne Castle stood proud on its rock. On the other, the sandstone arch of the ruined priory showed above a meadow. The picture postcard perfection, boats rocking on the blue water, seemed unreal after what had gone before.

He still remembered that mixture of anger and alarm as the tide mounted around the Cavendishes. He was only beginning to be relieved that the lifeboat had arrived in time.

Karen had been airlifted to hospital. The 4x4 had struck her a crushing blow on her shoulder and ribs, but that last-minute swerve as the helicopter came over the ridge had meant that the wheels did not run over her. She was in pain, but conscious.

Melangell licked the dribbles round her ice cream cone. She looked up at Lucy with her head on one side and relented.

"I didn't have to get away from them, because I wasn't *with* them. When Karen ran away, they forgot all about me and chased after her. So I ran away and hid, in case they came back."

"I'm sorry," Aidan exclaimed. "I should never have left you with them. I had no idea. They seemed such a harmless pair."

"I tried to tell you. But you went running after Lucy and you wouldn't listen."

His ears were burning now.

"Tell me what?"

"Well, you know the police kept asking us if anybody had a white jumper, or if we'd seen anyone else wearing one?"

"I thought that might have been Gerald's cricket sweater," Lucy said.

Aidan shot her an amused glance. "People talk about cricket whites, but that was cream. But I did notice Karen had a blue-and-white one."

"Not Karen, silly," Melangell protested. "And it wasn't a sweater at all. I'd been puzzling as hard as I could, and then this morning I remembered. It wasn't just because Mr Cavendish makes me feel creepy. Mrs Cavendish was always knitting something. The day we came, she was making a little white jacket for a baby. Then next day, after Rachel died, it was a blue one."

She left a triumphant silence. Into Aidan's photographer's memory came the image of Frances's ageing fingers making the needles dart in and out of the fluffy white wool.

Lucy gasped. "You know, that never occurred to me! You mean *that* was what they used to... to stifle Rachel?" She looked down in sudden concern at the child between them, then up at Aidan. "I wonder where they did it? Did they find her alone on the beach? Was it in the guesthouse, and they somehow smuggled her out in the back of their car? But there's no doubt about the reason. They might not have realized who Rachel was at first, but she must have recognized them. Everything changed for her after that. If only I'd known! If only she'd told me." She turned her attention back to Melangell. "But if they went after Karen without you, what were you doing out on the dunes with her when we found you?"

"*Well*, I was hiding in the bushes when they came back from looking for her. And they were really angry. Mr Cavendish said something about going after her, and they went to get their car. So I ran to the back of the garden where Karen went, and I saw her running down the field. And I went after her. She's, well… she's not very clever sometimes, is she, when she's had a lot to drink?"

Aidan and Lucy's eyes met over her head.

"No, love. So what did you want her to do?"

"Phone the police, of course. I told her. She had to tell them what she was going to tell Lucy. She didn't want to. I don't think she likes the police. Only then we saw their big red car coming down the road. And we just ran. It was hard for Karen, because she didn't have any shoes on. But then the ground got all sort of lumpy, and we couldn't see the road and they couldn't see us. I thought we'd got away. But we didn't know where we were going. We couldn't see the sea without going up to the top of the dunes, and that would mean they could see *us.* Then I heard the engine stop. And that was *really* creepy. I knew they were looking for us."

Her face had paled beneath the freckles. Aidan took her hand.

"I was just saying to Karen that if we ran back the way we'd come, they wouldn't know where we'd gone. And then I heard you shout. I've never been so glad to see you, Daddy."

He hugged her hard, wordlessly.

"Will Karen be all right?"

"Yes, I think so. It was lucky the mist lifted when it did. The police helicopter came just in time. That was your doing. If you hadn't made Karen ring the police, they wouldn't have known where you were. You saved her."

"Did I?" Her eyes were suddenly bright again. "I wanted to."

Aidan stood up. His eyes found Lucy's. "You can't have expected a week like this when you advertised your course. We've been a bit like the ten green bottles sitting on the wall. How many of us are there left now?"

"There's you and Melangell, and Elspeth and Valerie. Oh, and Peter."

They started to walk along the beach.

"We never did find out why James came back with his head bleeding and concussed. I really thought he'd been in some sort of fight with Rachel. A seduction gone wrong, perhaps, and he'd killed her, perhaps unintentionally. But maybe his head wound was just a common or garden accident after all. He fell in the castle garden, as he said."

"What do you think will happen to Elspeth, now I've told the police she gave Rachel cocaine? Will her university get to hear of it?"

He shrugged. "Not necessarily. It had nothing to do with Rachel's death. There's no reason why it should come up at the Cavendishes' trial. And if they prosecute her for it, the hearing will be a long way from Oxford."

"Unless the press get hold of it."

Something in Lucy's voice arrested Aidan. He looked up at her face. Melangell was skipping along the shore ahead of them.

"That's what happened to you, isn't it? The papers printed a story about Rachel's death, mentioning you. And your ex got hold of it."

Lucy's hand strayed to her neck, where the bruises still showed above the white silk scarf.

Had that really been only in the small hours of this morning?

He took her hand and squeezed it. "I'm sorry. The Cavendishes had driven it out of my mind. But you still have to face this. I wonder if they've arrested him."

Her clear eyes met his. "I thought they wouldn't find any evidence. He's clever. It would have been my word against his. But he can't hide the bruises you left on him. I owe you twice over."

"He took a gamble. With Rachel dead, he must have figured the police would think it was the same killer who went for you. It was just luck that I woke up." He was still holding her hand for reassurance. "He won't try a second time."

Her grave face flowered into a smile. "Once was bad enough. Thank you."

He had to let go of her hand. He had no right to be holding it. He had only known her three days. And he was still mourning Jenny. But he felt an overwhelming urge to protect her.

"I thought... Well, I thought two things really. When I first saw you with Brother Simon, it was obvious that you two... But then I came across the pair of you in the church, and I had an idea he might be a danger to you."

Lucy stopped dead on the beach. "You thought… Me and Simon! Yes, we go back to when I'd just left Bill. He picked me up when I was at my lowest. But he's celibate. I mean, it's really important to him. And he'd never hurt a hair of my head."

"I know that now. But a thing like this makes you suspect everybody."

Lucy was unaccountably blushing. "Well," she said, with an attempt at lightness. "We ought to get back to St Colman's and bring the rest of them up to speed."

"Peter will be glad they've caught them. It hit him hard."

"I hadn't realized how much he cared about her."

"No," Aidan said. "Sometimes these things take you by surprise."

They walked in silence, side by side, towards the village, watching Melangell skipping in front of them.

"I have to give it to you," Elspeth told Lucy in a gruffer voice than usual. "I only came here to humour Val. But, well… it's not everyone who would have carried things through, under the circumstances. Good show. I shall read the Venerable Bede with different eyes in the future. And that was right, what you told us last night. Your monks didn't just give up after the Vikings. They took Cuthbert's body away to begin again somewhere else. And in time, the Benedictines moved in to start over again on Lindisfarne. Life has to go on."

Valerie came forward and put her hands on Lucy's shoulders. She bent forward, rather awkwardly, and dropped a dry kiss on her cheek. "I'm sorry. I know you did what you had to."

Lucy murmured embarrassed denials of their need for thanks or apologies. She watched the two women loading their cases into the elderly Bentley.

It was over, she thought, with a strange sense of astonishment and relief. Somehow she had got to the end of this week.

She looked over her shoulder to find Aidan and Melangell coming out of the house. Aidan was in shorts, with a loaded rucksack on his back. Melangell was skipping beside him carrying a smaller, bright pink knapsack.

Lucy started to raise her hand in farewell. Then she hesitated.

"Are you sure you want to do the pilgrim thing again and walk back over the sands? I could give you a lift across the causeway."

She saw a flash of something unreadable in Aidan's eyes.

"What do you think, partner?" he said to Melangell.

The girl put her head on one side. "We… ell, I suppose the monks sometimes rode horses."

"And we've got a long drive south ahead of us when we get to the other side. Yes, please, if you've got room for us."

Lucy felt an unexpected lift of her heart.

The Bentley was already pulling out on to the road. Elspeth stuck a hand through the open window and gave them a cheery wave and a toot of the horn.

There were only four of them left in the car park of St Colman's. Inside, Mrs Batley had given Lucy a surprisingly affectionate goodbye.

Peter had the boot of the VW open. He stood back to make room for Aidan and Melangell's bags.

"You drive," Lucy said, on a sudden impulse.

Peter's heavy eyebrows shot up. "Are you sure?"

"You can take us down the A1 and along Hadrian's Wall. I'll take over when we reach the motorway."

She settled into the front seat, with the Davisons in the back. It would have been a long hike for them along the line of posts that led from Lindisfarne to the mainland. By car, the journey would be over all too quickly. Why did she feel she wanted to prolong it as long as possible?

Peter took them cautiously out of the car park and swung right along the coast road. Lucy's throat tightened as she recalled that gut-churning drive along this same road in the fog. They came to the bend in the road where they had discovered the Cavendishes' 4x4. She half-turned to see if Melangell was remembering that chase too.

But the child's face was eagerly alive. "We're like King Oswald, riding back to Bamburgh after visiting St Aidan."

They ventured out onto the narrow strip of tarmac which was all that distinguished the causeway from the surrounding sands. The tide was out, and the flats shimmered with occasional pools. The refuge box loomed ever closer. Then they were over the deep-water channel and the mainland was speeding towards them. Peter pulled into the small car park on the right.

All this time, Lucy had not found anything to say to Aidan, though she had chatted to Melangell. She felt a wall of obligation standing between her and the red-bearded photographer. She owed her life to him. It made impossible the normal friendship that might have developed after their abrasive start. Now that the time had come to bid him goodbye, she did not know what to say to him. Yet, as father and daughter got out of the car and retrieved their bags, she felt a wrenching sense of loss.

The two of them stood, meeting each other's eyes, at a loss for words. It was Melangell who rescued them.

"Shall we see you again?"

Lucy caught the start of surprise in Aidan's eyes. He looked from his daughter back to Lucy.

"Well, we don't live far apart," she found herself saying. "You could come over some time, if you like."

"Yes, please! When?" Melangell cried.

Lucy turned more gravely to Aidan. "They released Karen from hospital yesterday. I'll be conducting Rachel's funeral when I get back. It won't be the jolliest of parties, but it would be good to have someone there who knew her, who saw what happened. I'd be glad of the support."

She held her breath.

"Of course I'll come. But maybe later… if Melangell wants to…"

Lucy's heart dropped a little in disappointment. Would he only come because of Rachel, or Melangell?

His hand closed over hers, warm and firm. "Thanks," he said, "for a lot of things."

She ought to give him her enormous thanks for saving her life. But she stood, tongue-tied, conscious of the pressure of his hand, his skin against her own, the steady light of those grey-blue eyes, the colour of the North Sea behind him.

Too soon, he dropped her hand. They stood awkwardly in silence. Then he shouldered his rucksack and began to move towards their car.

Melangell lingered for a moment. She looked up at Lucy conspiratorially. "He likes you," she whispered. "He's sad about Mummy, but he likes you too." She ran forward and put her arms round Lucy's waist. "And so do I."

Lucy told herself it was the wind whipping tears into her eyes as she watched them board their car. Then she slipped back into the passenger seat and let Peter drive her south along the road the monks of Lindisfarne might have carried Cuthbert's body. Into a new and still unforeseeable reality.

Questions for Groups

1. Lucy leaves the police force to be ordained. How does the attitude of a police officer to a crime differ from that of a minister?

2. How much would eight-year-old Melangell understand about what was going on?

3. Are the stories about seventh-century Northumbria relevant to the modern plot?

4. Is there anything that could have been done to help or protect Rachel?

5. Is the portrayal of the apparently successful pastor James fair?

6. Is there a danger in taking a site that is sacred to many people and making it the scene of a violent crime?

7. How important is the setting of the novel? Would the story have been the same if it had been set on the mainland?

8. How did you find the device of telling the story through alternating viewpoints?

9. Did you feel that Aidan was being true to Jenny's memory?

10. Is it possible for a crime novel to have a happy ending?